PRAISE FOR THE BOOKS OF NANCY HERRIMAN

"In this latest Mystery of Old San Francisco, justice is served in ways that will leave readers thoroughly satisfied and have them cheering at the end."
—Alyssa Maxwell, author of the Gilded Newport Mysteries

"Nancy Herriman has penned a clever, atmospheric mystery with interesting, diverse, and compelling characters that transported me right back to late-19th-century San Fransisco! I can't wait for the next book!"
—Colleen Cambridge, Agatha Award-nominated author of *Murder at Mallowan Hall*

"Clever and ever-capable nurse Celia Davies once again finds use for her considerable skills in this compelling series addition. *No Refuge from the Grave* is a tightly plotted, engrossing mystery that is rich in historical detail and vividly brings to life 1860s San Francisco."
—Ashley Weaver, Edgar Award-nominated author of the Amory Ames Mysteries

"Highly recommended!"
—Historical Novel Society, Editors' Choice on *Searcher of the Dead*

"You'll love the intrepid heroine, nurse Celia Davies."
—Victoria Thompson, bestselling author of the Gaslight Mysteries, on *No Pity for the Dead*

"A tremendously riveting read . . ."
—*Newport Plain Talk* on *Searcher of the Dead*

"Skillful storytelling . . . a standout historical mystery."
—*Publishers Weekly* starred review of *A Fall of Shadows*

BOOKS BY NANCY HERRIMAN

Mysteries of Old San Francisco

No Comfort for the Lost
No Pity for the Dead
No Quiet among the Shadows
No Darkness as like Death
No Refuge from the Grave
No Justice for the Deceived
No Rest for the Departed
No Mercy for the Innocent

Bess Ellyott Mysteries

Searcher of the Dead
A Fall of Shadows

Stand-Alone Novels

Josiah's Treasure
The Irish Healer

NO MERCY
for the
INNOCENT

NANCY HERRIMAN

BEYOND THE PAGE
PUBLISHING

In memory of my mother

✄ CHAPTER 1 ᘒ

"You can't know how much it means to me that you and your cousin agreed to accompany us on our little vacation, Mrs. Davies," Mrs. Merrill said.

The woman stood just inside the doorway to Celia's clinic room, crowding the opening with her voluminous indigo-floral cotton skirt and fluttering black lace shawl. She resisted stepping all the way into the room, her dark-eyed gaze darting about and never settling for long on any particular item. Instead, it skipped over Celia's cabinet of medical supplies, her examining table, the stethoscope out of its box and laying atop Celia's desk alongside a roll of bandaging. Elnora Merrill was either uncomfortable with the implements of a nursing practice or censorious of the woman who might make use of them. Or both.

"You were very persuasive, Mrs. Merrill," Celia replied, folding her stethoscope back into its walnut box. "And I have been considering a visit to the mineral springs for a while. For Barbara's sake. The waters might offer her some relief."

"Yes, your cousin's foot," she said. "I'm aware that it pains her sometimes, which is why I came up with the idea to include you both."

An invitation Celia would have declined if not for her friend Jane offering to cover the cost. "I appreciate you thinking of us."

"I trust, though, that my last-minute request didn't prove to be a bother for you."

"Not in the least," Celia replied, smiling even though she'd had to rearrange appointments. "I only hope that my patients can tolerate my absence."

"I expect they will be fine, Mrs. Davies."

Celia was nowhere near as certain. She glanced at her notes, carefully stacked atop her desk, each one written in crisp black ink, observations and treatment plans for each of the women she tended to. She'd never been away for more than a day or so previously. But Barbara's health was important, too, and Celia would genuinely welcome a holiday.

"I should add, of course, that Cassandra is grateful for an additional companion," Elnora Merrill said, fidgeting with the straps of her reticule, twined around her wrist. She'd been fidgeting with them for the past several minutes. "She's tired of my company—she misses her mother, you see—and will enjoy having a young woman near her own age in our party."

Even if that young woman was half Chinese? Someone who Cassandra Weaver barely knew, having met Barbara only a few times at scholarly events that their mutual tutor held. A strange choice of traveling companion, if Celia was being honest.

"Furthermore, my niece admires Miss Walford," Mrs. Merrill continued. "Cassandra finds her to be intelligent and courageous."

"How very kind of her."

"Yes," she said, unwinding the straps. Possibly because her fingers had gone numb from the constriction. "Well, I do hope your cousin is also looking forward to the trip."

"We both are," Celia replied, even though Barbara's reaction, when told about the proposed holiday, had been brusque and short-tempered. She'd announced that she had no interest in seeing hot water spurting from the ground or bubbling up in noxious pools. Being forced to be a "part of a whole troop of people," as she'd put it, had not increased her interest. Celia had spent several hours expounding the benefits before Barbara had agreed to go.

"Good. Very good." Mrs. Merrill stopped fidgeting with her reticule to pluck at her skirt, trying to drag it away from the doorframe; a ruffle had tangled in one of the hinges. "Very good."

Celia peered at her. "Mrs. Merrill, is everything quite all right?"

"Why wouldn't everything be all right?" she replied, releasing her hold on the indigo floral cotton with a snap of her wrist.

"You appear troubled, if you don't mind my saying."

"Well, I'm not."

"Are you certain?"

She drew in a lengthy breath, which seemed to calm her restlessness. At least temporarily. "I suppose I can tell you. We will be joined at the hotel by a fellow who . . ." Her mouth puckered with distaste. "A fellow my brother-in-law would like Cassandra to marry."

"But you do not care for the man."

"I do not know what to make of him, actually."

"Does your brother-in-law know of your reservations?"

"Yes, and I do not think he cares," she said. "He is too wrapped up in his business concerns, frankly, to spare a thought for my opinion."

"Ah." A family dispute. How pleasant.

"In fact, Mrs. Davies, I believe I would welcome your impression of Mr. Thaddeus Thompson."

My *impression*? "I do not know what I can discern in the handful of days we will be at the geysers, Mrs. Merrill," she said. "That is insufficient time to form a thorough impression of an individual."

However, she had to admit to herself that she had formed opinions in shorter periods of time.

"You are clever," she replied. In a tone that was not necessarily complimentary. "I trust you will discover if I should be worried about the man or not."

"Truly, Mrs. Merrill, I do not know—"

"I would greatly appreciate it, Mrs. Davies," she insisted. "Please. I do not want Cassandra to end up unhappy. She reminds me of her mother, my dearest sister, and I care about Cassandra as I would my own daughter. If I had one."

Celia opened her mouth to protest but didn't; the woman clearly needed her. Perhaps Cassandra needed her, as well. "All right."

"Thank you," she said, visibly relieved. "We shall see you at nine tomorrow morning, then. Yes?"

"Yes. You shall see us at nine. At the Vallejo Street dock."

"Until then." She turned, her broad skirts swirling, and nearly bumped into Addie, who'd been waiting behind her in the entry hall. *Eavesdropping* behind her in the entry hall.

Celia's housekeeper showed her out and scurried into the clinic room as soon as she'd dispensed with the woman.

"What was she all in a fidge about?" Addie asked.

"She claims she is concerned about her niece, Miss Weaver, and a man she might be marrying." Celia sat at her desk, sighing over her files. "She decided that she would like my opinion about the situation, since he will be joining us at the geysers."

"Hmph. Seems chancy to me, ma'am."

Celia glanced over her shoulder at her housekeeper; she was scowling. "A trip to the geysers seems chancy?"

"A trip with folk in a fidge like she was, ma'am, and who ask for your opinion about a 'situation.'"

Addie's concern was infectious, and she regretted not pressing Mrs. Merrill for more details. A more thorough explanation for her misgivings about Mr. Thaddeus Thompson.

"Nothing bad will happen, Addie."

She harrumphed. "Perhaps I should hurry over to my astrologer's and ask what you should do," she said.

"Maybe you should ask your astrologer whether or not you should be marrying a police officer, Addie," said Celia's cousin, squeezing past Addie and flouncing onto the chair Celia reserved for her patients. "Sounds potentially dangerous. Agreeing to Mr. Taylor's proposal."

Addie's soft cheeks flared a red the color of ripe apples. "He's nae proposed, Miss Barbara."

"Yet," Barbara countered.

"I've dinner to prepare." Addie jutted her chin and marched off.

"Don't tease her about Mr. Taylor, Barbara. Her nerves are on their last thread waiting for him to ask her to marry him." *Mine are, too. What will we do without her?*

"Well, if he hasn't already asked her, he will the moment we are out the door. So we don't have to worry that her nerves will fray beyond repair for much longer," she said. "Did Mrs. Merrill come here to let you know their plans have changed and we don't need to go to the geysers with them after all?"

"She wanted to confirm that we still intend to leave tomorrow."

"Oh." Barbara leaned down to massage her aching foot.

"Is it bad today?" Celia nodded toward her cousin's foot.

Barbara abruptly stopped massaging and sat up. "Nothing that some mineral springs won't fix, I've been told."

"They might help, Barbara."

"So I have to endure a trip on a steamer, then a train ride, then an overnight stay in a dusty hotel in the middle of nowhere, followed by a teeth-rattling ride over a mountain in a stagecoach to get to those springs," she retorted. "All in hopes an hour or two of soaking my club foot might help."

"Barbara, if you really do not want to go, I can send a message to Mrs. Merrill immediately that we've decided to cancel."

"I don't know what I want to do." She stood, crossing to the examining table. She started to work her way through a stack of clean bandaging that Addie had placed there, rolling each length into bundles. "Other than not be forced to spend several days with Cassandra Weaver and her family."

"Will the trip actually be so terrible, Barbara?" Celia asked. "Besides, I think Miss Weaver truly likes you."

"Likes me? Nobody likes me, Cousin Celia. Besides Addie. And you," she hastily added.

Celia joined Barbara at the table. "And Owen and Mr. Greaves and Mr. Taylor. And, of course, Jane and Grace," she said, listing all the people in their lives who cared dearly about her cousin. About them both. "There are many people who are fond of you and you know it. You are an intelligent, talented, and a lovely young woman, Barbara. Anyone who cannot see and appreciate that is a fool." Or hopelessly prejudiced.

"I still think it's all strange," Barbara said, having to rewind the last bandage roll so that it was tidy. "Don't you think it's strange? The Weavers wanting us to accompany them on their trip?"

"No, I think it is very sensible," Celia said. "Mrs. Merrill has observed that you might benefit from a visit to the hot springs, and her niece could use the company of a friend while she seeks a treatment for her skin rash. Not in the least strange."

Her cousin looked over. "You don't honestly believe it's not strange, do you?"

"I do," she stated, rather than give in to her own doubts.

"Well, I can't understand why you're not more suspicious, Cousin," she said. "You're always suspicious."

Celia Davies. The "lady detective." Perhaps even Barbara had come to accept the label a newspaperman had slapped on Celia after the third—or was it the fourth?—time she'd become entangled in one of Nicholas's murder investigations. How he rebelled against them calling her a detective. Hated when her suspicions led her into trouble.

"Not this time."

Barbara narrowed her eyes. "You *are* suspicious. Admit it."

Am I? Perhaps I am.

"I am *curious*," Celia said, rather than admit her true concerns. Which were growing by the minute, now that Barbara was just as convinced that the reason behind the invitation might not be all that it seemed. "That is all, Barbara. Nothing more. I am curious."

"I'll bet," she replied and smirked.

• • •

"You're asking me for a favor, Greaves?" Captain Eagan leaned back in his desk chair and folded his arms. A gold signet ring flashed on his right hand, catching the morning light provided by the office's tall windows. When had he taken to wearing one like a banker or a real estate mogul?

"It's not a favor to consider finally promoting Mr. Taylor to detective, Captain. There has been an opening for the past three months." Ever since one of the detectives had been convicted of accepting bribes from smugglers. Among other crimes. "He deserves the job. He works hard and has been an invaluable assistant to me."

"You're biased, Greaves. Taylor is your friend and you're biased toward him."

"Is there somebody better on the force? Somebody more qualified?" Nick asked.

"I have my eyes on one of the men."

Eagan was being obstinate just to infuriate Nick. Which he was succeeding at.

"Taylor is going to be getting married soon." He hadn't asked Addie Ferguson to marry him yet, but he would soon. And she'd accept without blinking. "He'll have a wife, sir. He'll need the extra income."

"We pay our police officers well. He can support a wife on his salary."

"It's only fair."

Eagan's gaze narrowed. "Are you saying that I'm not fair, Greaves? Is that what you're saying?"

I wish like hell I could say exactly what I think of you. Eagan should've been accused along with the others who'd been jailed for helping smugglers sneak goods into the city. But Nick had no proof of the captain's involvement, just a feeling. Any accusation he'd make would risk his position on the force, and he needed the job; he might be getting married himself soon. If he'd ever summon the courage to ask Celia for her hand.

"I just want you to consider it, Captain," he said.

Eagan rubbed the knuckles of his right hand down his thick—magnificent, as Celia had once described them—black sideburns. "Is there anything else?"

Apparently not.

Nick exited Eagan's office and stormed through the building and over to the stairs leading down to the basement police station.

"There you are, Mr. Greaves." The booking sergeant, standing at his desk by the door to the cells, noticed his arrival. "Mrs. Davies is here to see you," he said, smirking.

"Take that expression off your face, Sergeant."

He smirked more. "Why, yes, Mr. Greaves."

Nick marched into the detectives' office. It was empty, except for Celia, occupying the chair in front of his desk.

"Celia, what brings you here?"

He'd like nothing better than to kiss her, bury his face in the soft honey-colored hair hidden beneath her bonnet, inhale the smell of lavender that lingered on her skin, her clothes. But he'd intentionally left the door ajar, not wanting to add gossip to the booking sergeant's amusement, and merely took the gloved hand she extended.

"I thought you were heading to the geysers this morning. It is Monday, isn't it?" He hadn't previously noticed Eagan's signet ring; maybe he had his days confused, too.

"I cannot have turned up out of a superstitious need to have you wish me a bon voyage, Nicholas?" She smiled and squeezed his fingers before releasing them.

"Bon voyage," he said, realizing how much he was going to miss her. *Only a week, Greaves. Only a week.* He tossed his hat onto his desk, not as cluttered with papers as usual, and sat down. "But I'm guessing there's more. Since I'm also guessing that Miss Walford isn't finished packing and you should be at home supervising her."

"I am hoping that, in the hour we have left before we need to head to the ferry dock, she will finish," she said. "As an insurance policy, I left Addie to stand over my cousin and make certain that she is ready to depart when I return."

He had no doubt Addie Ferguson wouldn't budge until the task was completed. "You must have an important reason, though, for coming here when you're so short on time."

"I am likely being ridiculous."

"Celia, you are many things, but you are never ridiculous."

She smiled. The expression lit her pale, clear eyes.

"Thank you for saying so, Mr. Greaves," she said. "Anyway, Elnora Merrill stopped in to see me yesterday to make certain that we still intend to join them. She was agitated. I pressed her, and she finally admitted that she is uneasy about a man who will be joining us. A fellow her brother-in-law, Hiram Weaver, intends for his daughter to wed. Mrs. Merrill wants my opinion on the fellow."

"Your opinion?"

"On if she is wrong to be concerned about him."

Nick sat forward. "Is he dangerous?" *And are you going to get yourself into trouble again?*

"Mrs. Merrill gave no indication that he represents a danger to anyone," she said. "Merely that he may be unsuitable for her cherished niece, Miss Cassandra Weaver."

"What can I do?" And wouldn't Eagan love to hear that Nick was spending time looking into the background of some rich young woman's potential husband.

Celia leaned forward. "Have you ever heard of Thaddeus Thompson? Any Thompson, for that matter?"

"Do you mean, has one of them ever been in the station accused of a crime?"

"I suppose I do."

"Not that I can recall." He'd have to ask Taylor and the other men.

"What about Hiram Weaver? He will also be traveling with us," she said. "Mrs. Merrill made a comment about her brother-in-law that led me to believe his business might be in trouble. Just a feeling. Nothing more definite."

Hiram Weaver wouldn't be the only man with a failing business in the city. "Haven't heard anything about him, either."

"Well, that is a bit of a relief," she said. "I do, however, wish that Jane was in town. I'd be requesting her assistance in collecting any gossip about the two families, if she were. But she and Frank and Grace have gone back East to visit his ailing mother."

Thank God the Hutchinsons were away; Jane had been injured more than once while helping Celia investigate.

"I'll see what I can do, Celia, but don't expect me to learn anything between now and when you leave."

"I'm not expecting a miracle, Nicholas," she said. "If you do learn something concerning, I trust I'll be able to receive a telegram up at the hotel."

"Hopefully in time for you to be able to do something with the information."

"There is no need to be sarcastic, Mr. Greaves."

"I wasn't being sarcastic, Celia," he said. "But be careful. Please." How many times before had he warned her? He was losing count.

"Believe me, Nicholas, I shall try my very best."

℘ CHAPTER 2 ℞

The Vallejo wharf bustled with activity. Numerous carriages pulled up with passengers, parking alongside wagons loaded with cargo, their goods bound for the countryside north of the bay and into the hills. Stevedores shouted over the din of rigging slapping against masts and barrels being rolled up planks. The steamer ferry itself puffed away at dock, its decks crowding with both travelers and crew. Celia had learned from the man at the ticket office that the journey to Petaluma, where they would disembark, took only four hours. She glanced at Barbara, her cousin's bonnet pulled tight around her face to shield it from unwanted stares, the ribbons rippling in the wind. Her cousin was already looking green at the notion of that much time spent on the water. She'd never endured a voyage across the ocean in steerage like Celia and Patrick and Addie had done. Before that journey, Celia had thought herself a hardy traveler; she'd learned otherwise.

Barbara sensed Celia's attention and looked over. "Where are the Weavers?" she asked. "Have they already boarded? I thought we were to meet here onshore then board together."

"I don't know." Celia shielded her eyes against the morning sun, which peeked through a skim of fog, with her hand. "Ah, there they are."

A carriage pulled up with Mrs. Merrill, Cassandra Weaver, and two men aboard. Cassandra spotted Celia and Barbara. She scrambled down from the carriage and ran across the wharf to join them, her skirts flapping.

"Cassandra, be ladylike!" her aunt called after her.

"I'm so glad you're here," she said to Celia and Barbara.

She was small and thin, her tailored green traveling dress covering her arms to the wrists, its neckline taut against her jawline. Every inch of excess material hid the rash that blemished her skin. The high collar had the benefit, though, of accentuating her heart-shaped face and its fresh loveliness. She looked so much younger than her eighteen years. Young and innocent.

"We told your aunt we would be, Cassandra," said Barbara. A trifle impatiently, but Cassandra didn't appear to be offended.

"We were worried that we'd somehow missed you, Miss Weaver," Celia said.

She frowned at the occupants of the carriage, who'd all disembarked and were fussing over their luggage, the driver slowly unloading it from the conveyance. "We had to wait for Cousin Denny."

"The one in the cream-colored linen suit?" asked Barbara, peering at him from beneath the brim of her bonnet.

"Well, he's not actually my cousin. Not by blood. But I'm supposed to call him Cousin," she added.

Celia eyed the fellow. He'd stopped bothering with the luggage and stood back to smoke a cigarillo. A grin on his suntanned face, he watched the older gentleman Celia presumed was Mr. Weaver bark orders at the driver. The man's suit was bound to get dirtied during the dusty stage trip ahead of them; perhaps he'd packed another one.

"He can be so annoying," Cassandra announced. She noticed her aunt striding their way and grabbed Barbara's wrist. "We should go, Barbara. We need to find a place in the saloon to sit before all the best spots get taken. I can't wait to get this trip over with. The last thing I want is to be uncomfortable."

Barbara grabbed her carpetbag, and Cassandra pulled her toward the gangplank. Escaping just as Mrs. Merrill arrived at Celia's side.

"I do not understand what is going on with Cassandra today," Mrs. Merrill said.

"She does seem eager to get the journey underway, Mrs. Merrill," Celia responded, watching the two young women cross to the ship, Barbara struggling to keep up with Cassandra.

Her eyes flicked to Celia's face. "She's rarely eager about anything, Mrs. Davies."

"Ah, the inimitable Mrs. Davies." The fellow in the ivory linen suit had managed to creep up unnoticed, startling Celia.

"Mrs. Davies, this is my stepson, Dennis Merrill. Denny, Mrs. Davies," Elnora announced flatly.

"I've heard so much about you." His voice was smooth as a cream custard, though his general appearance was rumpled and rough. Which reflected the actuality and which the affectation, his voice or his attire? He took her hand and bowed over it, his grip not so strong as to violate courtesy, then released her fingers.

"You have me at a disadvantage, Mr. Merrill, because I have heard nothing about you and did not realize that you were to accompany us," she replied. "And I recommend that you not believe everything you read in the newspapers or hear in parlors about me."

He plucked his cigarillo from his mouth and laughed a full-throated guffaw. Beneath his broad-brimmed straw hat, the brightest of blue eyes sparkled with humor, and his hair was the faded brown that came from a great deal of time spent in the sunshine. He was handsome, and he was fully aware of the fact.

"I'll keep your excellent recommendation in mind, Mrs. Davies."

He smiled without revealing his teeth. Perhaps they were stained from frequent cigarillo smoking and he was too vain to show them. His smile, however, appeared genuine. Why had Miss Weaver labeled him "annoying"? Celia presumed she'd come to understand eventually.

"I see Hiram has succeeded in convincing the driver to cart all of our luggage over to the boat, so shall we go?" Mrs. Merrill asked. "We have a long trip ahead of us."

She strode off, leaving her stepson behind.

"Let me find a porter to help you with your trunk, Mrs. Davies," Dennis Merrill said. "And I'm hoping in exchange for my chivalry, you'll regale me with details of your adventures in police work at some point on our little vacation."

"I'd hardly wish to bore you, Mr. Merrill."

"Trust me when I say I would find such conversation far from boring, Mrs. Davies."

He hurried away to locate a porter, and she watched him go, the cold wind off the water causing Celia to wrap her shawl more tightly around her shoulders. *Look like the innocent flower but be the serpent under't.* A morsel of advice from Lady Macbeth that, perhaps, Mr. Merrill followed. Although he hardly looked innocent.

But a serpent, Celia? She *was* being suspicious.

• • •

"I've got some information on Thaddeus Thompson, sir." Taylor stepped inside Nick's office and dropped onto the chair against the wall. "Or rather, his father. He's a city supervisor."

An upright citizen of San Francisco. "But nothing on his son."

"Nope," he said and hunted through his coat pockets for a cigar. He turned up empty-handed. "That's good, isn't it, sir? Mr. Greaves?"

"Better than discovering he's wanted for murder, Taylor."

"Yes, sir," he said.

"What about Hiram Weaver?"

"Working on him next, Mr. Greaves," he said, starting to hunt for a cigar again and remembering he didn't have any on him. "Umm, sir, I've got a question for you."

"Does your question have to do with Addie Ferguson, Taylor?" The usual reason for his awkward hemming and hawing these days.

He lifted his eyebrows. "Would you help me look for an engagement ring for her?" he asked all in a rush.

Everything around Nick seemed to go quiet and still. He stopped noticing the ticking of the clock on the wall, the noise out in the station, the clatter of wheels on the road beyond his window. His pulse thudded and he felt sick. *I'm happy for Taylor. I knew this day was coming, and I'm happy.*

"Nothing fancy, sir. No diamonds like is getting popular these days," Taylor stammered, bothered by Nick's silence. "Just a plain gold ring, or maybe something with a little stone in it. That's what I'd like your advice on. Help me find a ring that's good enough for Miss Ferguson."

What would Celia want? Diamonds? Or just a plain gold ring? Her husband . . . her *deceased* husband had given her a plain gold band. Might've been all that Patrick Davies had been able to afford. Might've been all that Celia had wanted.

"A nice ring that's not too flashy," Nick said.

"Exactly." He nodded, taking Nick's response as an agreement to help. "And, sir, would you be my best man? At the wedding. If Addie . . . if Miss Ferguson accepts me."

He drew in a breath; his hesitation was ridiculous.

"She'll accept you, Taylor." He had no doubt about her saying yes; he'd seen the way she looked at him.

Taylor's brow furrowed. "Well, will you, sir? Mr. Greaves? Be my best man?"

"I'd be honored, Taylor," he said, meaning every word.

And before that day, he'd figure out how to not feel sick. How to be fully happy.

• • •

After the predicted four hours, they steamed up Petaluma Creek and arrived at the landing, which was, Celia was informed, two miles south of Petaluma itself.

"Are we almost there?" Barbara asked, leaning over the deck railing. The chop of the bay combined with the confinement of the saloon had proven too much for her stomach. Or maybe it had been Cassandra Weaver's company that had wearied her.

"Only a few more minutes, Barbara. I see the harbor up ahead."

There was more to both the harbor and the town itself than Celia had been anticipating. From their vantage point on the deck of the steamer, she could make out several mills and manufactories, and at least six church steeples rose above the buildings—mostly of wood but some of brick—crowding the shoreline.

"Mrs. Davies, Miss Walford," Mr. Merrill said, crossing the deck to join them at the railing. His linen suit remained pristine. But then, the worst of the journey was ahead. "Are you both ready for the next phase of our adventure?"

Barbara noticed Miss Weaver exiting the saloon. "There's Cassandra. I'll see you onshore, Cousin. Mr. Merrill," she said and walked off, looking back once before hurrying onward.

"My cousin is apprehensive about the stagecoach ride, I'm afraid," Celia said, steadying herself against the abrupt slowing of the ferry as it pulled into dock.

"Hiram has hired two coaches to take us to Healdsburg. It's the trip from there to the geysers tomorrow morning that is worth being concerned about," he said. "I've heard that Mr. Foss, the owner of the stage line to Geyser Springs, can be aggressive in handling the horses. Although as far as I know, none of the extras have ever plunged off the side of the mountain."

Something to be grateful for, she supposed. "'Extra'?" She'd never heard the term before.

"A large, open carriage with three rows of seats." He looked down at his clothing. "Won't be wearing this suit tomorrow, Mrs. Davies." He winked.

The steamer bumped against the dock and one of the crew scrambled to moor the boat, tossing a rope to the fellow ashore. Seagulls circled and screeched overhead. Beyond the town, rugged hills rose against the hazy blue sky. The sun overhead was warm, and a trickle of sweat made its way between Celia's shoulder blades. She'd given Barbara the sun parasol and was beginning to envy Mr. Merrill's cool linen suit.

"Mr. Merrill, if you do not mind my asking, what brings you to join us on this trip?"

He grinned as though he'd been anticipating such a question from the "lady detective." "I've never been to see the geysers, Mrs. Davies. It's as simple as that. And Hiram is paying the way."

"Are you and Mr. Weaver closely acquainted?" she asked. "Aside from you being his sister-in-law's stepson."

"We have discovered that we have an interest in common. A desire to form another city baseball team. A hobby of mine," he said. "The sport is going to be big someday, I predict."

"Ah."

His blue-eyed gaze moved from focusing on Celia's face to tracking the movements of Miss Weaver and Barbara as they walked over to the gangway, being extended toward the pier and landing with a thud when the plank found it. Perhaps baseball was not all he and Mr. Weaver had in common.

"And Miss Weaver?" Celia asked.

He chuckled. "You're wondering if my interests also extend in her direction."

"She is a very lovely young woman, Mr. Merrill." And the daughter of a well-off man.

"That she is," he said. Somewhat wistfully. "Maybe I hope to impress her with my particular charms on this trip."

"I was under the impression that her father has another man in mind for her."

He winked again. "May the best man win."

Indeed.

• • •

After a quick pause in Petaluma to refresh themselves, the coaches were brought around to continue their journey, and they all climbed aboard. Celia and Barbara accompanied Mr. Weaver, while the rest took the other coach. They journeyed past fields of grain interspersed with vineyards, grasses browning in the heat, and stands of scrubby oak trees. An hour or so into the trip, the hard, upright seat backs began to make Barbara squirm. Mr. Weaver appeared indifferent to the discomfort of the jolting ride. He frankly appeared indifferent to everything, including Celia and Barbara.

She considered the back of his head—the graying hair where it showed beneath the brim of his hat, the stern set of his neck and shoulders—and leaned forward to tap him on the shoulder.

He shifted in his seat to stare at her. "Yes, Mrs. Davies? Do you need the driver to stop?" he asked coolly, his tone expressing his lack of interest in slowing their journey.

"No, Mr. Weaver. I have no need to stop," she answered, grabbing the iron bar screwed to the back of the front seat to steady herself against the carriage's swaying. "I only wish to thank you personally for allowing my cousin and me to accompany your party to the geysers. I've not yet had an opportunity."

She could sense Barbara's sideways glance, likely wondering why Celia had bothered to thank the man. Especially when he'd appeared so keen to avoid conversation with them.

"Elnora insisted. She said my daughter would enjoy your cousin's company, Mrs. Davies," he said. "I didn't have a reason to refuse her."

Barbara rolled her eyes and resumed leaning against the corner of the black canopy, drawn over the coach to shield them from the sun.

"I was surprised to discover that Mrs. Merrill's stepson was accompanying us," Celia said. "He seems a pleasant enough fellow. He tells me that you two are both interested in starting a baseball team. How intriguing."

"Denny Merrill has plenty of ideas, Mrs. Davies. Not all of them smart."

"Do his unwise ideas include your daughter, Mr. Weaver?"

He frowned. "My plans for my daughter are none of your business, Mrs. Davies."

He turned around again. Barbara leaned over and jabbed her elbow into Celia's side.

"Why do you insist on antagonizing people?" she hissed.

"'Nothing is so oppressive as a secret,' Barbara." A quote from a French poet whose name escaped her. "And there are secrets aplenty among our traveling companions."

"But do you have to root them out?"

"I find that I apparently do."

• • •

"I'm looking for someone to help me," a man at the door to the detectives' office said. He was dressed in what appeared to be a rarely worn suit, maybe aiming to look as businesslike as possible, and nervously scanned the interior of the room. Nick was the only one in the room. As usual. "I was told by one of the officers out there that you might be able to." He jerked his head to indicate the main room at his back.

"Do you want to report a crime?"

"More like a complaint," he said. "Up to you to decide if it's a crime or not, Officer."

"Detective. Detective Greaves." Nick pushed aside the case notes he'd been writing—trying to write and not actually getting anywhere with—and indicated the chair in front of his desk. "Please, have a seat, Mr. . . ."

"Mr. Kott." He took the chair and dragged his bowler hat off his head. His brown hair was slicked with pomatum and didn't need fixing, but he ran thick fingers through it anyway.

"How can I help?"

"Well, I'm a coal and wood supplier. Have been for near onto five years now," he said proudly. "I've been supplying the city for its steam fire engines, in fact. Was expecting to get my contract renewed this year."

"But I take it that it wasn't renewed."

"No, and I can't get an explanation as to why not."

"Mr. Kott, it's not my job to negotiate disputes between the city and a supplier." Did it look like he wasn't busy? He had stacks of paper on his desk. *Which you're not focusing on because you're too worried about Celia, Greaves.*

"Somebody's been bribing the city supervisors, Detective. Looking into that *is* your job, isn't it?" he asked. "A bribe is the only explanation for why my bid has been passed over this time."

"Is that your belief, or do you have more solid information?"

"I know a fellow who's one of the clerks," he said. "He's heard rumors about underhanded dealings."

"Rumors aren't much to go on, Mr. Kott."

"You gotta start someplace, don't you?"

Nick had started with less. "Tell me about the rumors," he said, hunting for a blank piece of paper and a pencil.

"One of the owners of a wood and coal company has been cozying up with a city supervisor, Detective," he said, craning his neck to see if Nick was taking any notes. "I don't know which supervisor."

Very helpful. "You are going to tell me the name of the coal company owner, though, right? The one you suspect."

"Oh, sure," he said. "It's Hiram Weaver."

Damn.

• • •

The remainder of the ride passed in chilling silence. They arrived in Healdsburg and disembarked in front of the Sotoyome Hotel. It was a three-story, flat-fronted white hotel with a suggestion of a balcony more meant to provide shade to those passing on the pavement below than to ever support the weight of someone standing on it to catch the air. They ventured inside, Mrs. Merrill fussing over Cassandra, the both of them looking as windblown and dust-covered as Celia felt.

"We should go inside, Cousin," Barbara said, her arm sagging under the weight of her carpetbag as she trooped after the Weavers and the Merrills.

The shadowed ground-floor room was cooler than outside but choked with cigar and cigarillo smoke from the occupants of the saloon. The man at the reception desk showed them to their accommodations on the first floor, announced when supper was to be served, and left them to freshen up.

"I won't be surprised if Mr. Weaver sends us packing back to San Francisco tomorrow morning, after you insisted on asking him about Mr. Merrill and Cassandra," Barbara stated the moment the door closed behind him. She prodded the mattress of the narrow bed nearest the window and frowned. "He was very annoyed."

"I do not much care if I annoyed Mr. Weaver, Barbara." Celia removed her shawl and bonnet and hung them on one of the hooks by the door.

"I don't think I like Mr. Merrill. Too . . . self-confident."

Smug. "He is definitely interested in Cassandra Weaver." Celia peered into the porcelain pitcher set on a wobbly dressing table. It held water, which she poured into the supplied matching basin. Clear water, thankfully. Celia wet a clean cloth and wiped her face and neck. "Too late, though, if Hiram Weaver has this Thaddeus Thompson fellow in mind for his daughter."

"Maybe he's hoping she'll defy her father and choose him instead." Barbara peeled back the bed's thin coverlet and dropped onto it. "And Mr. Merrill will one day get all her wonderful money."

"How very cynical, Barbara," she said. Although possibly an accurate assessment. "I believe I shall stretch my legs before supper. No need to accompany me."

"After that ride, I don't want to budge."

Celia stepped into the passageway outside the rooms. The air was warm and stuffy. The proprietor had promised that it would cool "delightfully," as he'd put it, once the sun set. Her back ached so much she wondered if she'd sleep no matter how cool the sleeping room got.

A gaunt fellow in blue jean trousers and a duster coat strode down the hall toward her, his spurs chinking as he walked. He politely tipped his sweat-stained hat as he passed.

"Ma'am," he drawled with a half smile.

"Sir," she replied, looking away before he might conclude that her response was an invitation. She should have brought her black dress, despite the daytime heat and no longer being in mourning. The gown's color usually succeeded at warding off unwanted greetings from men.

She turned the corner where the staircase wound its way through the building. Before she descended, though, the sound of upraised voices in a nearby room stopped her. Familiar—and angry—voices.

"She came to the house looking for you, Denny," Elnora Merrill hissed. "It's embarrassing."

"It's none of your concern, Elnora. I'll take care of it."

"None of my concern?" Her skirts rustled; perhaps she'd moved closer to him. "Of course it's my concern. Tell me she was lying, Denny."

"Would you believe me if I professed my innocence?"

"I would like to," she said.

Celia could hear Elnora breathing, wheezing gasps of breath as though she was an asthmatic, accompanied by the rapid flapping of her fan.

"What are we to do?" she asked.

"What are *we* to do? You can always move back to St. Louis, Elnora. Frankly, my father never should've brought you out here," he said. "But you won't move back, will you? You have life too good here. As for me, I intend to proceed as we planned, because that woman lied to you. Just don't tell Hiram."

"He'll find out," she said. "She's not going to give up, Denny."

"I'll take care of it, Elnora. It will all be fine."

She made a low noise of complaint. "Between you and Hiram, I don't know who to worry about more."

"You should probably worry about yourself."

The rapid flapping of her fan ceased. "What do you mean by that comment, Denny?"

He exhaled, likely breathing out a lengthy stream of cigarillo smoke. "I'm only wondering what's going to happen to you, Elnora."

"We don't offer a tea service in this hotel, Mrs. Davies, if that's what you were heading downstairs for."

The man's voice, suddenly booming behind her, made Celia jump. She was growing lax, allowing so many people to sneak up on her lately. The fellow, one of the staff, had also been heard by the occupants of the room; Mr. Merrill and Elnora had stopped talking. *Gad.*

"And it's not time for supper yet," the staff member continued. "Not for another fifteen minutes or so. Maybe not having somebody sound a gong confused you."

"Oh, thank you for clarifying," she said, pulse thumping, expecting that, at any moment, Dennis Merrill or his stepmother would charge into the hallway to confront her. "I shall return to my room and wait, in that case."

She turned on her heel and tried not to run.

⍥ CHAPTER 3 ⍥

"Everything aches," Barbara said.

She stared mournfully at the carriages—the "extras," as Mr. Merrill had referred to them—waiting on the dirt road outside the hotel. Three rows of hard benches, the frontmost one higher and occupied by the driver and anyone else who dared sit up there, were fully exposed to the elements. The wheels were painted brilliant green and *Geyser Springs* was emblazoned across the body of the coach. Four horses had been put in harness. Whenever they shook their heads, the gleaming brass fittings jingled and the vivid tassels attached to their bridles swung, causing folks in the street to look over. Although Celia had to believe they'd often seen the spectacle.

"That bed was—"

"Hard as a board," Celia said, using a finger to loosen the collar of her dress. The early morning air was refreshing, but the sun promised another day of heat. Would the canyon where the Geyser Hotel was located be cooler? Celia doubted it. "I wonder if the Weavers have abandoned us," Celia said, looking around.

She and her cousin were the only members of their party who'd yet to make an appearance on the hotel porch.

"If they have, then we can go back to San Francisco immediately," Barbara said hopefully. "And I can sleep on a comfortable bed tonight, instead of what I'm afraid awaits us at the Geyser Hotel."

"I wonder if their delayed appearance has anything to do with the argument between Mr. Merrill and his stepmother that I overheard last night."

"An argument?" Barbara whispered.

"Yes. About a woman who approached Mrs. Merrill with a 'lie,' as Mr. Merrill characterized it. He does not want Hiram Weaver to learn of what that woman told Elnora," she said. "That's about the extent of it, and I do not know what the 'lie' is."

Barbara wrapped her arms around her waist. "I don't like this at all, Cousin."

A lanky fellow, dressed in a checked summer suit with a vivid scarlet waistcoat, strode out from the hotel, preventing Celia from responding to Barbara's comment.

He paused on the front steps not ten feet from them and looked over. "Excuse me, ladies." He tipped his hat. "Are you two bound for the geysers?"

"Yes, we are," Celia answered.

He grinned broadly, a pleasant smile revealing that most of his teeth were in place. "My name is Parker Young. I believe I have the pleasure of joining you on our sojourn this morning," he said. "I'm headed there as well."

"My name is Celia Davies, and this is my ward, Barbara Walford."

Mr. Young's assessing look gave the impression he was intrigued by Barbara's ethnicity but not bothered by it. For that, Celia was immensely grateful.

"Have you traveled to the geysers before, Mr. Young?" Celia asked.

"Never had cause to before. But the injury I suffered during the war is paining me again." His left arm hung limply at his side. "I'm hopeful the waters can provide a cure." He glanced over at a man out in the road. "Well, there's Old Chieftain himself."

"Who?" Barbara asked.

"Colonel Foss. That's what some folks call him," he explained. "Heard he drives his carriage like the very fiends from hell are after him."

Mr. Foss, a robust man whose great height was made greater by the massive gray top hat he wore, pulled on fringed gauntlet gloves as he strode toward the carriages. He was as much a spectacle as the sight of his conveyances and horses. He called to the other driver, his booming voice reverberating off the flat-fronted wood buildings crowding the street on either side.

"There's that voice, too." Mr. Young chuckled. "Makes him all the more fearsome, don't you agree? Heard tell that one lady, discovering that she was going to have to ride with him, refused to go. Neither of you look to be timid as that. You're not, are you?"

Barbara jutted her chin. "Certainly not. I'm not afraid."

"All right then, miss. Ma'am. Be ready for the ride of your lives." He tapped the brim of his hat with his long fingers and strolled off.

Porters carrying luggage exited the hotel, hauling the trunks and bags over to the carriages for loading onto the baggage racks behind the drivers' seats. Miss Weaver scurried out onto the porch behind them, followed by her aunt. Interestingly, Mr. Young went over to speak with Elnora. A very brief and somewhat tense conversation, from what Celia could observe.

"Mrs. Davies, Barbara," Cassandra said, anxiously gripping the handle of the parasol she carried. "I'd like to ride in your carriage, if possible. Father insists on riding with Mr. Foss, and I don't want to go with him or that Mr. Young. I saw you speaking with him, Mrs. Davies. What did he have to say?"

Barbara slid Celia a look.

"Trivialities about the excitement ahead of us, Miss Weaver. That is all," Celia said, smiling at her. "You are certainly welcome to ride with us."

"Thank you."

"How is he able to function?" Barbara muttered to Celia as Dennis Merrill pushed through the front door and headed their way. "He was so drunk last night. Out in the street and singing at the top of his lungs."

"He was?" Celia asked. A bout of drinking he'd engaged in after an argument with his stepmother. How interesting.

"There you are, Miss Weaver," Dennis Merrill called out. He'd tied a red bandana around his neck, a bright blot of color like a slash across his throat. *Gruesome, Celia.* "I see we're about to get underway."

"Do you mean to travel with the famed Mr. Foss, Mr. Merrill?" Celia asked.

"No, I thought I would ride with you ladies," he replied pleasantly, giving no indication that he was aware that she'd overheard the argument he'd had with his stepmother last night.

He glanced at Cassandra, who turned her back to him and made a great show of observing the comings and goings on the road. *How very unsettling.* Very, very unsettling.

• • •

"I don't know anything about engagement rings, Mr. Taylor," Owen said, striding alongside Mr. Greaves's assistant.

"Well, Mr. Greaves acted awkward about helping me hunt for one, so I thought I'd ask you."

"Why not Mr. Mullahey?" He was one of the other officers, and Owen had always thought he and Mr. Taylor were friends.

"If you're not keen on doing this, Owen, just let me know."

Mr. Taylor sounded hurt. "No, no. That's not it at all," Owen protested. "Just confused because you've never asked me to do anything with you before."

"This is different. Isn't it?"

Was it? "I suppose."

They crossed the road, and Mr. Taylor paused outside a tobacconist's shop. He took one look at the smokes on sale and ducked inside. The store smelled spicy and earthy and fruity all at once. Owen decided he liked the aroma, almost as much as he'd liked the smell of the candy store when he'd worked there.

"Don't say a word to Miss Ferguson that I went in here, got it, Owen?"

"Okay, Mr. Taylor." First a request to help him search for an engagement ring and now a request to keep a secret. Maybe Mr. Taylor had suddenly realized that Owen wasn't a kid anymore, and he was going to start to treat him like a man.

Owen's chest swelled over the idea.

"And you don't have to keep calling me Mr. Taylor. You can call me Jerich, Owen."

"That's your Christian name?" Not even Mr. Greaves knew Mr. Taylor's Christian name.

Mr. Taylor flushed. "What's wrong with it?"

The tobacconist watched them from behind the main counter. Since Mr. Taylor had his policeman's uniform on, Owen supposed the fellow wasn't going to complain too quickly about them blocking folks from coming through the door.

"Nothing. Nothing at all," he said. "I've just never heard a name like that before."

"Actually, it's Jericho, but I don't let *anybody* call me that. Anybody aside from my ma, that is."

"Not even Addie?"

"Nope." He marched over to the counter, purchased a couple of cigars, had the owner trim the end of one of them, and marched back out of the tobacco shop.

They walked a while without talking, battling the usual crowds on the sidewalks. It was a warm day and people were not in the best humor. Mr. Taylor wasn't, either. *Shoot. I hope I haven't made him too mad.*

Owen summoned the courage to speak up. "What are you thinking of getting her?"

"Something simple."

Mr. Taylor paused to strike a match against the brick wall of a former fur dealer's store. The place had been vacated, workers inside clearing out the rest of the fixtures and whatnot. Owen always felt sorry for the fellows whose businesses failed, but it seemed to happen every day.

"Or do you think she'd like something fancy?" Mr. Taylor asked. He used the match to light the trimmed cigar, puffing heavily until the tip flared orange. "Something with nice gemstones in it, maybe."

"Don't think Addie would want anything fancy, Mr. Taylor." He would never be comfortable with calling him Jerich. It was best to just stick with what was familiar.

"You're probably right, Owen."

He dropped the match onto the sidewalk, stomping it out quickly, and nodded at the worker staring at him through the store's big window. Owen started to move on, but Mr. Taylor hadn't budged.

"What is it, Mr. Taylor?"

"Dennis Merrill." He used the cigar to point out the name that had been painted on the window glass. One of the workers had started to scrape it off but hadn't finished the job. "Mrs. Davies and Miss Walford are traveling with a Mrs. Merrill to the geysers. Wonder if this fellow is related."

Owen wasn't sure why it mattered if he was related, but Mr. Taylor seemed concerned about it. "So?"

"Probably doesn't mean anything, Owen," he said and tucked the cigar into his mouth. "Now, let's go find a ring."

• • •

Barbara and Cassandra had secured the middle bench for themselves, leaving Celia alone in the back while Mr. Merrill sat up front with the driver. They climbed ever upward for several hours, the coach bouncing over every pit and stone in the road with enough force to loosen a person's teeth. But there were calmer moments, between the jarring, when Celia could enjoy the glorious blue of the sky stretching above the surrounding mountains. Moments permitting her to revel in the crisp smell of pine and laurel. Marvel at the sight of a hawk gliding on the rising currents of warm air, searching for a victim scurrying for the cover of a clump of brush.

"Shake! Shake one!" Mr. Foss shouted in the carriage ahead of theirs, his command sending his horses into a frenzy as they surged onward. The road was straighter and flatter for this stretch.

Their own driver, less of a daredevil, muttered in Spanish and cracked the whip over the heads of the horses to speed them. Cassandra clutched her bonnet to keep it from being torn from her head.

Mr. Merrill pulled down the bandana, which had been covering the lower half of his face, and looked over his shoulder at them. "Enjoying the ride?"

"Not really," Barbara replied.

"How much longer to the hotel?" Cassandra asked no one in particular.

Their driver answered. "We reach Hogback Ridge soon. Over the top and then a few miles still. But quick."

Celia expected him to return his attention to his horses, but instead he continued to look at them. "I should warn you all. About these mountains. They are dangerous."

Dennis Merrill chuckled, restored the bandana over the bottom half of his face, and resumed facing straight ahead.

"Why do you say that?" asked Barbara.

"Because of the wild animals, señorita," he replied. "I warn you. Do not wander off the paths. There are grizzlies, and wild cats, too. In the chaparral."

He nodded toward the thicket of shrubs dotting the slopes. Celia believed the greatest danger they faced came from the driver's inattention to the road.

They continued on, upward toward a ridge beyond which Celia could see only sky. How steep the descent was on the other side, she didn't care to speculate on.

"Way down," Mr. Foss called, his horses halting on the proverbial dime.

They had arrived at the ridge, and their driver reined in the horses. Up ahead, Mr. Foss raised one gloved arm to point out the scenery. It was magnificent, a river far below them glistening in the sunshine like a silver ribbon as it twisted through a gorge, towering pine trees climbing either side. In the distance, more mountains rolled away, every shade of green blending into the tans and burnt umbers of the earth. They had scant time to enjoy it, for Mr. Foss was ready to proceed.

"We go fast now," their driver said.

"Now? Weren't we already going fast?" Cassandra asked, her voice trembling.

They began the descent, trees looming overhead to saturate the trail in shadows. Somewhere in the distance, a dog barked, the sound of civilization. The noise would be reassuring were it not for how near to the edge of the roadway the carriage came, the wheels clattering stones down the face of the hillside.

"We're going to get killed, Cousin," Barbara hissed between clenched teeth and clutched Celia's arm.

After more twists and turns, they slowed at a small rise. The stink of sulfur hung in the air. Seconds later, a blast like a great steam whistle echoed off the rocks and shrubs.

"What was that?" asked Barbara, startled.

"Steamboat Geyser," answered the driver.

"How often does it make that hideous screech?" she asked.

"Only God controls the geysers, señorita." He slightly turned his face toward them. Celia could see the hard set to his jaw. "Or the devil."

• • •

Celia, dizzy from the breakneck descent, was afraid the white building at the base of the ravine was only a mirage and not their destination. However, it thankfully was the Geyser Hotel, two wooden stories of shaded balconies laid out in an L shape, a handful of outbuildings sprawling across the yard. Mr. Foss trotted his carriage up to the front of the hotel at a dignified pace, their driver following suit.

"I think I'm going to get sick, Cousin," Barbara moaned. At her side, Cassandra looked no better. The heat bouncing off the rocky walls of the ravine and the heavy smell of rotten eggs, sulfur rising from the many geysers exhaling on the hillside opposite the hotel, was only making matters worse.

They all climbed down, Cassandra evading Mr. Merrill's attempt to assist her. Mrs. Merrill and the others clambered down from Mr. Foss's carriage, Mrs. Merrill straightening her bonnet.

"That was absolutely awful, Hiram."

Her brother-in-law didn't acknowledge her complaint. "Thank you, Colonel Foss. The trip was as exhilarating as advertised."

"You are welcome indeed, Mr. Weaver," he announced.

An individual who looked as though he was the hotel proprietor, based on his air of possessiveness and ready smile, hurried up to greet them.

"Ah, here are my Tuesday arrivals. Welcome, everybody." He peered quizzically at Celia and Barbara, trying to solve the puzzle of their relationship. "You didn't need to bring your servant with you, ma'am. We've got good staff here."

Barbara muttered under her breath.

"She is not my servant," Celia replied stiffly. "She is my cousin."

"Ah. I see. Well, I'm Mr. Shafer, and you're just in time for lunch," he said. "Most of our guests are in the parlor waiting for the meal. And I hope you didn't mind that notice that I put in several of the newspapers, Mr. Weaver, about your party joining us here at the Geyser Hotel. Like folks to know that we have discerning clientele."

"Not at all, Mr. Shafer," Hiram Weaver replied.

The fellow smiled, relieved. "I suppose you'd all like to freshen up before joining the others in the parlor. You're all on the second floor. Rooms up there catch the breezes better. Everybody except for Mr. Young. Yes, Mr. Young," he said as the fellow separated himself from the group. "Got your telegram last night about meaning to stay with us. Pleased to tell you I have a room. You're right over there."

With a flick of his head, he gestured for a servant, who'd been standing to one side, to show Mr. Young to his room.

"We usually have a lot of folks on their honeymoon this time of year," the proprietor continued. "Gettin' away from the bustle of the city and all. Had a whole passel come by coach from Calistoga recently, in fact. But it's a bit more quiet this week."

A young woman, her long dark hair a braided twist down her back, arrived to start hauling trunks to the upper floor. She surveyed the group before collecting any of the bags. Her gaze slowed when it passed over Mr. Merrill's face, and he winked in response.

"Would you ladies care for something cool to quench your parched throats?" Mr. Shafer asked. "Our spring out back gives nothin' but the purest water around. Plus, it's icy cold, which might be hard to believe in this here area but it's true."

Barbara scrunched up her nose. "Does the spring water smell like rotten eggs, too?"

"No, no, not at all!" The host sounded offended. "And you'll get used to the smell. Heck, I never notice it at all. So, water? Or would you like something stiffer?"

"Cool water would be very pleasant," said Celia.

"Has Mr. Thaddeus Thompson arrived yet?" Cassandra asked him.

Out of the corner of her eye, Celia noticed Elnora Merrill frown.

"Indeed he has, miss," he answered. "Water for you, too? And you, Mrs. Merrill?"

"Yes," Elnora replied, shifting her attention from Cassandra to Dennis Merrill, who'd wandered off into the shade of a massive pine tree to have a quick smoke.

"I'll tell Gabriella."

Mr. Shafer hoisted their carpetbags, one in each of his thick hands, and led the way. Cassandra lagged behind. Mr. Merrill finished his cigarillo and charged ahead, taking the stairs two at a time. He caught up with the dark-haired young woman. Maybe he'd already moved on from wanting to win Cassandra's affection.

"Don't think you've ever been to the geysers before, else I'd remember," their host said to Celia and Barbara. "Are you here to take in the mineral springs? We've got iron springs, alum springs, tartaric acid."

They passed the ground-floor sleeping rooms on their way to the exterior stairs tucked into the corner of the ell.

"Ammonia, magnesia," he continued his litany. "Even a lemonade spring to clear spots from your skin. A few guests are here to treat rashes and whatnot."

Like Cassandra. "We do intend a visit to the hot mineral springs, but we are also here to enjoy the sight of the geysers," Celia replied. "I've heard so much about them."

"We have bathing huts adjacent to several of the hot springs, if you'd like privacy while partaking, ma'am."

They reached the steps, and Mr. Shafer climbed ahead of them, struggling to keep their baggage from bumping against the railing. A scattering of chairs occupied the veranda, hindering his passage. Celia glanced down at Cassandra, busy studying the grounds. Searching for Mr. Thompson, perhaps. Her anointed suitor.

"You won't be disappointed in the sights we have on offer, I can guarantee that," Mr. Shafer said. "I'll get you set up with some geyser ponies, for when you make the hike."

"Geyser ponies?" asked Barbara.

He chuckled. "That's what we call our walking sticks, miss. Climbing over those rocks can be tough going. Don't want you falling into a steaming spring and burning yourself. Gabriella," he said to the young woman who'd carried up the bags. "Those three rooms are for the Weavers and the Merrills. Mr. Merrill, you're lucky we have spares so that you can enjoy a room to yourself."

"I'll never get this dust off," complained Elnora, scowling at Cassandra, who'd finally joined them. "You need to wash your face, young lady."

"I am not a child any longer, Aunt. I don't need to be told." She swept past her and into the room they'd be sharing.

The proprietor stopped before the last door along the veranda, set down Celia's and Barbara's carpetbags, and produced a key from a pocket in his waistcoat. He unlocked the door and toed it open.

"Here you go, ladies."

Two unpainted bedsteads, a small looking-glass hanging crookedly on the whitewashed wall, two plain cane-seated chairs, and a pine table with a washbasin were the sum total of the furnishings. Thin muslin curtains stirred in the breath of air fighting its way through the open window. It was clean and tidy, though. Something not every hotel in a remote location, or even in the center of a thriving metropolis, could claim.

Barbara went to sit on the farther bed. The ropes holding up the thin mattress sagged beneath her weight.

"The best time to see the springs is first thing in the morning. The steam from the fumaroles rises like a cloud. Mighty impressive, if you ask me," said their host, leaving the key upon the table. "Tours depart not long after sunrise. Although for you folks, we've delayed tomorrow morning's tour for an hour later than usual."

Barbara groaned at the earliness. Even though, for them, the tour was to get underway at a more reasonable time.

"If you find yourselves impatient to see the sights and would like to take a stroll after lunch, the river is always shaded and cool," Mr. Shafer said. "You can find the entrance to the path on the other side of the yard. It's a steep decline down to the water but manageable. Just don't get caught out by sunset. Gets dark down there mighty quick. Wouldn't want anything bad to happen to any of my guests. Wouldn't want that at all."

✂ CHAPTER 4 ⊃

Knuckles tapped on the detectives' office door, and Mullahey stepped into the room. "Have you time, Mr. Greaves?"

Any distraction was better than staring at paperwork while wondering what Celia was doing. If she was being careful.

Nick gestured for the officer to come in. "What do you have for me?"

"Mr. Weaver has recently opened a coal and wood supply company, Mr. Greaves," he said. "It's not gotten off to the best start, however."

"Close that door, Mullahey."

A conversation about one of the members of the city board of supervisors wasn't one he wanted to share with everybody, even if there weren't that many officers out in the main station at this hour. Eagan got touchy about any of his men investigating city officials who might be using their office to profit. Probably, as Nick had often suspected, because the captain hadn't been above using his own position to enrich himself.

"Have you confirmed that he *is* the one who's been awarded next year's contract instead of our Mr. Kott?" Nick asked.

"It took a bit to convince the city clerk to give me the details, but he finally admitted that Mr. Weaver will be providing the city's steam fire engines with wood and coal next year," he replied. "The news will be in the papers soon enough. Can't be saying why the clerk was reluctant to part with the information."

"Because he likes annoying the police, maybe," Nick said. "What have you or Taylor found out about Weaver and Thompson? Are they friends?"

Mullahey grinned, the movement of his mouth making his crooked nose, damaged during a brawl, look even more crooked.

"Indeed they are, Mr. Greaves," he said. "Our Mr. Weaver and Mr. Julius Thompson are regularly seen in each other's company. Both are members of the Odd Fellows, or at least they used to both be members. Before they got too rich to be a part of the organization is what I'm guessing."

Maybe they'd found Masons more to their taste. "No surprise, then, that Thaddeus Thompson and Miss Weaver might be getting engaged."

"Happens all the time, doesn't it? Rich men marrying off their children to each other."

Business arrangements didn't make the best foundation for a marriage, though. He supposed that was what Mrs. Merrill was worried about for her niece.

"Any proof that money changed hands in order for Weaver to get that city contract?" Or was Miss Weaver going to be the payment?

"I've not found the proof, Mr. Greaves. Not yet."

"Keep digging, Mullahey."

In the meantime, Nick needed to send a telegram.

• • •

The common room of the hotel was split into two spaces, one serving as what Mr. Shafer had termed the parlor and overcrowded with various mismatching chairs, a billiard table that appeared new, and an upright piano. The other beyond it held multiple large oak tables where numerous individuals were seated, including the Merrills. Several of the guests had been served and were busy eating, the young woman—Gabriella—moving between tables and pouring out coffee.

Elnora Merrill noticed their arrival and waved them over, indicating the two empty chairs at her end of the table. Cassandra and her father had yet to put in an appearance.

"Mrs. Davies, Miss Walford," said her stepson, politely rising to his feet as they took their seats. "Glad you could join us. Those chairs were looking pretty lonely."

"Denny here has been regaling me with the sights he thinks I need to visit while we're here," Elnora said, her attention never wandering too far from the doorway. "The . . . what are they all again?"

"Places that have the most fanciful names," he replied. "The Devil's Teakettle, the Witch's Cauldron, Pluto's Punchbowl, and the like."

The sort of thing that appealed to tourists.

"Oh, there Hiram is at last," Elnora declared.

He strode up. "Sorry I was delayed, Elnora. Mrs. Davies, Miss Walford. I was caught up in conversation with Mr. Shafer about the future of Sonoma County. A lot of potential here." He fingered the chain fob of his pocket watch as though reminding himself, and any who noticed, that the watch was gold-plated and he was a man of substance. He looked around the room. "Ah, there's Thompson."

Miss Weaver's beau. He'd taken a table in the corner of the dining room and had risen to his feet when Mr. Weaver had arrived.

He came over to their table. Tall, with eyes the color of hazelnuts, he was an earnest-seeming man with a plain but equally earnest face, all sharp angles and watchful eyes. Thaddeus Thompson was also older than Celia had expected Miss Weaver's suitor to be. She guessed he was nearly forty years of age.

He greeted the occupants of the table.

"Mr. Thompson," Mr. Weaver said. "Glad to see you were able to join us."

"I finally had the opportunity to get away from Calistoga, Mr. Weaver. So many investment opportunities there to look into," he said, his gaze scanning the occupants of the table, stalling briefly as it passed over Celia and Barbara. Noticing, of course, that Cassandra was not with them.

Hiram Weaver introduced those at the table who were not already acquainted with the fellow. "This is Mr. Thaddeus Thompson. His father and I are associates. We met through the Odd Fellows."

"Which is perhaps how you also became acquainted with Miss Weaver, Mr. Thompson?" Celia asked. Family members were often invited to the organization's events. "Forgive me if I am overstepping, but I have heard that you two are . . . particular friends."

"That is how they met," Elnora said, her voice brittle. "At that Odd Fellows' picnic last summer you took her to, Hiram."

"Did Miss Weaver not accompany you here?" Mr. Thompson asked.

"No, she's around. Someplace," her father replied.

"I'll tell her you were asking for her," Barbara volunteered, drawing Elnora's scowling attention.

"Thank you," he said and departed, rather than return to his seat.

Over the brim of her coffee cup, Celia considered the others at the table. Hiram Weaver, self-satisfied. Elnora Merrill, staring after Thaddeus Thompson. Dennis Merrill, smirking.

And Mr. Young, whom she'd not noticed until that moment, getting up from his table and trailing after the man.

• • •

"Do you intend to mope all day, Mr. Greaves? Because I'm not sure I want to see you again at dinner if you're going to keep acting like this."

Mrs. Jewett slapped the plate of ham and potatoes onto the table. "Or is your sour mood a temporary malady?"

He grabbed up his fork and skewered the nearest piece of meat. "I'm not moping, Mrs. Jewett."

She stood back and fisted her hips. "You haven't been living under my roof these past few years, Mr. Greaves, without me being able to tell whether or not you're moping."

"Taylor's going to ask Miss Ferguson to marry him while Mrs. Davies and her cousin are away," he said, which caught her unprepared.

"Is *that* what's bothering you?" she asked. "I thought it was because you're missing Mrs. Davies already."

He chewed a mouthful of food to avoid having to answer.

"You can admit that you're missing her, Mr. Greaves."

"I've gone days without seeing her plenty of times in recent months, Mrs. Jewett," he said. "I can survive a week of her being off and climbing around mineral springs." And hopefully not getting killed by a grizzly or getting scalded by a geyser.

Or running into trouble of the human-caused kind.

"You think you can survive that week, Mr. Greaves?" his landlady asked. "That's not what I see from here."

"I can't go chasing after her, Mrs. Jewett. My job doesn't allow for that. Plus, I can't afford the cost," he said, skewering more meat. "I'll just have to sit here and suffer. And you're gonna have to stand there and watch me do it."

"I can hardly wait." She reached for the coffeepot and topped off his cup, even though he hadn't drunk any. "What if I give you some money? It's funds I've been saving for a rainy day, and this day is pretty rainy from my perspective. What do you say to twenty dollars? Should safely get you there and back."

"I won't take your money, Mrs. Jewett."

She set down the coffee and straightened, a look of sheer determination on her face. "We'll see about that."

• • •

After finishing a strained meal, the party went their separate ways. Mr. Merrill departed to hunt for the trout-fishing implements and the bend in the river that Mr. Shafer had declared to be prime fishing territory. Mr. Weaver chose to go for a stroll. And Elnora Merrill announced that she intended to return to her room to search for Cassandra, who'd never joined them. Celia and Barbara decided to take a walk along the treed banks of the stream. The shade was dappled and cool, as promised.

"Can we stop up ahead?" Barbara asked, grabbing an overhanging branch to steady herself on the uneven ground. "There's a rock there we could rest against."

Taking Barbara's elbow, Celia guided her over to a boulder that stood half in, half out of the stream. Rushing water churned around the stone, casting sprays of droplets to sparkle in the air. The smell of the sulfur springs was not as strong as it was near the hotel, a reprieve Celia was grateful for.

Barbara leaned against the rock and bent to untie her boot laces. "I wonder where Cassandra went to," she said, sliding her bare feet into the stream with a sigh.

"Off to have a private rendezvous with Mr. Thompson, perhaps."

"I don't know who'd be more displeased about that—her aunt or Mr. Merrill."

Celia tilted her head back. A wren called in a nearby tree. Steamboat Geyser let out its high-pitched whistle, which echoed off the rocks. "Or both of them equally."

"Excuse me," a man said. "Didn't know you two ladies were here."

The noise of the geyser had muffled the sound of his approach. With a splash, Barbara jerked her feet beneath the concealing skirts of her petticoat.

Celia straightened. It was Mr. Young.

"I didn't mean to disturb you," he said.

Bareheaded, he tugged the strands of brown hair drooping over his forehead in greeting. She found the gesture old-fashioned and disarming. Barbara was not charmed, however, and frowned at her skirt, the hem dragging in the river and getting soaked.

"A nice spot here, isn't it? More pleasant than up by the geysers, that's for sure," he said. "But I didn't mean to disturb you, so I'll leave you two ladies be. Good afternoon."

He continued up the river, a whistled tune floating behind him.

"What is he doing down here?" Barbara asked, staring after him. "He didn't have any fishing gear with him."

"Enjoying the coolness of the river. Just like we are."

"Well, I'm not enjoying it any longer," she said, Mr. Young's unexpected appearance having spoiled their exploration of the river. "Can we go back to the hotel, Cousin? I'm tired."

"Of course."

Barbara practically ran all the way back to the hotel and retreated into their sleeping room, Celia trailing her at a more composed pace.

Rather than disturb her cousin, who'd curled up on her bed to rest, Celia decided to read a novel out on the veranda. The breeze had shifted, blessedly dispersing the smell of the springs. She couldn't concentrate on her book, however, her attention endlessly drifting to the fumaroles steaming in the gorge across the way.

An empty coach arrived in a swirl of dust. Mr. Shafer, baggage in hand, hurried out of the hotel. A cluster of departing passengers followed him and climbed aboard. By the white picket fence, a grizzled fellow who tended the vegetable garden stood talking with the hotel's cook, a Chinese man. His presence surprised Celia, though it ought not. The host's brindle dog loped over to sniff at the hem of the gardener's canvas trousers. Cassandra, her head down, dashed across the yard and headed for the end of the hotel at Celia's immediate right.

How curious.

"You have a telegram, Mrs. Davies." Gabriella hurried along the veranda, the message in her outstretched hand.

"Thank you," Celia said, taking it from her. The young woman eyed the telegram before turning and heading back the way she'd come.

It was from Nicholas and typically succinct.

> Weaver and Thompson Sr friends. Weaver possibly bribing Thompson to get city contract. *Be careful.*
>
> N

Was Elnora aware of the crime—the *possible* crime—her brother-in-law was committing? Perhaps Thaddeus Thompson's character was not what concerned Elnora, but rather the character of his father. Although apples and trees and all that.

Celia folded the telegram and tucked it into her book. Out in the yard, all the passengers had boarded the coach, and Mr. Shafer waved at the driver to go. The clack of billiard balls and laughter rose from the direction of the parlor, momentarily muffled by a fresh blast from

Steamboat Geyser. Dennis Merrill, returning from his fishing expedition and another cigarillo clamped in his mouth, strolled through the archway in the picket fence just as Hiram Weaver stepped into the yard from beneath Celia's spot on the veranda. Dennis Merrill gestured for Mr. Weaver to join him in the shade of a nearby tree. A few rooms down from the one Celia shared with Barbara, a door clicked open. Mrs. Merrill stepped through. She gripped the wood railing of the balustrade as she stared down into the yard, seemingly oblivious to Celia's presence on the veranda.

Should I clear my throat and make myself known?

Mr. Young chose that moment to stride across the yard from the general direction of the outbuildings. He must have found another path back from the river. Elnora recoiled upon spotting him and hurried back inside her room.

Just then, Mr. Weaver looked up at the hotel and noticed Celia. She inclined her head. He returned her nod, said a few words to Mr. Merrill, and strode across the yard, bound for the parlor. Perhaps he wished to join the billiard game in progress.

Dennis Merrill grinned, dropped his cigarillo to the dirt, and crushed it beneath his boot heel. A few feet away, Mr. Shafer's dog had taken to scratching at fleas, his hind leg beating a swift rhythm. The cook called to the animal to come with him to the kitchen. After collecting his fishing gear and leaning it against the nearby fence, Mr. Merrill strolled off in the direction that Cassandra Weaver had gone. Which left the yard empty, save for a twist of dust caught by the wind.

Celia sat back and tapped the edge of her book against her chin. Something was amiss, she could feel it.

By a divine instinct men's minds mistrust ensuing dangers . . .

"Just so, Mr. Shakespeare," she murmured aloud.

• • •

The next morning came far earlier than Celia was prepared for. Somehow, Barbara looked to still be sound asleep. Yawning, Celia climbed out of the lumpy bed and reached for her wrap. She tied it over her cotton chemise, went to the window, and pushed aside the faded yellow muslin curtain to look outside. The sky was the pale purple of the hours between night and morning, the fumaroles on the hill beyond the ravine spewing steam that condensed in wisps in the clear air. Though it was an hour before the delayed tour to the geysers was scheduled, Mrs. Merrill stood near the archway set in the picket fence, the sign tacked to it indicating the path to the geysers. Why was she out there so early? Just then, Mr. Young appeared, strolling over from the direction of the outbuildings, his bright scarlet waistcoat making it easy to note his progress across the yard.

"What are you looking at?" asked Barbara from right behind her.

"You didn't need to get up, Barbara," she said. "We have another hour yet."

"So fortunate for us." Barbara squeezed in next to Celia. "Mrs. Merrill is down there already?"

"Early."

Mrs. Merrill glanced around and proceeded through the gate and onto the path.

"She's going alone?" Barbara asked, alarmed.

"Maybe she is impatient to get her hike underway."

"But it's not safe to walk up there alone, is it?"

"I'd not attempt it." Grizzlies and wild mountain cats aside, Elnora Merrill was risking an injury with no one to help her until the scheduled tour climbed to wherever she might be.

"Well, I'll be surprised if either Mr. Merrill or Mr. Thompson join us this morning," her cousin said. "Not after what took place last night."

Celia stepped back from the window, letting the curtain drop into place. "What do you mean?"

"They had a terrible row while Cassandra and I were playing cards in the parlor after you and I had tea," she said. "One minute they were playing billiards, the next they were shouting at each other. Something about Mr. Thompson being a fraud. That was when Mr. Thompson hit Mr. Merrill." She acknowledged Celia's astonishment with a wag of her eyebrows. "Mr. Shafer had to intervene. It was all very embarrassing."

"A fraud." Celia looked out through the muslin curtain at the yard again. The only person presently outside was the gardener, hiking poles in hand, readying for his additional role as tour guide. "What an interesting accusation."

"The fight upset Cassandra, which was understandable," Barbara said. "She ran off, even though we weren't finished with our game yet. And I was winning."

"I did not realize that Mr. Merrill and Mr. Thompson knew each other well enough to have developed an animosity that might devolve into a shouting match."

"Maybe Mr. Thompson was defending his claim to Cassandra," Barbara proposed, making Cassandra Weaver sound like a vein of gold. "It's not as if Mr. Merrill is hiding his interest in her."

"Indeed."

Barbara covered a yawn with her hand. "Well, after I've had some breakfast, I'm going to the bathing hut to soak my foot. Enjoy the hike. Maybe Mr. Merrill will take you aside next to an alum pool and whisper an explanation of what that argument was about."

"Not likely, Barbara."

After washing up and dressing, they went outside.

"An ominous sight, don't you think, Mrs. Davies?" asked Mr. Weaver, exiting his room at the same time. He nodded at the hill rising above the tree-covered ravine beyond the hotel's grounds.

"Ominous, Mr. Weaver?" she asked.

"The Devil's Cauldron and the Devil's Teapot and all that," he said. "Mighty sinister-sounding."

"I wonder if they will prove to be worthy of their titles."

"I expect they will be fully impressive, Mrs. Davies. They're world-famous, after all." He tucked his thumbs into the pockets of his plaid waistcoat and surveyed the landscape as if personally responsible for the geysers' impressiveness. "I am glad our host decided that, despite the wonders of seeing the geysers at six in the morning, seven's just as good and a whole lot more civilized hour to be wandering around in the wilderness."

"Mrs. Merrill mustn't have recalled the delayed departure, because she was down in the yard at least a half hour ago." Perhaps even longer.

"She was?" He surveyed the yard as if needing to verify her comment.

"Is Cassandra up yet, Mr. Weaver?" Barbara asked.

"If my sister-in-law has already dressed and gone down, I assume my daughter is up as well, Miss Walford," he said. "You'll probably find her in the dining room, having breakfast."

"Thank you. I think I'll go and join her." Barbara made her way along the veranda and down the stairs.

"What of Mr. Merrill, Mr. Weaver? Does he intend to join us?"

Celia asked. "After his altercation with Mr. Thompson last evening, I confess I was questioning if he might desire to return to San Francisco early." Or Mr. Thompson depart for Calistoga.

Mr. Weaver's expression darkened. "I heard about their argument. Bad taste to be brawling like hooligans," he said. "And there's Denny now."

Mr. Merrill, looking none the worse for wear after his fight with Mr. Thompson, was standing in the yard. He'd rolled up his pants legs in preparation for their hike to the geysers, revealing brown leather brogans.

He looked up at them and tipped his hat. "Mornin', Hiram. Mrs. Davies."

"Up already, Denny?" Mr. Weaver called back.

"I've been up a while, just enjoying the view."

He gestured toward the hillside, far more visible from Celia's vantage point than his. The areas not concealed by intervening trees were deserted at the moment, however. She briefly wondered where Elnora was. Perhaps she'd not climbed very far.

Dennis Merrill lit a cigarillo and resumed his regard of the scarred and steaming rocky hillside. What was it he found so interesting? For Celia doubted that Dennis Merrill was someone who might simply be admiring the rough beauty of their surroundings.

Perhaps he was, though, and her dislike of him was unfounded.

His admiration of the scenery was disrupted by Gabriella crossing the yard from the direction of the hotel. More movement caught Celia's eye. It was Barbara, nibbling on a piece of toast and heading for the trail that would take her to the bathing hut. Cassandra was not with her. Mr. Thompson was nowhere to be seen, either. Other guests had begun to gather near the archway, though, their chattering sounding like a flock of excited sparrows in a hedgerow.

"It appears that your cousin will not be joining us," Mr. Weaver said.

"The hike would likely be too difficult for her, so she has chosen to visit one of the bathing huts where she can soak her foot in privacy."

"Ah, yes. I've heard it's deformed."

Celia winced at the coarse, but accurate, description. Mr. Weaver was no longer looking at her and did not observe her reaction.

Mr. Merrill finished smoking and crushed his spent cigarillo under his boot heel. Whoever was responsible for maintaining the cleanliness of the yard was destined to find a number of Dennis Merrill's stubs, at the rate he was discarding them. He strolled off toward the ravine, slowing to acknowledge the other guests, and passed beneath the arch. He disappeared into the shadows of the trees.

"Mr. Merrill is not accompanying us either, it seems," she said.

"My impression of my sister-in-law's stepson is that he's not one to ever do what is expected of him. Drives Elnora mad." He tapped fingertips to the brim of his hat. "I'm going to the dining room. Are you coming down?"

"In a few minutes. I will see you then."

She stepped back into the room. The bodice and skirt she'd chosen were going to be too heavy for the heat. Thankfully, Addie had packed Celia's old clay-colored chambray dress. After changing and putting her hair back in order, she hunted for her cousin's sun parasol. It was not on Barbara's bed, though, or propped in one of the corners.

"Wherever did you toss it, Barbara?" she asked aloud, as though the skewed mirror or the rag rug might provide an answer. Given the small size of the space, the parasol should be easier to locate than was proving to be the case.

She was bent down to search underneath her cousin's bed when the door opened. It wasn't Barbara but Gabriella.

"Oh!" the young woman said. "I am sorry, ma'am. I did not think you were in here."

Celia grabbed the parasol from beneath the bed and straightened. "Were you planning on tidying the room?" Not that she had any cleaning items with her.

"Oh. Yes," she answered. "But I can return later."

Suddenly, a screech rang out across the canyon, sounding through the door Gabriella had left open.

"Ay," she muttered. "That horrible sound."

The screech repeated, spiking Celia's pulse. "That is not a geyser, Gabriella."

Celia dropped the parasol and sprinted from the room and across the veranda. The few guests who'd arrived early for the hike were looking at each other in confusion. One of the men split off from the group and started running toward the sound.

Toward the screams.

Celia descended to the yard. Mr. Merrill appeared off to her left from among a stand of trees.

"What has happened, Mr. Merrill?"

"I don't know."

Celia reached the path and raced down it, sliding on loose stones and gravel. A slash of bright blue on the far side of the ravine caught her eye. It was Cassandra, bent over a dark shape sprawled between boulders partway up the hill. Water vapor rose like a veiling mist at her back.

"Miss Weaver!" Celia cried out as she and Mr. Merrill thundered across the rickety bridge that spanned the stream.

Mr. Merrill climbed the rocky trail more quickly than Celia could manage in her dress. Stones gave way beneath her boots, and she grabbed for the branch of a nearby manzanita to steady herself.

Cassandra turned and peered down at them. "Denny! Mrs. Davies!" She straightened. "Come quickly!"

Mr. Merrill reached her first and crouched by the body—for it was a body, wearing a heavy dark skirt and bodice—crumpled not far from a bubbling mineral pool. He glanced over at Celia, reaching the scene at last. "It's Elnora."

"Yes, Mr. Merrill. I can see that."

She stooped down next to him and peeled back the cuff of Elnora's right sleeve, feeling for a pulse in her wrist and not finding one. The hem of Elnora's skirts were soaked and stained with a yellow residue as if she'd stepped into one of the pools. Or slipped into one. What was left of her shoes and stockings told a more complete story. Her lower limbs had been badly burned.

"Dear God," breathed Mr. Merrill.

The pain of the scalding water would've caused her to jump back. She must have lost her footing and tumbled a short distance down the hillside. She'd come to rest against a boulder, her head twisted awkwardly to one side, a rivulet of blood oozing from beneath her bonnet. Her eyes were still open from the shock; Celia lowered their lids.

"Is she . . . ?" Cassandra asked, afraid to finish her question.

"Yes, Miss Weaver," Celia said. Dennis Merrill got to his feet, wiping his hands together to clear grit from them. Celia accepted his help to regain her feet. "Your aunt is dead."

⌀ CHAPTER 5 ⌀

The commotion had attracted the remainder of the hotel guests. They'd collected in a loose group on the other side of the stream, scattered about among the trees and straining for a view.

"It can't be. It can't be!" Cassandra Weaver sobbed. "She shouldn't have come up here alone. She shouldn't have."

Celia gathered Cassandra in her arms. She was shaking fiercely.

"You know how she is, Cassandra," Mr. Merrill said in a soothing tone. "How she was. Stubborn."

"But her heart," she sniffled into Celia's shoulder.

"She had a problem with her heart?" Celia asked.

"She did," Dennis Merrill answered. "She'd been taking medicine for it and thought she'd be all right to take this trip."

"It's so hot. That's what happened," Cassandra said, pulling free from Celia's grasp. "She was overwhelmed by the heat, became faint, and staggered into one of the mineral pools. It's . . . it's awful, Mrs. Davies."

The fellow who'd bolted up the hill ahead of them crashed through a nearby stand of shrubbery. "I thought I saw somebody else up here, but I couldn't find him." He glanced at Elnora Merrill. "Lord in heaven."

"You thought you saw someone?" Celia asked him.

"Thought I'd noticed a person cutting through the brush over thataway," he said, pointing. "Didn't get a good look, though."

"Did you see this person with my stepmother?" Mr. Merrill asked him. "Did they . . . could they have pushed her?"

"Denny, what are you saying?" Cassandra asked, her bonnet askew and tendrils of her pale hair straggling down her face.

"Mr. Merrill, we cannot assume Elnora's death was anything other than an accident," Celia said.

A cascade of stones drew Celia's attention upward. Standing farther along the hillside was Barbara. One hand pressed to her mouth, she gazed at them, her dark eyes wide and her face ashen.

"Barbara!" Celia shouted. "What are you doing there?"

Mr. Merrill's gaze followed hers. "I admit I'm wondering the same thing, Mrs. Davies."

Gad.

"Mr. Merrill, will you take Cassandra back to the hotel? I will escort my cousin," she said.

"But . . ." Cassandra peeked at her aunt's body. Mr. Merrill had taken off his coat to cover it. "Should we just leave her up here?"

"Others will come to collect her, Miss Weaver," Celia replied. She looked over at the other man. "And might you . . . I do not know your name."

"Fletcher. Obediah Fletcher," he replied, digging a handkerchief from his coat pocket to mop his high forehead, which shimmered with sweat.

"Mr. Fletcher, if you could, please inform Mr. Shafer that the coroner needs to be sent for."

"Should I also tell him to send for the sheriff?" he asked. "In case it wasn't an accident. In case that fellow I saw did have something to do with her fall."

"Mrs. Merrill had a bad heart, Mr. Fletcher," Celia insisted. "She fainted and fell awkwardly. A terrible tragedy."

He did not appear to be listening. "Mighty suspicious. Running off like he did."

"Either way, please inform Mr. Shafer," she replied, doubts beginning to creep in around the edges of her certainty. What if he was right? What if it hadn't been an accident?

Mr. Fletcher dashed for the hotel, risking a twisted ankle as he hurtled down the rocky trail.

Dennis Merrill considered Elnora's prone body. "Did your cousin tell you she planned to climb to where my stepmother was, Mrs. Davies?"

"What do you mean, Denny?" Cassandra asked.

"He is implying that Barbara could be responsible for your aunt's accident, Miss Weaver," Celia replied, glancing toward her cousin, who was slowly making her way over to them.

"That's absurd, Denny."

"Maybe, Cassandra, but if I've had the idea, others will too." He took her elbow. "Come along. You're looking faint yourself. Let's see if we can find some lemonade or cold water for you."

She accompanied him down the hill, pausing once to look back over her shoulder at Celia and her aunt's body.

Barbara finally reached where Celia was standing. "What happened?"

"I wish I could say for certain. Probably an accidental fall." They began the descent of the trail. "What were you doing so far up the hill? I thought you were headed to the bathhouse by one of the lower mineral pools."

"I wanted to prove to myself I could climb to the geysers," she said. "The steam in the bathing hut was too hot, so I decided to try to climb the hill, instead. Since nobody seems to think I could manage it." She cast Celia a reproachful look.

Mr. Fletcher had arrived at the narrow wood bridge crossing the river and scurried across it, shouting for Mr. Shafer as he ran. Two men, overcome by curiosity, decided to scramble up to where Elnora Merrill lay. They passed Celia and Barbara on their way, casting Barbara hostile looks.

"Did you see anyone else on the hill?" Celia asked her cousin as they continued down the path. "Mr. Fletcher claims to have spotted a man running off through the shrubbery."

"You mean it *wasn't* an accident?"

"Mr. Merrill has implied that others might think you had a hand in her death, Barbara," she answered. "You saw how those men looked at you."

She set her jaw. "They suspect me simply because of who I am," she said bitterly. "But if Mr. Fletcher saw a *man*, then nobody can think I'm responsible."

"The worst among them might believe he was confused." Preferring their prejudice to logic.

"Well, it wasn't me. But I don't think I saw anybody else." Her brow furrowed. "I don't know. Maybe I did. I can't think clearly right now."

They made their way to the bridge. "Barbara, was Cassandra in the dining room when you went down for breakfast?"

"No, she wasn't," she replied. "I didn't see her anywhere, so I turned around and left."

"Ah." *Where had you been, Miss Weaver?*

Barbara slowed. "Are you thinking Cassandra might've been responsible for Mrs. Merrill's death?"

"I am only asking a question."

"Because you actually *don't* think she died accidentally, do you?" her cousin asked. "Well, if anyone wanted to hurt Mrs. Merrill, it was her stepson, not Cassandra. You heard their argument."

And do not understand its meaning. His tone, his words, though, had been threatening.

"But Dennis Merrill was down by the river when I came running in response to Cassandra's screams," Celia pointed out.

"That doesn't mean he couldn't have pushed his stepmother into a burning hot mineral pool earlier, though."

"True."

Mr. Shafer and Mr. Weaver clambered down the trail from the hotel yard and thundered across the bridge. Celia pulled her cousin out of their path.

"What in hell happened, Mrs. Davies?" Hiram Weaver shouted.

He cursed again and climbed behind the hotel proprietor. They joined the two men already standing over Elnora's body. One had bent down to peek beneath the coat tossed over her, cringing when he caught sight of her burns.

Mr. Weaver did not volunteer to help lift his sister-in-law's body off the rocks where she'd landed, standing aside to watch the others labor. She was not as light as they'd been anticipating, and their feet slipped on the gravel as they shifted her weight. In the city, no one would dare move a corpse before a proper inspection had been conducted. Miles from the nearest coroner and with the day's heat ahead, they had no other option; Elnora Merrill would, sadly, be decaying soon. After a brief conversation, the men decided to use Mr. Merrill's coat as an improvised stretcher to carry Elnora's body.

"Speak to no one, Barbara," Celia whispered to her cousin. "I don't want to give anyone the opportunity to accuse you, and the best way to ensure that is for both of us to be extremely cautious."

• • •

"You bought a ring for Miss Ferguson yet, Taylor?" Nick asked his assistant, walking alongside him on the sidewalk.

"I, um . . ." He cleared his throat. "Haven't found the perfect one just yet, sir. Mr. Greaves. Sir."

The perfect one. Taylor would want the best for Addie Ferguson.

"Oh, sir. I had a chance to stop by the office of Mr. Weaver's company. Pretty small. Guess I was expecting it'd be nicer," his assistant said, looking for someplace to stash the butt of the cigar he'd finished and settling on a coat pocket. "A fellow there didn't have much to say about Mr. Weaver and Mr. Thompson, other than he'd heard they'd be getting the city contract and Mr. Weaver had given the go-ahead for money to be spent on improvements."

"Confirming what the clerk told Mullahey," Nick said. "We still need more, though. Actual evidence of a bribe, or at least of money changing hands."

"But do you think anybody at Mr. Thompson's bank will help us, sir?" Taylor asked.

"Guess we'll find out."

Thompson's bank was on Montgomery, like so many others were. He and Taylor stepped inside. Nick showed his badge, concealed beneath the flap of his coat, to one of the tellers protected by his counter-to-ceiling iron grill. The fellow spluttered but kept his head; he wouldn't want to alert the customers that a police officer had turned up in the financial institution of their choosing. Nick explained why they were there. The teller strode to the end of the room, stepped through a latched door in the counter, and gestured for them to follow him.

The bank manager was located in an office one floor up from the lobby, a cut-glass window occupying half the door, his name engraved on a brass plate alongside. Two knocks and Nick and Taylor were shown in.

"These officers are here to ask you about the account held by . . ." The teller swallowed, his Adam's apple sliding along his thin neck. "By Mr. Julius Thompson."

The manager waved for the teller to depart and for Nick to take a seat. Taylor opted to stand by the door, notebook at the ready.

"How can I help you?" the man asked.

"We are looking into business dealings between a Mr. Hiram Weaver and Mr. Julius Thompson."

"I do not comprehend how I can assist, Officers."

"Is Mr. Thompson a trustworthy fellow? Decent?"

The man tilted his head, peering at Nick down the length of his long and narrow nose. "He is a city supervisor, Detective."

Which wasn't much of an explanation to Nick's way of thinking. "A true pillar of the community."

"Absolutely," he replied, failing to hear the sarcasm in Nick's voice.

"Do your records show that a surprising sum of money has recently been deposited in Mr. Thompson's account? Say, within the last month?"

The manager scowled. "What are you accusing Mr. Thompson of?"

"I'm not at liberty to explain."

"And I am not at liberty to tell you the details of Mr. Thompson's accounts," he replied. "He is a valuable client, and I do not intend to damage our relationship by gossiping about his banking habits."

"It's not gossip," Nick said. "It's police business."

The manager drew in a lengthy breath, his nose whistling as though it had been damaged by taking too much snuff. Maybe that was what was in the small, ornate silver box sitting on his desk. The fingernails on his right hand were stained, too.

"Until you have a warrant, Detective, I'm under no obligation to divulge any details about Mr. Thompson's bank account," he stated. "Therefore, I will thank the both of you to leave. Now," he added, unless he wasn't clear. Which he was.

Taylor descended the stairs behind Nick. "Well, he didn't help."

"Not until I get a warrant." He wished folks would stop being so insistent on proper procedures being followed and just cooperate for once.

Nick thanked the teller as they strode past him.

"Officers," he hissed, beckoning for them to come over to his station. He glanced around, but the customers who'd been in the bank when Nick and Taylor arrived had left. "What do you want to know about Mr. Thompson's account?"

Nick slid a glance at Taylor, who lifted his eyebrows.

"Has he made any unusual deposits lately?" Nick asked. "Unusually large, that is."

"Not Mr. Thompson personally." He quieted when one of the other tellers walked by, waiting until the man was out of earshot to continue. "I can't provide the details, Officers. I'll just say an acquaintance came in and deposited a healthy sum of money into his account."

"A name would be nice."

"So is my job."

Great.

. . .

All the guests staying at the hotel, or so it seemed, awaited Celia and Barbara. A few clutched cups of coffee, roused from their breakfasts by the entertaining prospect of gawking at a half-Chinese girl found in the vicinity of a woman's dead body. From the dining room came the sound of Cassandra Weaver dissolving into a fresh round of hysterics. Mr. Merrill was not at her side comforting her, because he was climbing the stairs to the first-floor sleeping rooms. Might Mr. Thompson be with her?

Celia pressed a hand to her cousin's back. "Go straight to our room and stay there."

Barbara kept her chin up as Celia urged her forward. The crowd parted to let her pass, her limp pronounced as she headed for the stairs.

The men carrying Elnora's body had scrambled up the path between the hotel and the river, struggling to keep from dropping her corpse. Mr. Weaver noticed Celia and crossed to where she stood while the others took direction from Mr. Shafer as to where to take the body.

"What happened, Mrs. Davies?" he asked, his face flushed from the exertion of climbing the steep path. Or from heightened emotion.

"I do not comprehend why you keep asking me, Mr. Weaver, when I did not see what took place," she replied. "I was in my room at the time."

"Your cousin—"

"Barbara did not see, either, Mr. Weaver, and is not in any way responsible," she insisted. Out of the corner of her eye, she could see that various guests had paused their gossiping and coffee drinking to stare at them.

"I just don't understand. How utterly disastrous."

He turned away and headed for the hotel common room to attend to his daughter.

She overheard Mr. Shafer instructing the men carrying Elnora's body to take it to a shed at the rear of the garden, where an overhanging tree shaded the squat wood building from the worst of the sun's heat.

"Mr. Shafer!" she called out, halting the proprietor before he got too far away. "I need to have a telegram sent." She had to inform Nicholas that Elnora Merrill had died.

"I'll see what I can do once I'm finished here, Mrs. Davies." He gestured toward the men gripping Mr. Merrill's coat, Elnora's body sagging as they tired of carrying her.

"Please. It's urgent."

"All right. I need somebody to go to Santa Rosa!" he shouted, hurrying after the men and Mrs. Merrill. Her arm dangled off the edge of the makeshift stretcher, swinging as they hustled her along.

Celia turned and strode through the horde that refused to disperse.

You're a magnet for trouble, Celia, drawing it to you like a pile of iron shavings. She could hear Nicholas's voice in her head. Chiding, his eyes filling with concern.

Indeed so, Mr. Greaves. Yet again.

"I wonder who else might be coming from Santa Rosa along with the coroner?" asked one of the men in the crowd as Celia walked by him. "The sheriff, I'll bet you anything."

"The sheriff?" his companion asked, not bothering to keep his voice down. "But the lady had a bad heart, I've heard. That's what caused her to fall."

"Oh, we'll see about that, won't we?" the first man drawled.

As Celia threaded her way through the chattering guests, she noticed Hiram Weaver escorting his daughter from the dining room. Not long afterward, Mr. Thompson—*there you are at last*—exited the hotel as well and turned in the other direction. Mr. Weaver and Cassandra climbed the stairs, bound for the large double sleeping room she'd shared with her aunt. He nodded at Mr. Merrill, seated on the veranda, before taking Cassandra inside her room. Mr. Merrill resumed what he'd been doing, namely staring at the hillside opposite the hotel.

Celia climbed the stairs and crossed the veranda, her steps slowing as she neared him. "Know that you have my sympathies on the death of your stepmother, Mr. Merrill. I should have offered them earlier."

"Thank you, Mrs. Davies," he said, peering up at her. Not getting to his feet, as would be gentlemanly to do. "I haven't quite absorbed the shock."

"I expect you have heard that Mr. Shafer is having someone ride to collect the coroner," she said, studying his demeanor. He did not appear distressed by Elnora's death, but then he had been arguing quite angrily with her the other night. "You might also be happy to learn that the sheriff will likely accompany him. At least, that is what those who enjoy betting are gambling."

"All I want, Mrs. Davies, is for my stepmother's death to be appropriately dealt with."

"As do I, Mr. Merrill," she responded. "If your stepmother's death was not accidental or the result of heart failure, however, who do you think may have been responsible? You know my cousin was not."

"I only met you two a couple of days ago, so I *don't* know that, Mrs. Davies," he said. "Besides, you're the lady detective."

That, again.

"Where were you all morning, Mr. Merrill?" she asked. "You had arisen early. I noticed you out in the yard before you wandered off. Perhaps you observed a suspicious individual near the river or the trail." *Or you concluded your argument with Elnora. Permanently.*

"Shouldn't interrogations wait for the coroner?"

Indeed. "Why did she make this journey, Mr. Merrill? A woman with a weak heart."

"Elnora would never have permitted Cassandra to travel here without her personal supervision."

"What was it that Elnora was so keen to supervise?"

He peered at her. "She was afraid Cassandra had plans to elope," he said flatly.

The answer was not what she'd expected, but it did explain much. "Mr. Thompson."

He smiled. "Very good, Mrs. Davies."

"Your stepmother informed me of their relationship, Mr. Merrill," she said. "No 'detecting' required."

"She didn't approve."

"Was Mrs. Merrill encouraging you to pursue Cassandra for yourself?"

"I don't think I need to answer that," he replied. "And I didn't require much encouragement. Cassandra is sweet and pretty."

And the daughter of a rich man, as Barbara had noted.

Shouts erupted in the yard. One of the guests was running from the direction of the stables. He skittered to a stop in front of the hotel. "My horse is gone! Somebody's stolen my horse!"

Dennis Merrill, deciding this was worth standing for, got to his feet. "Here's a turn, Mrs. Davies."

"My horse is gone!" the man shouted again.

"I saw him," a woman called from beneath where Celia and Dennis Merrill stood on the veranda. "I saw him ride away."

Celia leaned over the banister, attempting to locate her. If Mr. Merrill wished to cause trouble, this would have been an excellent opportunity to push her over the railing, but he made no such attempt. Probably because he was likewise leaning out to see.

"Who?" he asked the woman. "Who rode away?"

She hopped down from the slightly elevated ground floor walkway and moved into view. She was one of the guests; Celia recognized her from supper last evening.

"Mr. Young," she announced. "Mr. Young took your horse. I saw him!"

Mr. Shafer, the shouts having summoned him from his supervision of the men transporting Mrs. Merrill's body, came running. "What's going on?"

The victim of the horse theft and the female witness crowded around him, excitedly relaying their stories.

"Well, now." Mr. Merrill straightened and looked over at Celia, a wry smile teasing his mouth. "What do you make of that, Mrs. Davies?"

"It would be logical to conclude that Mr. Young may be guilty of causing your stepmother's unfortunate death," she said. "We cannot, however, be absolutely certain of the motive behind his rapid departure."

He lifted an eyebrow. "We can't?"

A fellow clattered down the front steps of the hotel and hurried into the yard. "His things are gone. I checked," he declared, pointing in the direction of Mr. Young's room on the ground floor. "Everything. Cleared out."

"Well, well," Mr. Merrill said, sounding amused by the entire situation. He searched his pockets for a cigarillo and wandered off.

Celia descended to the main level of the hotel and followed the others eager to confirm that Mr. Young had vacated the premises. She slipped into his room behind them. Aside from a solitary shirt left hanging on a hook, he had removed all his belongings and taken them with him. When had he found the time after Elnora's body had been discovered? Maybe he'd previously packed, intending to depart that morning, hastily collecting his things and another guest's horse.

Actions that make you appear all the more suspicious, Mr. Young.

Satisfied, the majority of the guests took themselves off to the parlor, eager to gossip about how suspicious they'd been of Mr. Young all along, not liking his looks. Or his voice. Or his bum arm, which was probably not a war wound, one of the gentlemen guests suggested. The only ones deciding to not join them were those most affected by Elnora Merrill's death—the Weavers, Mr. Thompson, Mr. Merrill, and Celia and Barbara.

After composing her telegram and handing it to the rider bound for Santa Rosa, Celia requested that a tray of food be sent to her sleeping room and went up to join Barbara.

"Mr. Young has departed with another guest's horse," she said to her cousin, slouched at the table in front of the window.

"I heard," Barbara said. "Does that mean I'm no longer suspected in Mrs. Merrill's death?"

"Likely so."

"Well, thank goodness for that."

The food and coffee arrived. Celia had no appetite, despite not having eaten that morning. So she joined her cousin at the table and stared out the window. What might Mr. Young's motive have been? He'd met Elnora in Healdsburg only two days ago, so far as Celia knew, which hardly seemed enough time to cultivate a homicidal grudge.

Barbara finished a piece of toast that had accompanied the cold ham and colder potatoes and got to her feet. "I'm going to lie down. I'm tired."

"While you're resting, I believe I shall take a brief walk outside," she said. "You don't need me in here, trying to sort through my thoughts and muttering to myself about what happened."

Barbara dropped onto the bed. "So you're instead going to walk around and mutter? Or are you going to go collect some clues?"

"Why might I seek to collect clues, when it appears certain Mr. Young is responsible?"

"Because you always like to collect clues, Cousin," she replied. "Even when the case looks to be cut-and-dried."

"It is a 'case' now, Barbara?"

The expression on her cousin's face could only be described as a smirk. "Somebody died unexpectedly and rather suspiciously. Of course it's a case."

✄ CHAPTER 6 ☜

The yard was unoccupied, as Celia had hoped. She crossed the bridge and began the climb to where Mrs. Merrill had suffered her fatal injuries. It would be at least five or six hours before the coroner arrived. Plenty of time to collect clues—*yes, Barbara*—should there be any to discover.

The heat of the early afternoon sun radiated off the surrounding rocks, and the rotting stink of sulfur grew stronger the higher Celia hiked. She scanned the ground as she climbed, hoping for . . . what? Evidence that an individual had pushed Elnora into a mineral pool and dropped an incriminating item in their rush to escape?

She took another step, her boots sliding on a patch of loose stones.

"Blast!" she muttered. *I shall be just as unfortunate as Elnora Merrill if I am not more careful.*

She steadied herself and resumed climbing, arriving at the spot where Elnora had been found. Springs bubbled in all directions, fumes rising from the hottest ones and leaving the surrounding rocks coated with deposits. Cakes of minerals had formed crusts over some of the pools, appearing deceivingly solid enough to walk upon. Hissing filled the air, the noise occasionally punctuated by the piercing whistle of Steamboat Geyser.

"What an ungodly place." At so close a distance, the sinister names given to the various springs and pools seemed accurately descriptive and less amusingly fanciful.

A yellow-orange crust skimmed the surface of a nearby pool. The overtopping layer was cracked as though someone has stepped on it. Elnora's clothing had been stained yellow. Perhaps this was the pool she'd plunged into. It certainly steamed hot enough to have caused the horrible burns on her legs.

A few feet ahead, Celia noticed a smear of yellow on the ground. Someone other than Elnora had tracked the mineral residue to that spot; her body had been found down the hill from the pool, not up from it. But had that mark been caused today or at an earlier time? She'd have to ask Mr. Shafer if any of his guests had recently reported damaging their shoes or being burned. But how quickly might a mineral pool's crust form again?

"Mrs. Davies."

The voice startled her, and she slipped again. The man behind the voice grabbed her. He was strong, his intervention rescuing her from a perilous fall.

"Be careful, there, ma'am," said Mr. Thompson.

"Thank you, Mr. Thompson," she replied, her heart pounding. "I did not hear you approach."

"All that hissing and squealing of the steam."

"Of course." She shot a glance at his shoes. No incriminating yellow, but by now he would've had time to change into another pair, if he'd brought more than one.

"What are you doing up here?" he asked.

"Letting my curiosity overwhelm me, Mr. Thompson," she said, accepting the offer of his arm as he supported her descent down the trail. Her examination of the scene of Elnora's death was concluded, it seemed. "I confess I find it shocking that Mr. Young could be responsible for Mrs. Merrill's fatal fall."

"I hope the sheriff locates him and justice is served," he said. "I only wish I'd been anywhere nearby when Mrs. Merrill died so tragically. I might have prevented Mr. Young from killing her."

"I cannot begin to fathom why a stranger might have wished to harm her, Mr. Thompson. The thought truly bothers me."

"I don't know the man, never even heard of him before this morning, and have no idea why he would've done this to Mrs. Merrill."

"The mysteries of people's actions, I suppose," she said. "If it wasn't him, can you think of anyone else who might have wanted to harm Mrs. Merrill?"

She snuck a sideways glance at him. The muscles along his jaw had tightened.

"Why wouldn't it have been him?" he asked. "He ran off. He has to be guilty. I expect that the coroner's jury will name him as the suspect."

"No doubt they will. How is Cassandra faring, by the way? The shock of finding her aunt's body was very distressing." Had her balmorals been yellow-stained? Celia could not remember.

"I presume you're asking me about Miss Weaver because you've heard that we are hoping to get married."

Planning to elope, according to Dennis Merrill. An elopement that would no longer occur, at least not at present, given that Elnora had so tragically died and the Weavers would be in mourning. An outcome Mr.

Merrill might profit from. Which was an intriguing thought.

"I confess that I've been listening to talk," she said, stepping around a branch that had broken off a trailside shrub. "Your family must be pleased by the prospect. Miss Weaver is a lovely young woman."

"My father and Mr. Weaver have been friends for a long time."

More than friends, if the information contained in Nicholas's telegram was accurate. Which she assumed it was.

"But now for this tragedy to have occurred," she said. "Any engagement will have to be delayed, I suppose."

"What else would we do, Mrs. Davies?"

"Only what is proper, I'm certain," she replied. "Although—I know this is bold of me to say—Mr. Merrill might be pleased by the delay."

He dropped his arm to his side, breaking her hold on it and forcing her to stop. "What do you mean by that?"

"Only that I gather he is interested in securing Miss Weaver's affections himself." *May the best man win,* after all.

"Miss Weaver isn't interested in him, so he's not going to secure her affections, no matter how hard he tries."

They neared the bottom of the ravine. Across the way, the Geyser Hotel came into view on its plateau above the riverbed. The cook shuffled out from behind the hotel to dump a large pot of water onto the ground. A commonplace scene that suggested normality, though the reality was far different.

"Then the argument you had with him last evening had nothing to do with his interest in Miss Weaver?" Celia asked.

"No, Mrs. Davies. It didn't," he said. "It was only a misunderstanding. Dennis Merrill has a hot temper and became angry over our billiard game."

"He called you a fraud. Why?"

His eyes, so notably intense, stared at her like a hawk noticing prey. "You ask a lot of questions, Mrs. Davies," he said. "And I don't understand what a rude comment from a snake like Dennis Merrill has to do with anything."

"My apologies, Mr. Thompson. I have overstepped with my inquisitiveness."

"I trust you can make it the rest of the way back on your own," he said curtly. "I need to see how Cassandra is doing."

He marched off, his heavy steps making the bridge shake beneath him.

"So, what next, Celia?" she muttered to herself.

The cook had returned to his kitchen, and Mr. Thompson climbed the short flight of steps to the main hotel entrance and went inside. A small collection of guests chattered as they took picnic baskets to some leafy glade nearby. Once they'd disappeared down the trail, a strange quiet fell over the grounds. Quiet enough that Celia could hear the padding of Mr. Shafer's brindle dog as he crossed the yard, bound for the shade of the trees near the rear garden. Perceive the sound of a warbler trilling from the shelter of one of the pine trees. The remaining guests must either be dozing in their rooms or still lingering in the parlor, likely partaking of refreshing lemonade and titillating gossip in equal measure.

Leaving the hotel grounds absent any onlookers who might observe her clandestine appointment with a dead body stored in a shed.

• • •

"This just came for you, Mr. Greaves." One of the officers stepped into the office, the light yellow envelope of a telegram pinched between his fingers.

Nick took it from him. He tore open the envelope and pulled out the telegram. It didn't say much. What it did say was maddening enough.

> Mrs. Merrill is dead. Suspicious?
> *C.*

"Damn it, Celia!"

Taylor picked that instant to walk into the office, his brows climbing up his forehead as high as was possible. "Sir?"

"I knew this would happen." He threw the telegram onto his desk.

"What's happened, Mr. Greaves? Is Mrs. Davies okay? What about Miss Barbara?"

"You don't have to look so alarmed, Taylor. They're both fine." *I think.* "It's Mrs. Merrill. She's dead and Celia decided to add a comment that she thinks the woman's death is suspicious." *Great.*

"It can't have anything to do with Mr. Kott's complaint against Mr. Weaver, can it?" his assistant asked, his eyebrows not yet returning to their normal position on his face. "Although, what if Mrs. Merrill had found out about Mr. Weaver's shady business dealings, sir? She lives with him and his daughter, doesn't she? What if he didn't like her knowing?"

"And now Celia is up there, with Weaver, poking around and likely getting into trouble." He grabbed his Colt and holster out of the drawer where he stored them. "I need to get to the geysers and stop her from getting herself killed."

"Do you think you'll be able to make the afternoon steamer to Suscol, sir?"

"I'm going to try, Taylor," he said, securing his holster on his belt.

"What should I tell the captain?"

"That I've suddenly taken ill. Sicker than you've ever seen me."

"I've never seen you sick, Mr. Greaves."

Nick slapped his hat onto his head and charged out of the office. "Then tell Eagan anything you can think of that he might believe."

Taylor hurried after him. "He'll sack you for sure if he finds out you've left without his permission, Mr. Greaves."

"At the moment, I don't much care."

"Do you want me to go with you, sir?"

Nick stopped by the steps leading up and out of the station and into the alley. "Eagan will sack us both if you did that, Taylor, and you can't afford to lose your job now," he said. "Plus, Addie Ferguson is going to need you, because she'll definitely become upset when she finds out that Mrs. Merrill has died, possibly suspiciously, and Celia's up there."

Taylor's face puckered, conflicted over who he wanted to protect more—his boss or his soon-to-be fiancée. He sensibly chose the latter. "If you're sure you won't need me, Mr. Greaves."

"As sure as I can be, Taylor," he said. "I only hope I can get there fast enough to prevent something else happening."

"Mrs. Davies will be all right. She always is, sir," Taylor replied, trying to reassure him. "She's lucky like that."

"Well, here's to her luck not running out."

• • •

Celia's sojourn across the yard, done with her pulse pounding in her head, was accomplished without notice. She was not as fortunate when she arrived at the shed. The moment she reached for the latch, the door swung open. The Chinese cook stood on the other side, his eyes wide.

Gad.

"You want something, ma'am?" he asked.

I want for my heart to stop attempting to leap out of my chest. "Can I trust you?" she whispered.

Whatever thoughts went through his mind, he carefully concealed. "What do you want me to do?"

"I would like to examine Mrs. Merrill's body. In private." She nodded at the shadowed depths of the shed at his back. "Without interruption by any of the guests or by your employer. I will only require a few minutes. Can you help me do that?"

He narrowed his gaze. "The girl with you . . . some think she killed her. Even though Mr. Young leave."

"What do you believe?"

In response, he stepped out of her way.

Celia hurried inside the building. "Before you go, I have a question for you," she said before he walked off.

"Yes?"

"Have any hotel guests recently ruined their shoes or burned themselves in one of the hot mineral pools?" The cook should know the answer; the supplies needed to tend the wound—a linseed oil and lime water liniment for less severe burns, a fomentation of heavy linen soaked with boiling water and turpentine for worse—would likely be stored among the kitchen goods.

He shook his head. "No," he added. "Not for a long time."

Suggesting that the break in the yellow mineral pools crust was recent. Likely caused by Elnora, along with an additional individual who'd also gotten yellow mineral residue on their shoes. Was that individual responsible for Elnora Merrill's death, though? Or were they merely a witness unwilling to come forward with what they'd seen?

She thanked the cook, and he shut the door, leaving her alone with the shadows and the body of a dead woman.

Slivers of sunlight worked their way through chinks in the wood plank walls and a gap in the shutters covering one dingy window. The space had already begun to take on the tang of death. Or maybe it was her imagination. Elnora had not been dead long enough to smell.

Celia waited until her eyes adjusted to the dimness before moving. Barrels and gardening implements were stacked along one wall, buckets and wheelbarrows elsewhere. A tiny four-legged creature skittered among the items unseen. And upon a moldering pile of hay rested Elnora's body, her stout figure covered by a brown wool horse blanket. Celia wondered what had happened with Mr. Merrill's coat, for it was gone. Perhaps someone had taken it to Gabriella to clean before returning the coat to him, whether he might want it back or not.

Celia hurried about her task. She lifted the edge of the blanket where it covered Mrs. Merrill's legs and feet.

She squinted at the woman's shoes. "Bloody . . . what I would not do for a lamp right now."

There were the stains she'd previously noticed, along with the damage to her dress, the hem eaten away by the acidic nature of the mineral pool she'd plunged into. Her stockings had sloughed off, along with some of the skin on her lower limbs. A horrid injury to endure. If her heart *had* been weak, the pain could have caused a fatal attack.

A sudden fit of coughing pulled her up short. But whoever strolled by the shed didn't open its door, and the sound of coughing faded.

She considered Elnora's body. Why had she gone up the trail an hour before the tour—the *delayed* tour—was scheduled?

Celia rolled the blanket up and out of the way. There was no other visible damage on her body. Although . . . She leaned down to examine Elnora's right wrist where it protruded from the cuff of her sleeve. The first signs of bruising were evident, as though someone had gripped it not long before she'd died. Evidence of a struggle? Or an attempt to rescue Elnora from her fall, an attempt that had failed?

She stepped back, scanning Elnora one last time, and noticed a bulge in one of the pockets sewn into the seam of her skirt. Celia reached inside and pulled out a linen handkerchief and a scrap of heavy paper, shoved deep inside.

Celia held the paper up to a shaft of light leaking through the nearest gap between boards, particles of dust floating on the beam. It was a menu card from the hotel, torn in half, with writing upon the back.

Fifty bucks and I stay quiet.

But—*blast it all*—the note was frustratingly unsigned. Not even an initial to offer a clue to the writer's identity.

Stuffing the note into her own pocket, Celia searched for the fifty dollars and came up empty-handed. Either Elnora had paid the individual or she'd not had the funds to give to them. It was a substantial sum of money, and Celia doubted that Mrs. Merrill would have had the cash on her person. Not on a trip to the geysers where Mr. Weaver was paying her expenses.

"Mrs. Davies, what are you doing in here?"

Celia's pulse jumped. Yet another person had managed to creep up on her and catch her unawares.

She hastily dropped the blanket over Elnora's legs. Why had the cook not stopped Miss Weaver? "I am visiting your aunt, Cassandra."

"But why were you looking at her legs?" she asked, coming to Celia's side.

Think quickly, Celia. "I was wondering if the heat had indeed overwhelmed her and she misstepped upon the rocky path, causing her to break her ankle. Such an injury would've kept her from stopping her fall."

Cassandra stared down at her aunt's legs, covered by the horse blanket. "Is one broken?"

"No."

"She still could have fainted and fallen, though. Right, Mrs. Davies? I mean . . . it had to have been an accident. Mr. Young wouldn't have a reason to push her. Despite him running off and all," she stated. "My aunt's death was an accident, nothing more. She grew faint and fell in the worst spot possible. Nobody would have wanted to kill her. Nobody!" she insisted, as though desperate to protect Mr. Young, a man she'd only met the other day.

"Cassandra, if you have any information that can help, please tell me. You can trust me. You know you can."

"There's no need for me to help, Mrs. Davies. It was an accident."

"Do you *truly* believe that?" Celia asked, watching the young woman's reaction.

"Yes, I do," she said firmly.

Outside, a woman started shouting, interrupting them. "I do not know where he went! I do not!"

Celia shot a look at Cassandra and rushed over to the shed's door. She eased it open and peered out through the gap. Gabriella was standing at the bottom of the hotel's steps, surrounded by a crowd.

"But I saw you," a fellow, one of the guests, shouted back at her. "This morning. Coming out of his room, and right early. She's in cahoots with Young, all right."

"What's this about, Gabriella?" asked Mr. Shafer, above her on the porch. "What were you doing in the room of one of our male guests?"

"In the room of a man who's a murderer!" another guest clarified. On the off chance others had not already made the correction in their own heads.

A few women expressed their disgust at discovering a woman of easy virtue in their midst.

"Don't let her give him an alibi," another person shouted. "They're both crooked."

"Maybe it really was an accident, Mrs. Davies," Cassandra, at her side, whispered. "Just like I said. If Mr. Young was . . . otherwise occupied."

Had he been occupied? He was out in the yard when Elnora was making her way to the trailhead. Unless he'd returned to his room for an interlude with Gabriella without Celia having noticed.

"We may as well join the others, Miss Weaver. We cannot stand here forever."

They left the shed. Mr. Merrill, smoking one of his cigarillos, noticed them and cocked an eyebrow.

"Maybe it *was* an accident that caused Mrs. Merrill's death. If Mr. Young was, um, busy," Mr. Shafer said, his brain coming to the same conclusion Cassandra had. Finding that it liked the chance that his hotel would not become infamous for a murder. "Maybe so."

Cassandra took Celia's hand; her skin was cold and clammy.

"But if Young is innocent, Mr. Shafer, why'd he skedaddle like he did?" a fellow asked. "Huh? Why'd he do that? She's got to know where he's gone to."

"I do not know!" Gabriella insisted, her eyes scanning the hostile crowd surrounding her. She was trapped like a prisoner in an ancient Roman coliseum. All that was lacking was a lion to tear her to shreds. "But I do not think he killed that woman. I don't."

"Because you were together?" Shafer asked.

"Naw, she's lyin'," the fellow who'd begun all the shouting said. "I saw Young myself, running across the bridge like a rabid beast was snapping at his heels. *Before* the screaming started. Her and Young mighta been together all night, but they weren't when that poor woman died."

Before Cassandra had started screaming? The fellow's observation meant that the person Mr. Fletcher thought he'd noticed on the hillside could *not* have been Mr. Young. The timing did not work. But who had it been?

"What *were* you doing in Mr. Young's room, Gabriella?" Mr. Shafer asked, tension pitching his voice higher. "Not to clean it. You weren't supposed to be in any of our guests' rooms until after breakfast."

Except she'd also crept into Celia and Barbara's room before that time.

Gabriella wrapped her arms around her waist. "I am sorry, Mr. Shafer."

A collective outraged gasp swept over the crowd like a wind rustling a stand of trees.

"Mr. Shafer, what sort of an establishment are you running here?" one of the offended ladies asked him.

He scowled. "Gabriella, I will deal with you later. Don't expect to keep your position here."

"I am sorry," she repeated, burst into tears, and scurried off.

Just then, Mr. Weaver strode across the yard.

"I don't know what we're hoping to achieve here, but it seems to me it's best for us to wait for the coroner to arrive to settle the matter of Mr. Young," he said to the crowd, his confident tone quieting the murmurs. "In the meantime, we should all return to whatever it was we were doing."

"A wise recommendation, Mr. Weaver," Mr. Shafer said.

"Cassandra, you should get to your room and rest. Now," her father ordered.

Celia released her hand, and she went to join him. Each step Cassandra took revealing a narrow smear of yellow on the heel of her left boot.

CHAPTER 7

"I've barely got time to catch the three o'clock steamer to Suscol," Nick said, stuffing clothing into a carpetbag Mrs. Jewett had located in her attic. The bag was dusty and moth-eaten, for which she'd profusely apologized, but he wasn't planning a tour of the great sights of Europe, so he didn't much care. "From there, I'll hire a horse to take me to the geysers."

"Overnight? In the pitch black?"

"Not much choice, Mrs. Jewett."

"There's always a choice, Mr. Greaves."

"Are you suggesting that I shouldn't try to get to the geysers as soon as possible?" he asked, looking over from his packing. "When Mrs. Davies could be in danger?"

"All right, I don't want that. And here, Mr. Greaves. You've packed three socks and forgotten the fourth." His landlady pushed his hands aside. "Let me do this." She tossed everything out onto his bed and started over, carefully folding each item of clothing. Not that there were a whole lot of items. "And what are you going to say to her?"

"To who?" he asked, hunting through his chest of drawers for a clean handkerchief.

"You know who. What are you going to say to her?"

He glanced over. "That I'm worried for her safety? Hers and Barbara's?" Handkerchief located, he brought it over for her to pack. "This trip is not an opportunity to ask her to marry me."

"I don't see why not," she said.

"There's no hurry."

She fisted her hips. "I do not know what I'm going to do with you, Mr. Greaves."

He closed the carpetbag. "Feed Riley while I'm gone, that's what you can do." His dog lay faithfully at the foot of the bed, his gaze mournful. "I shouldn't be long, boy. Friday, Saturday at the very latest." Riley thumped his tail hopefully.

"Wait, Mr. Greaves. Here. Take this." Mrs. Jewett reached into the pocket of her skirt and pulled out a small leather purse. It clinked with coins. "It's the money I offered for your trip, because I expect you haven't taken the time to stop at the bank."

"I've got what I need."

"Take the money anyway." She held out the bag. "I'll stand here with my hand extended until you do."

He sighed. "Mrs. Jewett, you can be just as stubborn—"

"As Mrs. Davies?"

Yes.

He grabbed the coin purse. "I'll be back soon. Take care of Riley."

• • •

"Did you hear the uproar, Barbara?" asked Celia, gently closing the door to their room behind her.

Her cousin had been seated at the little table, trying to read. "It was practically impossible not to," she said. "Was Gabriella trying to give Mr. Young an alibi?"

"I cannot explain what she intended," Celia replied. "And we cannot be sure he was actually with Gabriella when Elnora died. I noticed him out in the yard before you arose this morning."

Barbara set aside her book. "He *is* guilty. Despite Gabriella claiming he didn't kill Mrs. Merrill."

"I am suspicious of her, Barbara. She came in here right before Cassandra began to scream. Pretending she needed to clean, although it was too early for a round of tidying, according to Mr. Shafer," she said. "What was she up to?"

"Well, whatever she was doing, she must have expected the room to be empty," Barbara said. "Because we were supposed to be assembled to hike to the geysers."

"You're right." Celia went to take a seat on the edge of her bed. "I did go to where Mrs. Merrill died to search for clues, Barbara."

"And?"

"I noticed that someone had stepped into one of the mineral pools," she answered. "It is a type that forms a crust, which had been broken, much like how the skim of ice on a puddle cracks when trod upon. Mrs. Merrill has stains on her shoes and the edge of her skirt. Yellowish-gold stains that match the color of the pool crust."

"She stepped in it," Barbara said. "And it burned her."

"Based on a separate set of marks on the ground, Elnora Merrill was not the only one who'd stepped in that pool, or at least very close to it."

"It had to have been Mr. Young, because it wasn't me. I was careful when I was hiking up there."

"Unfortunately, it is too late to learn if his shoes were damaged. I can, however, state that Mr. Thompson's shoes are in fine shape. Quite interestingly, he was on the trail when I was, giving me the opportunity to examine them. Clean," she said. "He had a vague excuse for his argument with Mr. Merrill, by the way. A disagreement over Mr. Thompson's billiard skills. He also refused to explain what Mr. Merrill meant when he called him a fraud. Mr. Thompson clearly despises him, though."

"You know, Mr. Young didn't look like somebody who'd harm a stranger," Barbara said. "Not to me."

And not to Gabriella either, apparently. "'False face must hide what the false heart doth know.'"

"I recognize that quote. It's from *Macbeth*."

"It is." Celia leaned forward. "But perhaps he—or another individual here at the hotel—is not so harmless. I found a note in the pocket of Mrs. Merrill's skirt. A request for fifty dollars in exchange for silence."

"A blackmailer."

"The note was not signed, so we cannot readily identify the author. However, it must be one of the guests," she said. "The message was written on the back of one of our hotel's menu cards."

Barbara's eyes widened. "I certainly *hope* Mr. Young is the author, Cousin, because I don't want it to be somebody else. Somebody who's still at the hotel and could be dangerous."

Worse, perhaps, than wild animals.

Celia considered her cousin. "There is one other individual we must consider in the question of who may have caused the break in the surface of the mineral pool." An individual perhaps presenting her own false face.

"Cassandra was up there. She found her aunt."

"Yes," Celia said. "And the left heel of her boot bears a telltale streak of yellow."

"She must have stepped on the crust around the edge of the pool in her panic," her cousin said. "She's lucky she didn't fall in too."

"It is a good ten or fifteen feet between that pool and where Elnora's body was found, Barbara," Celia explained. "No amount of panicked dancing about should have resulted in Cassandra stepping on a skim of yellow mineral deposits."

"There's an innocent reason for what you found. A reason that has nothing to do with her aunt's death," Barbara countered. "Maybe Cassandra had gone there at some other time but doesn't want anybody to know. Probably because she was with Mr. Thompson."

"That is a possibility, Barbara."

Her cousin peered at her. "Only a possibility? You want me to think that Cassandra is responsible, don't you?"

"I noticed a bruise on Elnora's wrist as though someone had squeezed it hard enough to cause one," Celia told her. "Perhaps she and Cassandra had been arguing about Mr. Thompson. Cassandra grabbed her aunt's wrist, Elnora lost her footing and fell. A tragic accident."

"Then it was an accident, and she shouldn't be worried about being accused of something . . . something terrible."

"Except she has not admitted to that being the sequence of events." Why not? Possibly because those had *not* been the sequence of events.

"Promise me you will be thorough," her cousin begged. "Promise that you won't share the information about Cassandra's boot with the coroner until you are positive about what that stain means."

Withholding evidence was a crime. But was she withholding evidence if she had no idea what the yellow streak on Cassandra's heel actually meant?

"The coroner and his jury will ultimately decide who should be considered the correct suspect, Barbara," she said. "If Mrs. Merrill's death is ruled a homicide and not an accident, that is."

She frowned. "Hopefully they don't decide on the wrong one."

• • •

By the time Nick disembarked the steamer in Suscol, news had reached the town that there'd been a "terrible happening" up at the geysers. He stopped for a quick supper in a saloon and heard the gossip, ricocheting fast as a shot. A woman had drowned. A woman had burned to death in one of the steam vents. A woman had fallen from one of the cliffs and broken her neck. There'd been an argument and a man had been shot. Nick could've told the saloonkeeper, who'd shared that particular version of the story, that he was definitely wrong.

"Can I rent a horse around here?" Nick asked the fellow instead of correcting him.

The saloonkeeper eyed him from his spot on the other side of the long walnut bar. "Sure. Where you headed to?"

Nick supposed his destination somehow made a difference. "Up to the geysers."

The saloonkeeper had been aiming to grab a fresh bottle of whiskey, but he paused mid-reach. "What's your business up there?"

"Oh, maybe I'm just curious about that terrible happening," he said. "Like to see for myself what went on."

"What you wanna do that for?"

"Guess I'm just nosy," he said. "The horse?"

"It'd be faster to take the train. You've got . . ." He shot a look at the watch tucked into his vest pocket; there weren't any clocks in the saloon. "You've got about fifteen minutes to catch it. Hire a horse in St. Helena after the train pulls in. Or take the stage that regularly leaves for the geysers from there or Calistoga."

Nick dropped the coins he owed for his meal onto the bar. "I'll do that."

He turned and walked out, eyes watching and whispers trailing after. Out on the street, the shadows were lengthening across the gravel road as the sun lowered in the sky. One of the shadows was man-shaped and not his; he'd been followed.

"Can I help you?" he asked the fellow, a grizzled old man who stooped like he'd once been a miner. A hazard of too much time spent bending over gold pans.

"You need to be careful, mister."

"Is it dangerous up at the geysers? Is that what you're talking about?" he asked. "I've never read in the San Francisco papers about any problems."

"A woman died, didn't she?"

"Her death could've been an accident, for all any of us know."

"That ain't the way things sound, based on what one of Colonel Foss's riders, who lives up in Calistoga, had to say to a fella who drives his delivery wagon into Napa every afternoon." He shook his head mournfully. "Nope. Weren't no accident at all."

"I guess I'll find out when I get there." The train whistle screeched at the station, warning passengers to hurry and get on board. "I need to buy tickets and catch my train."

"Just be careful you don't run into the fellow who done it."

"What fellow?"

"The one who done it," he repeated, exasperated. "Heard he hightailed it away from the Geyser Hotel like the devil himself was after him. Think I saw him in town. A stranger lookin' twitchety. Yep."

"Here? Already?"

"Might've gotten here, if he'd ridden hard enough," he said. "Either way, if I was you, I'd be careful. There's a dangerous man on the loose out there. Yep. Dangerous."

• • •

"Have you heard anything from Mrs. Davies, Addie?" Owen picked at the bowl of stew she'd handed him. It wasn't like him to not wolf down her cooking. But ever since he'd gone to the station to ask if Mr. Taylor wanted more help searching for an engagement ring and heard that Mr. Greaves had gone up to the geysers in a hurry that afternoon, Owen's stomach had been in knots.

Addie, her forehead creasing with that funny wrinkle it got when she was worried, pulled out a chair at the dining room table and sat down across from him. It was downright strange for the two of them to be seated at the table without Miss Barbara or Mrs. Davies there, too. Felt wrong. In fact, he'd never seen Addie sit at the dining room table at all. She was the housekeeper and housekeepers didn't do that sort of thing, as far as he knew. But this household was different and always had been. They'd welcomed him, a kid who'd been abandoned by his parents, hadn't they?

"Are you ready to listen now, Owen Cassidy?" she asked.

"What do you mean?"

"I could tell you were doing some hard thinking, laddie. Thought I'd let you finish before I spoke."

He pushed aside his plate. "I'm listening. Is it bad?"

Her hazel eyes were serious but not tear-filled. She hadn't heard any bad news. Or maybe she was just trying to keep the news from him. Shoot, he wasn't a kid anymore. He could take it. But in case he couldn't, he clasped his hands together on his lap and squeezed as hard as he could.

She leaned across the table. "Jer . . . Mr. Taylor has told me that Mr. Greaves has gone up to the geysers and was in a mighty rush to leave."

"I heard that, too," he said. "And that Mr. Greaves told Mr. Taylor to tell the captain that he'd fallen sick."

"He's not ill, laddie." She frowned, which made that wrinkle on her brow even more foreboding. "Mrs. Merrill has died."

"The woman who invited Mrs. Davies and Miss Barbara to travel to the geysers with her and her family?" *Shoot.* "Mrs. Davies must think she was murdered, if Mr. Greaves decided to go up there."

"Sadly so, Owen."

"I should go to the geysers. I could help."

He started to rise, but Addie stopped him with a brisk wave of her hand. "You stay right here, Owen Cassidy," she ordered. "I've enough to fret over with Miss Barbara up there, too."

"Okay, Addie."

He had to do something, though. He just had to.

• • •

The sun was setting, casting the ravine where the Geyser Hotel was situated into deep shadows long before the peaks of the mountains looming over the building and its occupants would be darkened. Lamps were flickering to life in several of the sleeping rooms, dots of light that had appeared charming and comforting last night, but which now seemed a desperate attempt to chase away the gloom.

A chill swept over Celia as she stood at the railing outside her sleeping room, and she drew her shawl more tightly around her, the fringe tickling the exposed skin of her forearms. Mr. Shafer expected the coroner to arrive at any moment, possibly with the sheriff in tow, and the expectant hush that had settled over the hotel and its grounds was as deep and dark as the shadows.

The door to Dennis Merrill's room opened, and he stepped onto the veranda with a cigarillo in hand. He lit it, tossed the spent match onto the ground below, and looked in Celia's direction.

"Good evening, Mrs. Davies," he said, pulling over the chair that sat outside on the veranda and taking a seat. "I presume you're waiting for the coroner like the rest of us."

"It appears to me that most people are actually hiding from the imminent arrival of the coroner, Mr. Merrill," she replied. "Including Mr. Shafer."

"They'll all be out of their rooms in a flash once they hear the man's horse trotting down the road and across the yard."

He leaned back, tipping the chair onto its rear legs, and propped his feet on the railing. Squint as she might, it was too dark to see from where she stood if there were any stains of yellow upon his boots.

The ends of her shawl clutched in her hands, Celia strolled closer to him. The tip of his cigarillo flared orange as he drew in a breath and watched her approach.

"I still do not know what to make of Mr. Young's speedy departure, Mr. Merrill," she said. "My impression of him was not that of a killer." Just that of a fellow who'd been behaving oddly.

He lifted an eyebrow and blew out a stream of smoke. "He's guilty of causing my stepmother's death, whether he meant to cause it or not," he said. "That's what you should make of his speedy departure."

"If he did not intend to cause her harm, why run off?"

"Involuntary manslaughter still carries a lengthy prison term, Mrs. Davies," he answered. "As I suspect you, in your capacity as a lady detective, already know."

"I have noticed you speaking with Gabriella once or twice," she said and shot another look at his boots. No apparent staining from having plunged into a yellow-crusted mineral pool. "She claimed that Mr. Young is not a killer. Why might she have sought to defend him?"

"The conversations I've had with Gabriella weren't exactly long enough to gain any insight into her character, Mrs. Davies."

Other than whether she might be receptive to his flirtations. "Why might Mr. Young have wanted to harm your stepmother, do you think, Mr. Merrill?" she asked. "Even accidentally?"

"You're asking me for my opinion again?"

"Every detective seeks others' opinions, Mr. Merrill. The good ones do, at least."

"He's a madman. Simple as that."

"And Elnora had the misfortune of being in the wrong place at the wrong time?"

He shrugged and pulled on his cigarillo. "Seems like it."

"Is it possible that they knew each other prior to our journey here?" she asked. "Did she ever mention him to you before?"

"They didn't know each other, far as I'm aware."

"So he could not have been attempting to blackmail her," she said.

"Blackmail?" he asked. "Elnora?"

"Just a thought, Mr. Merrill."

He stared at her over the flaring tip of his cigarillo. "I suppose I should tell you that right before we left Healdsburg yesterday morning, I noticed him approach my stepmother. Outside the hotel," he said. "She brushed him off, though, and I assumed Young was trying to get an introduction to Cassandra. The burden of being young and beautiful."

And wealthy.

She had noticed their interaction as well. A few brief seconds of conversation that now carried a greater import than Celia had conceived at the time.

"I'm curious about something else, Mr. Merrill," she said. "About the altercation you had with Mr. Thompson last night."

"An altercation?" He appeared amused by her choice of word; he was always amused. "It was just an argument, Mrs. Davies. Nothing so important as an altercation."

"It is my understanding that you called him a fraud," she said. "Why?"

"In my opinion, he's not at all what he appears to be."

"Oh? How so, Mr. Merrill?"

He winked. "I'm sure you'll figure it out, Mrs. Davies."

The man was exasperating.

"I hate to say this, Mr. Merrill, but your stepmother's death greatly reduces the likelihood that Cassandra will elope with Mr. Thompson, thereby providing you more time to charm her."

Dennis Merrill chuckled. "Oh, you don't hate to say that at all, Mrs. Davies."

No, she did not. His directness was overbold, however. A strategy, perhaps, to unbalance her. "You might be interested to learn that I made a curious observation earlier today. Close to where Mrs. Merrill had passed away."

"A more curious observation than Elnora's body?"

I find that I do so want to believe him guilty of killing her. A stepson full of resentment for the woman who'd become his father's second wife, perhaps.

"I observed a break in the crust that had formed over one of the

73

mineral pools," she said. "Stains on your stepmother's clothing, and the obvious burns on her lower limbs, indicate she was the one who stepped into the pool."

"All right. Go on," he said.

"Further exploration suggests she was not the only one to have done so," she continued. "I discovered residue on another patch of ground. It was at a location not in the direct path of Elnora's fall down the hill. The marks had to have been left by another person's shoes."

A fresh grin teasing the corners of his mouth, he lifted one foot at a time off the handrail, exposing the bottoms of his boots. "Feel free to inspect my boots, Mrs. Davies."

She made no attempt to; he would not have offered if he knew she might discover a stain. "Many hours have passed since the person damaged their shoes, Mr. Merrill. I expect it is too late for me to discover the individual responsible."

"Then why mention it to me?"

Because I am clutching at straws. And coming up empty-handed.

Just then, Mr. Shafer's dog dashed into the yard, barking in the direction of the approaching road. A horse and rider, the reason for the animal's excitement, trotted into view. As if backstage and hearing their cue, guests—the majority fully dressed, she noted—flung open their sleeping room doors and headed for the yard to greet the new arrival.

"And there's the coroner now, trying to look official even though he's covered in dust." Mr. Merrill rose to his feet. "Time to offer my services for his jury."

"But you cannot—"

"I cannot be a member of the jury because I'm one of your suspects?" he asked. "I can't be the only one you're focusing on. You've got to be considering others. I'd be disappointed if you weren't."

"Any person in particular I should be considering, Mr. Merrill?"

He stubbed out the cigarillo on the handrail, tossing the spent butt out onto the yard to join its many brethren that he'd flung there previously. "You should be grateful Mr. Young ran off like he did. I'd say he did you a grand favor."

And you as well, she could have stated. "You mean he did my *cousin* a grand favor."

"I guess I do," he said. "And Mrs. Davies, there really is only one suspect to accuse. Mr. Young. You should probably accept the fact."

✍ CHAPTER 8 ℞

"Any indication they're done yet?" Barbara asked. The coroner's jury, after having trooped into the shed to examine Mrs. Merrill's body along with the coroner, had sequestered themselves inside Mr. Shafer's personal room adjacent the parlor. Well out of sight, apart from the glow of a paraffin oil lamp behind the window's half-closed shutters. "Anything at all?"

She leaned over the railing alongside Celia, both hoping to spy the jury's proceedings from their observation post on the veranda. The location, however, was as useless as pacing outside the parlor windows had proven to be, which was where she and Barbara had begun their vigil. Until they'd realized that not only was the night air chilling, but wild animals rustled out in the woods hemming the property. Grizzlies, perhaps. Or wild cats.

"The lantern is still lit in Mr. Shafer's room," Celia said, irritably impatient.

Women could not participate in juries—too emotional, too unintelligent, purportedly—so she and Barbara were forced to wait, along with the other women and men not selected, while the coroner reviewed what scant evidence there was. Gabriella had been summoned to reveal what she knew. However, she must have finished, because she briefly appeared in the yard to speak with the Chinese cook, idling near the gardener's cottage, before returning to the hotel kitchen.

"What *was* she doing in our room this morning?" Barbara asked, her gaze tracking the young woman. "Have you thought of a reason?"

"No, I have not."

"Maybe she steals from the guests when the rooms are unoccupied," she said. "Maybe that's why she also was in Mr. Young's room."

"Do we look as though we might have possessions worth stealing?" Celia asked.

"I brought my nice silver hair comb with me."

"All I can say is that she did become very skittish when she realized I was inside."

A shaft of light broke across the main steps of the hotel, spilling down into the yard, and a handful of men exited the building. They were members of the jury. *At last.* Mr. Fletcher was among them, his assertion that he'd noticed a suspicious person on the hillside likely viewed as a key piece of information. Along with the individual claiming he'd noticed Mr. Young running across the bridge right before Cassandra had begun to scream. Two events whose timing was contradictory. But in the hurry to accuse Mr. Young, no one likely cared about the contradiction. Or that it implied that Mr. Fletcher had observed someone other than Mr. Young.

The men bid each other good night and headed for their rooms. Mr. Merrill strolled out of the hotel behind them, a lit cigarillo—he clearly had brought a large supply with him—pinched between thumb and forefinger. He wandered out into the yard to smoke it.

Around the corner from Barbara and Celia, one of the female guests, her curls tied in cloth wrappers for the night, leaned over the banister.

"What's the verdict?" she shouted down to Dennis Merrill.

"Thank goodness somebody decided to ask, because I was about to if nobody else did," Barbara said.

"Homicide," he answered.

Not ruled an accident. As anyone would honestly expect, given the few available facts.

"I knew it!" The woman had a carrying voice and appeared accustomed to using it at full volume. "That Young fellow. He's got to be responsible."

"He has been accused. And good night to you, Mrs. Davies. Miss Walford." He tipped an imaginary hat then wandered toward the gateway at the edge of the property, the one that led to the geyser trail. He must not be concerned about the wild animals rustling in the woods.

The woman in the cloth hair wrappers shot them both a fierce look, dismayed that other female guests had observed her indecorous bellowing, and stomped back into her room.

"Now what?" Barbara asked.

"A warrant for the man's arrest will be issued by the local magistrate, and the authorities will be on the lookout for him." Although he'd been on the run for around thirteen—Celia squinted at the watch pinned at her waist—more like *fourteen* hours. Who knew how far away he'd managed to travel in that amount of time? None of them were likely to ever see Mr. Young again.

"No, I meant now what do *we* do?"

"What can we do, Barbara? Mr. Young is suspected of causing Mrs. Merrill's death, and I anticipate that Mr. Weaver will want to leave as soon as possible tomorrow morning." With Mrs. Merrill's body placed in a carriage of her own, wrapped in blankets and packed in straw to conceal the aroma of death.

"So that's all? Well, thank heavens," she said. "I'm more than ready to leave, even if it means rattling in a stagecoach for hours on end."

"We may go via St. Helena, which will allow us to take the Napa Valley Railroad train for part of the journey."

"Even better," Barbara said and returned to their room.

Mr. Weaver had finished with the coroner and had clomped up the stairs and across the veranda. He stopped when he noticed Celia outside her room.

"We'll be leaving on the Calistoga coach, once it gets here in the morning, Mrs. Davies. We'll catch the train in St. Helena," he announced, confirming her assumption of their travel plans. "Please inform your cousin."

"I shall," she said. "Mr. Weaver, forgive me for asking, but are you content with the jury's conclusion tonight?"

"That Young is the responsible party? The villain who murdered my sister-in-law?"

"The coroner's jury did not conclude he murdered her, Mr. Weaver." That required a grand jury. "Merely that her death was suspicious and he may have caused it."

"Oh, he'll be indicted for murder, Mrs. Davies," he said. "The fact that he has beaten a hasty retreat speaks for itself."

"I suppose it does."

Hiram Weaver bid her good night and turned toward his sleeping room.

"Mr. Weaver, one more question," she said, stopping him. "Do you know anything about a message your sister-in-law received requesting a sum of money in exchange for keeping silent?"

"What are you talking about?"

"A note. Fifty dollars in exchange for keeping quiet about a secret or some other information that this person had become aware of."

His fingers twisted his watch chain. "How do you know about some note Elnora received?" he asked, his gaze narrowing. "Or maybe you're just meaning to cause trouble, Mrs. Davies. Is that what this is about? Because you're talking nonsense."

He yanked open the sleeping room door, abruptly dismissing their conversation. She did manage to study his sturdy leather shoes before the door slammed behind him. They were clean of yellow residue.

Blast.

• • •

"You're willing to take me overnight?" Nick asked the man at the livery stable. At this late hour, he'd been lucky to find one open.

"Sure. I've done it before," the man replied, turning aside to spit a stream of chaw onto the ground.

Nick should question how often the man had ridden into the hills with only moonlight to guide him, but if he learned the answer, he might change his mind. "How long will it take?"

"If we ride hard, we should get there in four or five hours," he said. "But it'll cost you extra."

"How much extra?"

The man wiped the back of his hand across his mouth, clearing a trail of greenish tobacco juice from his chin. He looked Nick up and down. "Two bucks."

More than the train ride to get here. He could show the fellow his badge, but it wouldn't mean much. St. Helena wasn't Nick's jurisdiction. Besides, he never cared for the unwanted, occasionally hazardous attention a police badge could bring. Even if showing it and stating he was on "police business" might lower the price.

"All right." Nick took the necessary funds out of his vest pocket; he'd separated the money he'd reluctantly taken from Mrs. Jewett to reduce losing it all to a deft pickpocket.

The man snatched the coins from him. "What're you in such a hurry for? Could always wait for the stage in the morning that heads to the geysers. There's a nice hotel in Calistoga, not ten miles up the road. Leaves from there pretty early."

"Just keen to get to the geysers. I hear they're spectacular at sunrise." He'd read that someplace. An advertisement in the newspaper, probably.

The fellow found a plug of chaw deep in one of his pants pockets and tucked it into a fold of his cheek. "A woman was killed up there this morning."

"Oh?"

"That's what I heard," he said. "Also heard that the fellow responsible for killing her stole a horse from the Calistoga postmaster, leaving the one he'd been riding half-dead in the road outside the postmaster's house."

Suddenly, those extra dollars were worth spending. "Anybody see the man? Could maybe describe him?"

"I heard he was skinny. Sorta little. Had a bum arm, too."

He'd heard quite a lot. "Anything else?"

"That he was headed south on the road to Napa," he said, a dribble of tobacco leaking from the corner of his mouth. "Coulda gone any direction after that, though." He eyed Nick. "Why are you so keen to know?"

He gave the same reason as he'd given to the saloonkeeper in Suscol. "Nosy, I guess."

An apparently satisfactory explanation, because the fellow nodded. "Ready to go?"

"Yes. I am."

• • •

Celia stared at the sleeping room window, the moonlight coloring the thin window curtain a pale gray. Elnora's death had sent her brain whirling, and she'd not been able to sleep. Barbara, however, had dropped off quickly, based on the soft snores that had begun emanating as soon as she'd rested her head on the pillow.

She eased herself off the cot, cursing the squeak of the rope mattress support, and collected her cotton wrapper. She searched her luggage and located the notebook, along with a pencil, she'd thought to pack. *How prescient of you.* Or superstitious.

Taking the notebook, the lantern, and matches out onto the veranda, she settled onto the chair left outside the room. The stars sparkled thickly white, inscribing a trail across the black night sky. How glorious a sight. It was often too foggy to see stars in San Francisco, or hazy from coal and wood smoke. More importantly, she was usually far too exhausted from her daily visits with patients to indulge in an evening spent staring up at the stars. Perhaps that might change, were she to marry Nicholas. Perhaps they would sit together in the cool evening air and stare up at the stars together.

"Do keep on course, Celia," she chided herself. Dreams of what their life together might be like needed to wait.

She lit the wick and set the lantern alongside the chair. She was not the only person awake past midnight; from one of the rooms on the ground floor came the sound of male laughter. Several of the guests had decided upon a long evening of cards and drinking. Disturbing their neighbors, no doubt.

Celia flipped open the notebook, thumbing through it until she found the first empty page, and took up her pencil. She tilted the book toward the lantern light and inscribed the names of all those she considered to be a suspect—Mr. Young, Cassandra, Mr. Thompson, Mr. Merrill, Mr. Weaver.

Where had they all been when Elnora had plunged into a mineral pool, either accidentally or otherwise? Which had to have occurred several minutes after Celia noticed her by the gate, which would have been around . . .

"Six?" Celia wrote that down.

Which meant she'd died sometime between six ten and no later than a few minutes before seven, when folks had been gathering in the yard in readiness for the delayed tour, only to hear Cassandra screaming.

Celia had to admit that the geysers made an excellent location to commit murder and hope to pass it off as an unfortunate incident. Although the subsequent actions of Mr. Young, if he was not actually the killer, had provided a perfect and unexpected cover for the true perpetrator.

As for her suspects' locations—Mr. Weaver was in his sleeping room until he'd gone down to the breakfast room when Barbara had done. Mr. Young had been in the yard prior to Elnora's death, but Celia could not say where he was at the critical moment. Dennis Merrill had been up and about, in the yard then disappearing into the ravine. Reappearing just as Celia was responding to the sound of Cassandra's screams. She'd not noticed Mr. Thompson until after Elnora had been found. Gabriella had first been in Mr. Young's room, then in Celia and Barbara's. And Cassandra . . .

"Was the first to arrive on the scene."

Cassandra. Motive—to remove an obstacle keeping her from the man she loved. A fellow her aunt had not wanted as a husband for her niece, for a reason she'd never explained to Celia. Perhaps she'd been arguing with Cassandra about Mr. Thompson, attempting to save her niece from heartbreak, but Cassandra had been stubbornly refusing to listen. How many disagreements had Celia had with Barbara where her cousin had reacted before allowing Celia a chance to fully speak her mind? Numerous ones.

At least she's never tried to push me into a scalding mineral pool, thank heavens.

Perhaps Cassandra, upset and not thinking, had lashed out and caused her aunt to lose her footing and fall, as Celia had said to Barbara. But she'd not been willing to admit her part for fear of being accused of wanting to kill Elnora. Most incriminatingly, her shoe bore a streak of yellow across its heel.

Mr. Thompson. Motive—the same as Cassandra's. Although why might either of them believe that Elnora could successfully interfere with their engagement? They must have done, which would explain why they'd planned an elopement. Or was a possible motive related to what Nicholas had uncovered? That Mr. Weaver may have bribed Mr. Thompson's father in exchange for his business receiving a city contract.

"A scandal, to be sure." And had Elnora discovered the scheme, threatened to expose it?

Celia wished she knew more about Thaddeus Thompson. Whether he was the sort of fellow who might kill someone to protect his name or his family's name. But she knew next to nothing about the fellow, other than Mr. Merrill considered him to be a fraud, a vague assessment he'd refused to clarify. Sour grapes, perhaps, over the man in the best position to win Miss Weaver's hand. Mr. Thompson's shoes had been clean of any yellow residue. Curious that he'd gone to see where Mrs. Merrill had died. Or, rather, to hunt for evidence he may have left behind. Was *he* the fellow Mr. Fletcher thought he'd noticed?

Mr. Merrill. Motive—ridding himself of someone he despised. Even Hiram Weaver had admitted that Mr. Merrill drove Elnora mad. Plus, there was the argument Celia had overheard, his threatening comment that Elnora should worry about herself. Mr. Merrill exhibited no particular distress over his stepmother's death. It was a common enough tale, the lack of affection between a stepchild and the mother who'd replaced their biological one. Jane worried constantly that her own stepdaughter, Grace, did not love her. That she pined for her deceased mother.

"Poor Jane," she murmured into the soft nighttime air and wondered how her visit to Frank's family back East was going.

However, Mrs. Merrill's death only increased the chance that Mr. Thompson would, in the end, marry Cassandra. She'd no longer be around to protest the arrangement. Did that mean Mr. Merrill did not have a motive to kill her? Or merely that his motive was unrelated to a desire to marry Cassandra Weaver.

Returning to her notes, she added one more item to Mr. Merrill's summary—the will his father had left. Would the amount of Dennis Merrill's inheritance increase because of his stepmother's death? Celia could not, however, walk up to Denny Merrill and bluntly ask him.

Well, perhaps I could, she thought and smiled.

Mr. Weaver. Motive—his bribery of Mr. Thompson's father. If Elnora had learned of it and she'd told him she knew, could he have become irate enough to have wanted to kill her? Or unintentionally caused her to fall? But he was in his sleeping room, then the dining room, when she'd died. Unless he'd *not* been in his sleeping room the entire time.

"However, he is not the fellow who stole a horse and fled," she whispered, her breath misting. She wished she'd thought to collect her shawl in addition to her wrapper.

Mr. Young. Motive—blackmail gone awry? Was he the individual seeking fifty dollars from Elnora Merrill? Perhaps she gave him the money, then he killed her to keep her quiet. A terrible crime to commit for not the greatest gain. His rapid departure was a significant indicator of guilt.

"What, though, was the secret worth blackmailing Elnora over?"

And then there was Gabriella.

Gabriella. Motive—unknown. She'd curiously decided to proclaim that Mr. Young could not be a killer, when silence about the fellow might have been a wiser course of action. She had been seen leaving his room, and there was her inexplicable appearance in Celia and Barbara's sleeping room. What had she been up to? Thievery?

As for murdering Mrs. Merrill, could Gabriella have left Mr. Young's room, climbed the trail and found a hiding spot to wait for Elnora, pushed her to her death, then returned to the hotel before Cassandra began to scream? So much to accomplish in a short period of time. Unless the witness was confused about when he'd observed her leaving Mr. Young's room.

Tapping her pencil against her chin, Celia exhaled and stared out into the darkness consuming the grounds of the hotel, the ravine, the sputtering fumaroles on the opposite hillside. Consuming everything except for the stars that sparkled overhead. She'd miss the spectacle when they returned to San Francisco.

Celia resumed staring at her notes. "But why kill Elnora Merrill, Gabriella? Had someone paid you?"

The sleeping room door behind her opened and Barbara stepped through. "I can hear you muttering out here, Cousin," she said, yawning into her hand. "You're not as quiet as you think you are."

"I apologize for waking you." Celia stowed her pencil inside her notebook and started to rise.

"I wasn't sleeping anyway. And you don't need to get up." Barbara leaned against the railing and peered into the blackness of the trees beyond the yard. "It doesn't smell as bad as when we first arrived."

"Perhaps the wind has shifted."

Barbara hugged her arms around her waist. She stood silently for a while, listening to the night sounds accompanied by steam hisses and the burble of the river, the yipping of a distant coyote quickly echoed by companions. "I should tell you something."

"Oh?"

Her cousin turned to face her. "I think I know why Cassandra has been so irritable and jumpy on this trip. It's not earth-shaking, so don't get that look in your eye as though I'm about to prove she killed her aunt."

Had she gotten "that look" in her eye? Could Barbara see "that look" on the shadowed balcony? Most likely, her cousin merely knew her well enough to expect it was there.

"Is she upset because of Elnora's concerns about Thaddeus Thompson?" Celia asked.

"There is that. Her aunt claimed he doesn't love her," she said. "That he's only her suitor because of an arrangement between her father and Mr. Thompson's."

Celia stood and walked to the far end of the veranda, away from anyone who might be overhearing their conversation from the privacy of one of the sleeping rooms. She signaled for Barbara to join her.

"Mr. Greaves has learned that Mr. Weaver may be bribing Mr. Thompson's father. Mr. Weaver wishes to obtain a contract with the city, it appears," Celia said. "I should have mentioned it to you as soon as I found out."

"But what has that to do with Cassandra?"

"Perhaps she is part of the bribe." An innocent possibly ensnared in a chess game where she was a pawn. "I wonder how she learned about her father's plans, if that is why she's been upset." Mr. Weaver certainly would not have discussed the situation with his daughter.

"From her aunt, maybe," she said. "I think Mrs. Merrill knew that he'd done something wrong, according to Cassandra."

"As I'd conjectured," she said. "I do wish Elnora had been more forthright when she came to visit on Sunday." *If I'd known, though, could I have averted the tragedy that ultimately occurred?*

"This gives Mr. Weaver a motive to want to silence his sister-in-law, doesn't it?" Barbara asked.

"How much of a threat did Mrs. Merrill present, though? He could have simply maintained that she was paying too much attention to idle gossip," she said. And he was in his sleeping room when she died. Unless he wasn't. "Although a motive for Mr. Weaver to silence Mrs. Merrill is also a motive for Mr. Thompson. They both stand to suffer if the scandal becomes widely known."

Barbara wrapped her arms more tightly about her waist. "There's more, Cousin."

"Oh?" Celia felt certain she had "that look" in her eye now.

"Like I told you before, I can't be sure if I saw anybody on the hillside this morning. But I might have smelled his cigar smoke," she said. "Or rather, his cigarillo smoke."

"Mr. Merrill." *I knew it.* "When?"

"When I was still in the bathing hut. Before I tried to climb the hill."

Which meant that Mr. Merrill was on the trail before Elnora was found dead. How clever of him to ensure that Celia encountered him by the river. As though he'd been there all along.

"Thank you, Barbara, but we will need more proof of his guilt. Proof, perhaps, that he was the one who'd left behind a yellow mark upon some rocks."

"How are we going to get that proof? By searching his sleeping room?" she whispered. "Wait, you intend to do that, don't you? But we're leaving as soon as a carriage gets here, aren't we?"

"Then I shall have to wake up even earlier in order to search it while he is at breakfast."

Her cousin shook her head. "It's too dangerous, Cousin."

"Once we've left this hotel, my chance to learn anything about either Mr. Thompson's culpability or Mr. Merrill's will be lost."

"And Mr. Weaver's."

"Searching three rooms will require more time than I have, Barbara." Searching one would be bad enough.

Suddenly, Mr. Shafer's dog began barking in its pen. Someone released it and the dog burst into the yard, frantically yapping in the direction of the road that led to the mountain pass. Downstairs, the men who'd been laughing over whiskey and cards quieted, and the door to their room flung open. The faint glow from a lantern bobbed across the road and lit the trees on the far side of the drive. The light became brighter as the individual carrying the lamp drew closer.

Mr. Shafer followed his dog into the yard, stuffing his nightshirt into a pair of trousers he'd hastily pulled on. "Who is it?" he called.

"Just me, Shafer," a man shouted back. "Got a fellow from San Francisco with me. Mighty keen to get here and didn't care about the hour. Hope you got room for him."

The two men on horseback trotted into view. Celia's pulse skipped. She'd recognize the second man anywhere, from any distance and any angle.

Barbara leaned over the balustrade alongside her. "Well, it looks like Mr. Greaves has turned up, Cousin."

"Indeed."

℘ CHAPTER 9 ℞

"What are you doing here, Nicholas?" Celia asked, her dressing gown discreetly tied over her nightclothes, the braid of her long blond hair hanging over her shoulder. Nick was finding it hard to think when she looked like that, soft and vulnerable. Soft and vulnerable aside from the consternation puckering her forehead. "Is Addie all right? Owen?"

"They're both fine. And I'm here because of the telegram you sent me today, Celia. Or should I say yesterday, since I'm pretty sure it's past midnight," he replied, moving aside to let the female servant take his bag into his room. "What was I supposed to do? Ignore it? Sit around San Francisco and just hope you weren't getting yourself killed?"

She glanced over at the young woman and lowered her voice. "I was not going to get killed, Nicholas."

Maybe. "Just tell me that you're okay."

"I am perfectly fine, as you can see."

He wanted to confirm that for himself. Grab her and hold her close, feel her warmth. Be positive that she was unharmed. But he didn't. Not here and not now.

She was smiling, gently, calmly. It was the best reassurance he could ask for.

"Thank you, though, for being so concerned and making the journey, Nicholas," she said. "But how did you manage to get away?"

"Eagan's been told I'm deathly ill."

"And how long will he believe that story?" she asked. "You have risked your career by coming here, Nicholas."

Probably. "How did Mrs. Merrill die?"

She glanced over at the servant again. The young woman might've been listening, or she might not have been. Too hard to tell.

"Somehow, she fell into a scalding hot mineral spring, suffered severe burns, and may have had a heart attack as a result," Celia said.

A terrible way to die.

"Could've been an accident, Celia."

"I know, but her death does not feel accidental to me, Nicholas," she said. "The coroner and his jury agree and have concluded that a man named Parker Young is responsible."

Celia paused as the servant finished preparing Nick's room. The young woman turned to leave, lingering in the doorway for a few seconds longer than necessary, and gave him a smile—she was pretty, no mistaking—before she strode off down the veranda.

Celia frowned after her. "Why is Gabriella still here? I thought Mr. Shafer dismissed her," she said. "For possibly being with Mr. Young overnight. Which she has not denied."

"Maybe Shafer's decided to take pity on her."

"Hmm . . ." Celia murmured skeptically.

"What makes Young the likely suspect?"

"He took one of the other guests' horses and fled right after Mrs. Merrill's body was found. I wonder how quickly he'll be able to ride, though," she said. "His left arm hangs limply at his side. Damage caused by a war injury was what he told me. It might make it difficult to control an animal on the roads that head down off this mountain."

"I know. I just came up from Calistoga." Hard riding. "A man in a hurry left a horse in Calistoga and stole the postmaster's animal. Might've been your Mr. Young. And he might've already made it as far as Suscol, if not farther."

"Then his arm has not hindered his escape."

"Seems like it hasn't."

"I've been attempting to discover his motive. However, by all accounts he was a stranger to everyone, including Elnora Merrill," she said. "I am not, however, convinced that Mr. Young is the culprit."

"Of course you aren't," he said, a grin tugging at his mouth. "And you're going to explain why you aren't convinced."

"Because it seems that every one of our traveling companions has a motive to have wanted her out of the way," she said. "Her stepson, Dennis Merrill, whom I overheard arguing with her while we overnighted in Healdsburg. Thaddeus Thompson, distrusted by Elnora. Cassandra herself, determined to marry the man despite her aunt's objections. And I should add Mr. Weaver, based on your telegram. She may have discovered his crime."

"We're trying to get proof that Weaver paid Thompson to persuade his fellow city supervisors to award Weaver's company a contract," Nick said. "It's not worth a massive amount of money, but it might save his flailing business. Having a city contract would look good to other customers."

"Rather like holding a royal warrant for supplying goods to the queen, I suppose," she said. "And Mr. Weaver would be eternally grateful, perhaps adding his daughter's hand in marriage as part of the bribe."

"What evidence is there against any of them?" he asked.

"Well, let's see." She rearranged her dressing gown, tying it more tightly around her waist. It was cold out on the veranda, but he didn't dare invite her into his room. Much as he might like to. "Cassandra has a yellow mineral stain on one of her shoes, the same sort of stain as on Mrs. Merrill's clothing."

She explained about some crust on a mineral pool and marks on nearby gravel and Mrs. Merrill's injuries so quickly that Nick barely caught it all.

"Also, Mr. Thompson decided to visit the site where her body was found, which I find curious. And Barbara may have smelled Mr. Merrill's cigarillo smoke near to where his stepmother suffered her fatal injury and around the same time she died. As for Mr. Weaver, he purportedly was in his sleeping room. He, however, is not sharing his quarters with anyone, so how can we be certain?"

"We can't."

"I do wish there wasn't a vacant room between my sleeping room and the others'. Otherwise, I might've heard one of them rustling about this morning."

Getting ready to bump Elnora Merrill into a boiling mineral spring. "Nothing definite, then."

"Unfortunately, we are running out of time to gather evidence," she said. "We depart as soon as the carriage arrives from Calistoga. Mr. Weaver is impatient to return to San Francisco. As is Barbara, I need not add."

"Which leaves a few hours to do some investigating before we depart."

"Is that enough time to uncover anything, Nicholas?" she asked.

"Does your question mean that you're not planning on doing more investigating before you leave, Mrs. Davies?"

A question she didn't bother to answer.

• • •

Celia had left the sleeping-room curtains open, hoping to rise along with the sun. Instead, she slept through the sunrise and only succeeded in waking before half past five because Barbara jostled her. Rather roughly.

"I thought you were going to get up early in order to poke around in folks' rooms while they were at breakfast, Cousin."

Yawning, Celia sat up and reached for her wrapper. "That was my intention."

"Well, waking up might've been easier if you hadn't spent half the night mooning over Mr. Greaves."

Her cheeks heated. "I was not mooning, whatever that word means, and it was not half the night," she replied defensively. "Why are you up already?"

"Because Mr. Weaver was bellowing for Mr. Shafer down in the yard, wondering when the coaches were going to get here," she said. "Which supposedly will be around seven, by the way."

Blast. So little time. "I wonder how many of the others are up, too."

"Most of our party, I'd guess. And they should be at breakfast," Barbara said. "Mr. Weaver wanted food made available early."

"Run down to the dining room and see if Mr. Thompson and Mr. Merrill are in there having breakfast." Thankfully, her cousin already had her travel costume on. "Without it being obvious that you're looking for them."

Barbara scowled. "I know how to be unobtrusive, Cousin," she replied and dashed off.

Celia was dressed and waiting out on the veranda when she returned.

She nodded. "All of them are there. Even Cassandra."

"Good. Wait here and keep an eye out for any of them," she said, indicating the chair on the veranda. "Alert me, should either of the men appear before I'm finished."

Celia strolled to Mr. Thompson's room first, which was the nearer of the two. Though Mr. Weaver and the rest of their traveling party were breakfasting, none of the other guests appeared to have arisen yet. Possibly still asleep after yesterday's exhausting excitement.

She checked the time on her Ellery watch. Only about an hour until the Calistoga coach would arrive, bringing a frenzy of activity with it. The Weavers and Mr. Merrill and Mr. Thompson would be sure to return to their rooms before it got here, in order to pack.

She pressed an ear to the door of Mr. Thompson's room. Not that she was expecting to hear any noise, given Barbara's report, but it always paid to be careful. After a quick glance around, she removed a hairpin from her chignon and unbent it. She slid it into the keyhole while testing the handle. It turned readily and her dubious lock-picking abilities thankfully wouldn't be required, for Mr. Thompson had left his room unlocked.

Tossing away the ruined hairpin, she went inside. His room contained a narrow bed, a small table, and two chairs, just like the one she occupied with Barbara. A dark frock coat hung from a hook on the wall, and the table was arrayed, in an orderly fashion, with the usual accoutrements of a well-off man—combs and toothpicks, a bone-handled toothbrush in a porcelain cup, a jar of hair pomade. A travel case stood open and at the ready, however. As soon as he returned to his room, it would be easy to sweep the contents of the table into it and be prepared to depart.

A pair of kip double-sole boots stood against the wall beneath the shirt. A hasty examination did not reveal any signs of a yellow mineral stain. They were either a new pair or they'd been thoroughly cleaned. The shoes he'd worn to breakfast were likely the clean ones she'd studied yesterday. Frustrated, she rearranged the boots on the floor the way she'd found them.

In addition to the table, Mr. Thompson's room had been additionally supplied with a compact desk. Its shallow drawer, which stuck when she tried to pull it open, was empty. In one corner sat a tidy stack of stationery, along with a packable inkwell and companion engraved silver pen. And sticking out from beneath the inkwell was a folded piece of paper. She slipped it out.

Fifty bucks for the item in my possession.

"Gad." Another note, but this time meant for Mr. Thompson.

She held the piece of paper up to the light coming through the window. Was the handwriting the same as on the note she'd found in Mrs. Merrill's pocket? Without doing a side-by-side comparison, she could not be sure. And she didn't have time to run back to her room and fetch the other one. She also didn't dare take this note with her; Thaddeus Thompson would notice its absence.

She returned the folded paper to its place, quickly scanned the room to be certain that everything looked the way it had when she'd stepped inside, and went back out onto the veranda. She lifted her eyebrows at Barbara, watching from where she sat.

Abruptly, Barbara's eyes widened. "Why, Mr. Weaver! Is the . . . is the coach here already?"

Celia spun to face the man, who'd come up the stairs behind Celia. "Good morning, Mr. Weaver." So much for searching Mr. Merrill's sleeping room.

"Were you in Mr. Thompson's room, Mrs. Davies?" he asked, his gaze taking turns sweeping over her and her cousin.

"I was hoping to speak to him about . . . oh, look! There he is now. Down in the yard. I shall see you in an hour, Mr. Weaver. Is that right?" she asked, moving past him. "Barbara, finish packing, if you would. Then join me in the dining room. We've not much time for a meal before departing."

Gad. Heart thumping, she grabbed her skirts and hurried across the veranda, feeling Mr. Weaver's watchful gaze until she turned the corner and passed out of his view.

• • •

Nick heard Celia pounding down the hotel's exterior stairs before he saw her.

He folded his arms and waited for her to reach where he stood at the far end of the building. "Been investigating, Mrs. Davies?"

"I've had a narrow squeak of it, Mr. Greaves." She released her grip on her skirts, patting them into place. "Mr. Weaver nearly caught me ferreting around inside Mr. Thompson's sleeping room."

"I'd guess he nevertheless suspects you were in there, because he's not stupid."

"Of course he suspects, but all he can say for certain is that I was standing outside of it when he came upon me."

"And did you discover anything?"

"Yes, I did. Firstly, Mr. Thompson brought two sets of footwear with him, unless he is in the dining room in stocking feet," she said. "The pair of boots in his room are, by the way, as pure as the driven snow."

"Unlike Cassandra Weaver's," he said. "I suppose you didn't have a chance to inspect Mr. Young's before he beat a retreat."

"No, and I've not been able to examine Mr. Weaver's shoes, either," she said. "As for Mr. Merrill, he was far too eager to have me look at his boots to expect I'd discover an incriminating stain. He is clever, though. I'll give him that."

She sounded admiring of the man, and Nick felt a spark of jealousy.

"I found something else very intriguing in Mr. Thompson's room, Nicholas." Celia hooked her arm in his, and they strolled toward the area of the hotel where they might find some breakfast. "A note with the following message—*Fifty bucks for the item in my possession.* What item, we must ask ourselves," she said. "I thought it unwise to take the note from his room, or else I'd show it to you."

"Somebody was blackmailing him?"

"Both him and Mrs. Merrill," she replied. "I found a similar note in the pocket of her dress. Which I forgot to mention to you last night, I now realize."

"You searched her body."

"Most certainly I did, Mr. Greaves," she said unapologetically. "Her note was also a request for fifty dollars. In her case, in exchange for silence. Neither of them was addressed to the recipient, nor was there a signature, unfortunately. Not even an initial to assist us, as has occurred previously. Perhaps the individual felt no need to sign the notes, because it would be obvious who'd composed them."

"If it was so obvious, why even compose one and deliver it in the first place?"

Celia came to a halt. "Perhaps prior attempts have failed and the individual has been forced to be more specific and direct," she said. "If I searched Mr. Weaver's room, I wonder if I'd find a note in there, as well."

"Don't get any ideas about doing that, Celia," he said. "He's onto you, after finding you outside Thompson's room."

"Ah, well." She resumed walking, their arms still linked. He liked the feel of her at his side, her skirt brushing his legs, the lavender smell of her hair drifting over. "I should add that Mr. Thompson's note was on a regular sheet of stationery, while Mrs. Merrill's had been scribbled on the back of a menu card from this hotel."

"Not an old note that she'd been carrying around, then," he said. "And which limits who our author might be."

"What about you, Mr. Greaves?" she asked. "Did you have a chance to question anyone?"

"I talked with Shafer this morning, trying to learn anything about the guests."

"And?"

"Only that Mr. Young's request for a room was made last-minute," he replied.

"I recall Mr. Shafer mentioning that when we arrived," she said. "How odd, do you not agree?"

"Yes, I do," he replied. "The remainder of the guests appear to be above suspicion, but I'm still confirming alibis."

"Ah, Mrs. Davies. Good morning." A fellow in a linen coat and pants descended the steps from the common rooms of the hotel and marched over to them. "Is this gentleman the notorious Detective Greaves?"

Celia exhaled. Loudly. "Mr. Greaves, this is Dennis Merrill."

The man grinned smugly. Nick distrusted men who grinned smugly. Especially ones Celia called clever.

"So, it's true," Merrill said. "Mr. Weaver thought you might be the police detective whose name is so often linked to Mrs. Davies's in the newspapers."

"Not *so* often, Mr. Merrill," she corrected.

Often enough, thought Nick.

"You're a little late, Detective, and out of your jurisdiction." The fellow assessed Nick as if hunting for weak spots. A chink in his armor. "The case of the mysterious demise of my stepmother already has a suspect, as determined by the coroner and his jury."

"My sympathies on her passing, Mr. Merrill," Nick said.

"Thank you. I'm still dealing with the shock of it, Detective," he said. "Mr. Young, as I've said to Mrs. Davies, must be a madman."

Nick considered him. "There's an indication that he might've been attempting to blackmail your stepmother, Mr. Merrill." A shot in the dark, since there wasn't any such indication, only a hunch.

"I can see that you and Mrs. Davies have had time to share your theories," he said, smirking. Nick hated men who smirked, too. "But even if Elnora had a secret worth keeping quiet, she wouldn't be able to pay whatever amount somebody scribbled in a note. She had a small income from my father's estate but managed to spend most of it every month. Not much money to spare."

"Then we must have been misled about a secret, Mr. Greaves,"

Celia said, turning to him. "And Mr. Young is simply an unwell man who murders innocent women."

"Seems so, ma'am," Nick replied.

"Well, Mrs. Davies, we'll be leaving soon, and I have to finish packing my trunk," Mr. Merrill said. "Will you be joining us on the journey, Mr. Greaves?"

"I haven't decided when I'm leaving yet."

"I hope you come with us, Detective, because I'd enjoy speaking more with you," he said. "As would the others."

That was not at all likely.

Merrill tipped his hat and strolled off.

Nick watched him go. "Did I mention a note, Mrs. Davies?"

"No, Mr. Greaves, you did not," she replied. "And neither did I when I asked Mr. Merrill about a blackmail attempt yesterday."

"Maybe he made a good guess."

"Perhaps," she said, not sounding convinced at all.

• • •

"I waited for you as long as I could in the dining room, Cousin," Barbara said, setting a plate with a piece of buttered toast and a fried egg on their sleeping room's table. "Breakfast offerings were sparse this early, and this was all I could collect, once I figured out you weren't coming down to eat. Where were you?"

"Outside with Mr. Greaves, speaking with Mr. Merrill. Who continues to deny that his stepmother could be the target of a blackmailing effort." Celia sat at the table. She took a bite of the toast and wished she had some of Addie's jam to accompany it. She was longing to return home as much as Barbara, it seemed. "Thank you, by the way."

Barbara took the opposite chair. "You're welcome."

Celia sipped some of the coffee Barbara had also carried up to the room. It was bitter and impossible to drink. In truth, Celia had never much cared for coffee, but she'd not be finding a well-brewed cup of oolong at the Geyser Hotel. Unless the Chinese cook had a stash of the tea someplace.

She set it down. "I found a second note looking for fifty dollars, Barbara. In Mr. Thompson's room," she said. "This time the demand was in exchange for some unspecified item the author has in their possession."

"You were right. Everybody seems to have secrets."

Knuckles rapped on the door, and it opened. Mr. Shafer poked his head through. "The extra is here, ladies."

"Thank you, Mr. Shafer. We shall be down in a few minutes," Celia replied.

"If they've brought an extra, that means we'll all be traveling together in one coach," her cousin said once he'd left. She picked up Celia's rejected cup of coffee and finished it off. "Except for Mr. Thompson. I overheard him telling Mr. Weaver that he intends to travel to San Francisco separately. I think he's leaving soon, if he hasn't gone already, actually."

"He's not returning to Calistoga?" Celia asked, eating the eggs as quickly as she could; it would be a lengthy ride this morning, and she did not know when they might have their next meal. "The town is on the way."

Barbara shrugged. "Interestingly, Gabriella was helping with breakfast," she said. "Mr. Shafer told her she needed to clear out once she was done in the kitchen, though, loudly enough for everybody in the dining room to hear. I wonder if he was hoping that the furor over her and Mr. Young would die down, but folks were still grumbling about it."

"I'd feel sorry for her if I did not remain confused about what she was doing in our room yesterday morning."

"She and Mr. Merrill are thick as thieves," Barbara said. "I saw them together again, when I was on my way back here with the food."

Mr. Merrill, who'd not hesitated to assume that a note had been used to attempt to blackmail his stepmother. And who smoked cigarillos.

Celia set down her fork. "How would anyone have known that Mrs. Merrill was alone by the mineral pools an hour before the scheduled tour?" she mused aloud.

"They'd seen her heading up there?" Barbara proposed.

Mr. Merrill might have observed her. "Or it was an arranged meeting."

Barbara frowned. "A meeting she shouldn't have agreed to."

ɸ CHAPTER 10 ଦ

"Mr. Weaver. Before you go, I'd like a word," Nick shouted. He angled across the yard, attempting to intercept the man before he escaped up the stairs and into his room. Weaver was more agile than his thick-bodied frame suggested, and Nick had to break into a run.

He halted and turned to face Nick. "We're leaving shortly, Detective. I don't have time to talk to you," he said. "Furthermore, you're out of your jurisdiction."

"Mr. Merrill has already reminded me of that fact, Mr. Weaver."

"Then I bid you a good day."

"Whoa. Hold on there," Nick said, stopping him from rushing up the stairs. "Just a quick question." Along with a quick glance at the man's shoes. No sign of yellow on them, as far as Nick could tell. "I've received a complaint about the city contract you've been granted. To supply coal and wood to the steam fire engines. Thought I'd ask you about it, while we're both here."

He jutted his chin. "I have an excellent company and the city supervisors saw the merits in my offer and awarded me that contract, Detective. Why wouldn't they?"

"A very specific city supervisor saw the merits, Mr. Weaver," Nick replied. "Mr. Julius Thompson."

"We are acquainted, and he would, of course, be the supervisor I'd approach. Nothing underhanded at all," he stated. "I believe we're finished here, Detective. I'm in mourning for my sister-in-law and in a hurry to return her body home. Have some respect."

"My sympathy, by the way," Nick said. "You know, it seems strange that Mr. Young could be responsible for her death. Any indication they knew each other?"

"No indication at all."

"Then why might he have wanted to harm her?"

He narrowed his gaze. "The police will have to ask him when he's found, Detective. Maybe you should be assisting the search, rather than pestering me."

"What was your impression of the fellow?" Young had cleared out his sleeping room completely, not leaving behind any clues that might allow Nick to form an opinion of his own.

"No impression, Detective. I did not interact with him."

"But you shared a carriage from Healdsburg with him, didn't you?"

"He seemed normal enough, but obviously he wasn't," he replied. "Now, if you don't mind."

He spun on his heel and charged up the stairs.

"Detective, I can tell you what *I* thought about Mr. Young," said a man who'd been lurking nearby. He rubbed the fingers of his left hand like they ached. Arthritic, maybe, and hoping for a cure from one of the mineral pools. "I'm Obediah Fletcher. I saw a fellow on the hillside right after that poor woman's body was found." He glanced over at the hill across the ravine in case Nick didn't know what poor woman he meant.

"Tell me your thoughts about Mr. Young, Mr. Fletcher."

"He was a shifty type. Noticed him trying to talk to several folks. The ones who came with Mr. Weaver, there." He gestured toward Weaver, who'd reached his sleeping room and had slammed the door behind him. "Seemed most interested in that tall fellow. He didn't like it, though. The tall fellow, that is."

"Tall fellow?"

"Thompson? I think that's his name."

Thaddeus Thompson had decamped right after breakfast, not giving Nick a chance to interview him. Maybe he hadn't needed to. "That's interesting, Mr. Fletcher."

"I thought so, too."

• • •

"I find it curious that Mr. Thompson decided to travel separately from us this morning," Celia said to Mr. Weaver, seated in front of her in the extra.

They'd finally arrived at a level part of the trail, allowing her to relax and question him after spending endless minutes clinging to the seat like a barnacle on the hull of a boat. She was afraid to look behind her at the cart carrying Mrs. Merrill's body, stored in a hastily constructed box, and discover that it had bounced out of the bed and onto the road somewhere along the way.

"Mr. Thompson would've been much more comfortable in the carriage than taking a horse," she added, though she wasn't certain that was true. Not at this rate of speed. Thaddeus Thompson had paid Mr. Shafer for the use of one of his horses and had ridden off a good hour before Celia and the others had departed. "Unless he does not intend to journey to Calistoga and then on to San Francisco, as we do."

Mr. Weaver's shoulders heaved with a deeply dramatic sigh. He'd said barely a word the entire journey down from the hotel, his reticence possibly due to having been cornered by Nicholas before they'd departed.

He turned in his seat to look at her. "Mr. Thompson is eventually heading to San Francisco but had business in Calistoga to attend to before continuing on. He was eager to get there before we're due to arrive," he said. "He intends to make his return trip to San Francisco tomorrow, I believe."

Celia slid a sideways glance toward Cassandra, seated on the other side of Barbara. She had her face averted, but she had to be listening to their conversation. It concerned her beloved, after all.

"Of course Mr. Thompson would provide you the details off his plans, you being great friends with his father. He is a city supervisor, isn't he? Most impressive." She noticed Dennis Merrill smirk; he'd been pretending to be asleep, but clearly he was not. "I am excessively curious, I admit. Ever since I emigrated to America, I cannot help but ask questions about all the interesting people I meet here. So different from England. So much greater energy and ambition." *Gad, Celia. Could you lay it on any thicker?*

The carriage hit a bump, jarring them, and delayed Mr. Weaver's response to her flattery of interesting Americans. The driver gave a hearty "gee-up" to spur the horses on, and the ride smoothed out again.

Mr. Merrill peeled open one eyelid. "Julius Thompson's position certainly impresses Hiram, Mrs. Davies."

Hiram Weaver frowned and resumed facing forward.

"Mr. Thompson senior sounds like a gentleman worth being associated with," Celia said.

"If you don't mind the costs involved in maintaining that association," Dennis Merrill replied and slid a look in Cassandra's direction.

The young woman stiffened, her hands clenching into fists on her lap. If Celia could peek beneath the concealing cover of her gloves, she might find that Cassandra's knuckles were white. How many people were aware of the agreement between Mr. Weaver and Mr. Thompson? Mr. Merrill appeared to be among the informed.

"What costs could those be, Mr. Merrill?" Celia asked, forcing a guileless tone.

A tone that did not dupe him. Instead, he guffawed and closed his eyes again. Based on the red of Mr. Weaver's neck, which showed between the bottom edge of his hairline and the top of his coat collar, he was incandescent with anger.

She sat back.

Barbara leaned into her. "What are you up to, Cousin?" she whispered.

"Just asking questions to bide the time, Barbara."

"You're upsetting Cassandra, in case you haven't noticed."

"I have noticed," she said.

"Furthermore, I don't think your questions have turned up any useful information."

"Haven't they?"

Barbara's brow furrowed. "No," she said, retying her bonnet ribbons, which had come loose in the wind stirred up by the carriage ride, with a snap of her wrists.

Am I causing more harm than good with my ceaseless prodding?

She'd not let herself believe that. She wanted to get to the bottom of what had happened to Elnora Merrill. Wanted to prevent Cassandra Weaver from making a terrible mistake with Mr. Thompson. Just as Celia had done with Patrick, despite the warning her own aunt had sent after she'd discovered that Celia had eloped with him. At the time, Celia had presumed the admonition had been delivered because Patrick was Irish. It was only later that she realized her aunt had foreseen the heartbreak. Sadly, the woman had passed away before Celia could apologize and tell her she'd been right to worry.

And here was Cassandra, possibly making a similar mistake. The one woman who'd attempted to warn *her* being carried in a wooden box on a long journey home.

• • •

Nick hadn't hung around in the yard to watch Celia and the others— minus Thompson—leave for Calistoga. They'd have a lengthy journey on the train that would take them to the ferry bound for San Francisco. Lots of time spent in close company with a potential killer. Maybe it was stupid to have let her travel with them, but Celia Davies wasn't somebody to order around. So he busied himself with questioning guests, collecting their opinions and their alibis, rather than think about her being in danger.

Folks were happy to talk about Parker Young. The general feeling was that Young had been congenial, at first, but his behavior hid a sneaky and shady side. There wasn't a speck of doubt he was guilty, according to the folks Nick spoke with. One or two suggested that Gabriella should be arrested as an accomplice. Maybe they were right.

"I'm looking for Gabriella," Nick said to the Chinese cook, who was scrubbing a pan on the steps outside the kitchen.

He gave Nick an expressionless look, maybe wondering what Nick wanted with her. More likely thinking he knew what most men wanted with her and expected that Nick wouldn't be any different.

"I'd like to ask Gabriella some questions, that's all. About Mr. Young," he said. "I'm with the San Francisco police."

The cook nodded toward a second rear entrance a few feet away. The door accessed a narrow hallway. Nick found Gabriella in one of the rooms branching off it.

The room, fitted with several large water basins and a copper boiler, was used as a laundry. Sleeves rolled up past her elbows, Gabriella had her hands plunged into a tub of soapy water and was scrubbing towels against a washboard. A stack of dirty linens waited for her once she finished with the towels.

"Do you have a minute, Gabriella?" he asked her.

She glanced over. "No, I do not."

"I won't take long."

"And I have work." She lifted the towel out of the water as proof. "I have to finish before I leave. I will not be paid if I don't finish."

Nick considered her. What would she do after she left this hotel? Would she find work elsewhere? Only if employers never learned of her connection to a horrible death at the geysers.

"Tell me about Parker Young," he said.

"He was a guest here. That's all I know about him."

"You weren't acquainted with him previously?"

She shook her head. "No."

"Then why were you seen leaving his room early yesterday morning, Gabriella?" Nick asked. "You weren't there to tidy it up, is my understanding."

She stiffened. "I don't want to talk to you."

"You've also claimed that Young didn't kill Mrs. Merrill," he said. "Why make that claim about a man you barely knew?"

She rubbed the towel down the length of the washboard before plopping it into the water again. "He seemed decent. Unlike others who come to this hotel."

He moved to better look her in the eye, but she wouldn't meet his gaze. "How much did he pay you to claim he was innocent, Gabriella?"

She threw the towel she'd been washing into the tub, a spout of soapy water splashing her and the ground. "What does it matter? The coroner has decided he is responsible for the woman's death. No one wants to listen to me. They'd rather think I am a liar than try to find out the truth."

"I'll listen to you, Gabriella. What *is* the truth, then?"

Her eyes examined his face. "I *was* with him, but he left to go walking. He came back soon after. He did not have enough time to kill Mrs. Merrill."

All right. This was better. "Folks have claimed they saw him on the bridge around when Miss Weaver started screaming. Which means he had to have gone out again."

"Maybe he did."

Great. "Anything else?"

She paused a long while before replying. "Mr. Merrill asked me to search that woman's room for a telegram."

What did that have to do with Parker Young? "Which woman?"

"The one they call the lady detective."

Celia's room. Of course. She hadn't told him about Gabriella poking around in her room, but then they hadn't had a lot of time together before she'd left. "Did Mr. Merrill explain why he wanted you to search her room for a telegram?"

"He did not," she replied, dropping her gaze. "And it does not matter, because I did not do what he asked. She was inside the room, and I couldn't."

"Failing doesn't make what you did okay, Gabriella," he said. "Why tell me about Mr. Merrill asking you to retrieve a telegram, Gabriella?

What does his request have to do with Mrs. Merrill's death? Anything?"

She turned away and resumed scrubbing the towel.

"If you're looking for me to pay you to answer my questions, Gabriella, I'm not going to. I'm a police officer." As if some police officers didn't pay for information. And Dennis Merrill might've simply persuaded her with a smile. He was charming enough. Nick couldn't speak to Young's charm, having never met the man.

Her frantic scouring of the towel slowed then stopped. "Mr. Young did go to the trail that leads to the geysers yesterday morning. It is true," she said quietly. "But he was not the only one who took that path."

"Who else, Gabriella?" When she didn't answer, he spun her to face him, the wet towel in her hand splattering water everywhere. "Who else?"

Just then, Shafer strode into the room with an armful of bedsheets. "More of the guests have decided to leave, after what's happened." His glance taking in Nick and Gabriella, he dropped the sheets onto the waiting pile of linens at her side. "Everything okay, Mr. Greaves?"

"I was just asking Gabriella about Mr. Young," he said. "She's been very helpful."

"Well, anyway, I'm glad I found you in here, Detective," Shafer said. "Your guide is ready to take you to Calistoga."

"Thanks."

Nick tapped the brim of his hat and strode off. She *had* been helpful. Why bring up Merrill if not to suggest that *he'd* been the other person she'd noticed near the geysers when Elnora Merrill had died?

• • •

Mr. Weaver ignored Celia's further attempts to engage him in conversation. Mr. Merrill, for his part, smirked the rest of the way to Calistoga, making her feel an idiot.

They shakily disembarked one coach only to transfer to a second one. It would take them the additional distance to St. Helena, the terminus of the Napa Valley train line. Mr. Weaver had decided they should wait for the afternoon train to Napa, a freight train with a passenger car attached, rather than hire a carriage and continue bouncing along at the mercy of leaf springs. Elnora's coffin would be loaded into one of the freight cars, where she'd pass the journey packed in insulating straw alongside crates of cheese and butter and grapes.

After a meal and an opportunity to refresh themselves in the facilities offered by one of the hotels, they boarded the train and settled into their seats. There were few passengers, and Cassandra found a bench all to herself several rows behind Celia and Barbara. Mr. Weaver and Mr. Merrill sat together, as did Celia and her cousin.

"How much longer?" Barbara asked once the train had chugged away from the station and the last remnants of St. Helena receded.

"The conductor informed me we should reach Napa City in less than two hours. We then journey on to Suscol to catch the ferry to San Francisco," she said. "We should arrive home tonight. Late, but still tonight." They'd set off for the geysers on Monday, and here it was only Thursday. Given all that had occurred, how had weeks not passed?

"Thank goodness," her cousin replied, nestling into the corner made by the outer wall of the train and the back of the bench. "I wish we'd never gone."

Celia patted her cousin's arm. "I'll be back in a few minutes, Barbara. You try to get some rest."

Steadying herself against the swaying of the car, Celia walked down the aisle to the seat Miss Weaver occupied.

"Do you mind if I sit with you for a few minutes, Miss Weaver?" Celia planted herself on the bench before Cassandra had a chance to answer.

Cassandra looked up from the book she'd been reading and glanced around, as if searching for an excuse that might allow her to say that she *did* mind. "Where is Barbara?"

"Oh, a few rows up ahead," she replied. "She enjoys having an entire seat to herself. She can relax a little more easily if I am not alongside, crowding her."

She lowered her book to her lap. "I suppose, then, that it's all right if you sit here, Mrs. Davies."

"Thank you. I won't keep you from your reading for too long," she said. "Your father was telling me all about Mr. Julius Thompson, your . . . Mr. Thaddeus Thompson's father. He seems the most remarkable man."

"I've only met him once. At an Odd Fellows' picnic."

"But he and your father are closely acquainted," Celia said. "I assumed that he would frequently visit your house to discuss business matters with your father."

"When I'm home, I'm usually in my bedroom or the morning room where I like to read and do my studies," she said. "I don't always know when visitors come by for my father."

"Miss Weaver, I should probably not admit this, but I have heard a rumor about your father. That he is attempting to seek a favor from the city for his business and has approached Mr. Julius Thompson with an offer of money," she said. "Your aunt was worried about him, wasn't she? If the rumor is true, your father is committing a crime."

Cassandra shot a look in the direction of her father, who was far enough away to not hear them. "I don't know what you're talking about."

"I think you do, Cassandra," Celia said. "Did you overhear a conversation at your house between the two men?" It was the most likely way for her to have learned about the arrangement.

"I don't make a habit of listening in on the conversations my father has with his visitors, Mrs. Davies," she said. "They're usually boring."

Perhaps Mrs. Merrill had not found those conversations boring.

"Why were you up on the hill so early yesterday morning, Cassandra?" Celia asked, noting that her question unsettled the young woman. "The guided tour was not due to start yet."

"I really don't want to talk about this, Mrs. Davies."

"Forgive me, but you must trust me when I say that I am asking for a good reason."

She drew in a long breath. "I saw my aunt heading for the bridge. I didn't understand what she was doing."

"Because she was supposed to wait for the tour, scheduled to get underway an hour later."

"It's not like her to wander off on her own. Especially in the heat. She did have problems with her heart," she said. "I thought it was strange, so I followed her."

"And what did you learn?"

Cassandra looked away to stare at the scenery sweeping past outside. The train clattered by brown patches of grass and stands of oak trees, lines of green grapevines arrayed on a nearby hillside, cattle browsing on another. A young boy riding a horse on an adjacent road tried to keep up with the train before slowing the animal and turning up a lane.

"My aunt was with somebody," she finally said. "I heard her talking and she can be quite loud. *Could* be quite loud," she corrected, frowning. "But I don't know who with."

Public and accessible to all the guests, the area near the fumaroles might make a good meeting spot. Although Elnora would have had to choose the exact location carefully. Much of the slope was visible from the hotel.

"You didn't approach your aunt and ask her?"

"I didn't have the nerve," she answered. "Aunt Elnora saw me coming up the trail—she was alone by that point—scolded me and told me to go back to the hotel."

"But you did not return to the hotel."

"I was going to, but I changed my mind and walked for a short way along one of the paths at the bottom of the gorge," she said. "But I couldn't shake my concern about her, so I went back and . . . It was terrible. I thought she'd had one of her fainting spells and would wake up if I shook her. But then I saw the blood and the terrible burns on her legs. And her eyes, wide open and unblinking."

Celia considered her. "Is it possible she'd been speaking with Mr. Merrill and he pushed her, Cassandra?"

She hesitated, although her delay in responding could have been a momentary reaction to the shuddering of the train as it passed over an uneven section of track. "Denny? No, it isn't possible. I didn't see him. Wouldn't I have seen him?"

"I noticed a stain on one of your shoes, Miss Weaver. It came from a mineral pool about ten feet from where you found your aunt's body," Celia informed her, perhaps unwisely. "Do you remember stepping in it?"

"I . . . I don't think so. I would've gotten burned."

"Does that mean you did not step into one?"

"I don't know."

"Of course," Celia replied, letting it go. "I should also tell you that I discovered a note in the pocket of Elnora's skirt."

"A note?"

Celia glanced at Cassandra's hands, twisting together in her lap. Forever twisting together.

"Yes. It was a demand for money," Celia replied. "Did she ever tell you about someone requesting funds from her?"

"No. Never. But then she might not have wanted me to worry. She did care about me," she said. "She often said that I reminded her of my mother. I miss her so much. And now Aunt Elnora is gone, too. It's just awful."

Tears began to slide down her cheek. Celia retrieved a clean handkerchief from her reticule and handed it to her.

"Mr. Thompson has received a similar demand," she said.

"He has?"

Did she look surprised? Celia could not tell.

"Yes," she said. "Cassandra, if you have any idea who is behind these blackmail attempts, you must tell someone, if not me."

A worried expression briefly pinched her face, then passed. "How would I know?"

How *would* an eighteen-year-old girl, naïve and protected, know? Perhaps it was wrong to imagine Elnora ever taking her niece into her confidence. Or for Thaddeus Thompson to admit that he might be the target of blackmail because of his father's illegal dealings.

"Mrs. Davies, if what you told me about my father is true, isn't it more likely that the note was meant for him?" Cassandra asked. "I don't know how my aunt got ahold of it, but doesn't that make more sense?"

It did.

"How might your father have felt about Elnora discovering his attempt to bribe a city official, Cassandra?" she asked. "Would he have been angry with her?"

She pinched her lips together and refused to reply. Perhaps she feared that if she spoke her agreement aloud, it would become the truth. Would make her father a killer.

❦ CHAPTER 11 ❧

"You sure Mr. Taylor isn't here?" Owen asked, looking around the station in case he came marching out of the detectives' office or strode through the door that led to the lockup.

The police officer who'd stopped him—Owen didn't recognize the man, and he thought he knew most of the fellows—folded his arms. "Do you see him?"

"No." The room wasn't so big that Mr. Taylor could be hiding someplace.

"Then I think you're finished here."

"Do you know where he is?" Owen asked.

The officer frowned. "If I did, why might I tell you?" he asked. "Who are you, anyway?"

"I'm his kid brother," Owen lied. He did feel bad when he lied, but it was always because he needed to, not because he liked to.

"Taylor has an Irish brother?" He roared with laughter, causing one of the other men in the station to look over. "Hey, is this boy Taylor's kid brother?"

"Him?" the cop asked, pointing his pencil at Owen. Unfortunately, Owen *had* seen him in the station before. "No. He's just a kid who likes to hang around and annoy us."

The officer who'd confronted Owen grabbed his shoulders and pushed him toward the alleyway door. "Time for you to leave and stop bothering the police. We're busy."

Shoot.

Owen stumbled up the steps and out into the alley. Now what? Wait for Mr. Taylor to return to the station? Wait for Mr. Greaves to get back to San Francisco? Or go do some investigating on his own?

He chose the latter. He was finished at the docks for the day and had the time. And since he'd already found the Weavers' address in the city directory stored at his boardinghouse, their house would make a good place to start. The woman who'd died at the geysers, Mrs. Merrill, was Miss Weaver's aunt and lived with her and her father. He'd learned that from Miss Barbara before she and Mrs. Davies had left for the geysers. He reckoned that Mr. Taylor probably had already gone to the Weavers' place to ask questions, but they might be more honest with Owen than with a police officer. Mrs. Davies always claimed that was why she got answers that Mr. Greaves sometimes failed to get; she wasn't a cop.

After a long walk from the police station, Owen climbed the steps to the Weavers' front door. Nobody had put any black crêpe on the knocker indicating that there'd been a death in the family. Maybe they didn't know yet. Or maybe they just hadn't gotten around to it. At least he didn't have to worry about one of the Weavers tossing him out on his ear, because they were probably still on their way home. Which meant he'd only have to deal with a servant who might not be happy about him snooping around.

He knocked and hurriedly straightened his cap and examined his clothes for dirt before somebody answered.

"We take deliveries around the side," the girl who answered the door said to him, even though it was obvious he didn't have anything to deliver. She was sorta pretty, with her reddish-brown hair peeking out beneath her cap and her clear skin, but he wasn't here to make her acquaintance.

"I'm bringing condolences from the family I work for," he said. "They are all sorry for your loss and will be sending a letter of sympathy soon."

She stepped back, deeper into the hallway beyond the door, where gleaming marble tiles stretched toward a fancy mahogany staircase. Rich folks always had the nicest, cleanest entryways. And flowers. They always had lots of flowers, which made Owen wonder where they got them from. Mrs. Davies's roses never bloomed for more than a couple of months, if they bloomed at all.

"What are you talking about? Nobody's died." She glared at him. "What are you about? Is this some sort of prank? Well, it's not funny."

The servants hadn't heard. But wasn't the news in the papers already? It should be, if Mr. Greaves had found out yesterday. Shouldn't it? Guess Mr. Taylor hadn't been to their place yet to ask questions, either. Meaning Owen was first on the scene.

He pulled his cap from his head, hoping his hair was clean. "Mrs. Merrill has passed away while visiting the geysers. We are awful sorry."

She gasped. "What a terrible lie! Go away and don't ever come back. Unless you want me to report you to the police!"

She made to slam the door on Owen just as another girl ran into the entry hall. "Mary! You won't believe it!"

Mary didn't look like a Mary, frankly. Not with her color of hair and eyes. But sometimes folks liked their servants to have simple English names, whether they were English or not. Maybe the Weavers hadn't been able to pronounce her real name. Maybe they hadn't even bothered to try.

"What won't I believe?" Mary asked.

"Mrs. Merrill has gone and died!"

Mary's glance darted between her and Owen. "What do you mean? Gone and died. How's that possible?"

"She fell. Up at the geysers. Cook was heading home from the Washington Market and got stopped by a police officer coming to bring us the news. So that we'd be prepared when the Weavers returned." She registered that Owen was standing in the doorway and looked over at him. "Who are you? We're not expecting any deliveries."

"He came from . . . Who did you say sent you?"

"The Davies family. They extend their deepest sympathies." *Dang.* Should he have come up with another last name? "My name's Owen, by the way."

"And you'll never believe this, Mary. A man is wanted in her death," the other girl continued. "She was murdered. Pushed down the hill and suffered awful, fatal burns from one of the steaming hot vents." She shuddered, imagining the damage. It did sound like a mighty gruesome way to go. Even he shuddered.

"Mr. Merrill, probably," Mary said, smirking.

Why'd she name him? She must have a reason. And hadn't the name of the fellow whose business had gone under been Merrill?

"Her husband?" Owen asked.

"No, her stepson. From what I've seen when he's been around, he doesn't like her," she said. "And the feeling was mutual."

Which sounded like an important clue.

The other, unnamed girl shushed her. "Mary, you shouldn't be speaking out of turn," she said. "And the officer told Cook that some fellow called Parker Young is suspected. Guess he's run off and they're searching for him."

"Never heard of a Parker Young."

"Mr. Young isn't somebody who's ever come to visit Mrs. Merrill?" Owen asked, grateful that, so far, they'd been willing to talk openly in front of him. Most folks were more cautious. Or maybe he was getting better at being an investigator. He sorta liked that explanation.

"Not as long as I've been answering the door," Mary replied.

"Wasn't Young the name of that woman who came wanting to talk to Mrs. Merrill the other day?" the other girl asked.

"No, her name was Gannon. Mrs. Gannon. Never seen her before, either," she said. "Although if *she'd* been at the Geyser Hotel with the Weavers and the Merrills, I wouldn't have been surprised to hear that she'd given Mrs. Merrill a good shove, as upset as she was when she came here looking for her. How she babbled on about letters she'd sent to Mrs. Merrill that never got a reply."

"What was in her letters?" Owen asked.

Mary scoffed. "Maybe *your* people tell you stuff, Owen, but Mrs. Merrill sure wasn't about to explain what the woman had wanted—not that I dared ask—and Mrs. Gannon also didn't explain. Just said she had an 'urgent matter to discuss.'"

"Didn't she say that her visit had to do with Mr. Merrill and to tell Mrs. Merrill that?" the other woman asked.

"Did she?" Mary asked. "I forgot about that. Must be why Mrs. Merrill finally agreed to see her."

"This is all weird, though, don't you think?" Owen asked. "I mean, some strange woman shows up here looking for Mrs. Merrill, and then not long after some strange man kills her." Could they be connected?

Mary was nodding her head in agreement. "You're right."

Just then, a woman hollered Mary's name from deep within the house. "Mary!" she repeated. "I need you back here now!"

"Have to go," Mary said and finally shut the door on Owen, leaving him standing on the stoop.

But he didn't mind being abandoned like an unwanted package. Not one bit. He only wished that Mr. Greaves or Mrs. Davies would hurry back to San Francisco so he could tell them what he'd learned.

• • •

Celia spent the remainder of the train ride mulling over what she knew and concluding that it was not much. Certainly not enough to arrive at a decision as to who may have killed Mrs. Merrill, if the perpetrator was not Mr. Young.

Giving up, she tried to doze. There was nothing to be gained by arriving in San Francisco exhausted. However, the rocking of the train made her feel slightly ill. And when they disembarked at Suscol and caught the ferry, the motion of the ship was no improvement. In the ferry's saloon, several men puffed on cigars, leaving the air chokingly full of smoke. So she went out on the deck to lean against the railing with Barbara and watch the sun set. It cast a golden glow upon the ruffled water, its light dimming as curls of fog stretched their fingers across the bay. It would be dark by the time they arrived home. How she longed for the comfort of her bed.

"You have truly upset Cassandra, Cousin," Barbara said, repositioning her shawl so that it covered her head. It was cold out here on the water. Bitterly so.

"I do apologize for that, Barbara. But in my conversation with her, she did propose an interesting idea," she said. "Concerning the note I found in Elnora's pocket. Cassandra has suggested that it may have been meant for her father, and her aunt had somehow found it."

"Blackmailing Mr. Weaver makes more sense."

"I agree, especially given the note I also found in Mr. Thompson's room. But who is the author? And how did this person learn of the bribery scheme?" she asked. "I do not think that Hiram Weaver is prone to blabbing, especially about such a sensitive topic."

"Somebody else might be." Barbara rubbed her hands together, trying to warm them. "Prone to blabbing, that is."

"But who?"

• • •

Nick rode hard, wanting to get back to San Francisco as fast as he could. He thought he might encounter Celia somewhere on the journey, but he didn't linger long enough in Calistoga to look for her and the others. Only as long as it took to catch a bite to eat and get a fresh horse for the rest of the trip to Suscol. Luckily for him, one of the Pacific Mail steamers had made an unscheduled stop at the port, meaning he could leave before the regularly scheduled ferry did. The ship's captain wasn't keen to take him aboard, but Nick's badge and some of Mrs. Jewett's money helped smooth matters.

He arrived in San Francisco not long after the sun had set. He pushed open the alley-side door to the police station and descended the short flight of stairs into the main room, his tired legs protesting every step. A new officer he didn't recognize and one of the sergeants who guarded the door to the lockup were the only ones there.

The sergeant nodded at Nick when he saw him. "Heard you've been ill, Greaves." He didn't look like he believed the story any more than Eagan probably had. "You've made a quick recovery, though."

"Feeling much better."

"You just missed that Irish kid," he said. "Guess he was here earlier, too. Looking for Taylor."

Cassidy. "Did he find him?"

"Taylor's been pretty scarce lately."

Probably trying to avoid getting asked any pressing questions about Nick and his "illness." Or occupied in a hunt for an engagement ring. "I'm sure he'll be around soon."

Nick found the door to the detectives' office unlocked. Inside, Mullahey was seated at Nick's desk, scribbling on a piece of paper.

"Leaving me a message, Mullahey?"

He got to his feet. "You're back, Mr. Greaves," he said. "Back early from your sickbed, that is. Glad to be seeing that you're better and all. Wasn't expecting you already."

"Well, here I am," Nick said. "What's in your note?"

Mullahey stepped out from behind Nick's desk. "I stopped in Mr. Weaver's office again. This mornin'."

Nick closed the door and took his chair. "Did you learn something new?"

"They are tight-lipped, the lot of them, that's for sure," he said. "Even worse than the first time I stopped by."

Anybody unwilling to talk with Mullahey was being stubborn for no good reason.

"However, one of the fellows told me something mighty interesting, Mr. Greaves," he continued. "Taylor mentioned that you'd learned about Mr. Thompson receiving a recent deposit to his bank account."

"We did," he said. "And I'm guessing that you're here to tell me that you've discovered the identity of the person who made that deposit."

"That I am, Mr. Greaves," he said. "It was the very fellow I was conversin' with at Mr. Hiram Weaver's office."

Excellent. "How did you get him to admit he was the one who'd deposited the money, Mullahey?"

The officer's mouth twisted with a grin. "Ah, Mr. Greaves, you don't want me to be confessin', do you?"

"Answer enough."

. . .

Celia was bone-tired by the time she and Barbara ascended the stairs to their house. Stairs that felt as though they'd increased in number since she'd last climbed them. Barbara lagged behind, her shoulders slumped under the weight of her carpetbag and small trunk.

"I want to sleep for an entire week," she declared.

Celia tested the doorknob, hoping Addie had received the telegram she'd sent from the telegraph station in Calistoga letting her know when they'd likely arrive home. The door swung open, but it wasn't Addie on the other side of it.

"Mrs. Davies, Miss Barbara, you're back!" Owen shouted.

"Owen, how can you be so energetic at this hour of the night?" Barbara moaned, dropping her baggage on the entryway floor.

"He's not been traveling since seven this morning, Barbara, that is how."

"Och, there you are, you two," Addie said, nudging Owen aside.

"It was horrible, Addie," Barbara said.

"And I've been sick with worry since Mr. Taylor told me about Mrs. Merrill," she said.

"We are home safely, Addie," Celia reassured her.

"Thankfully," she said. "Weel, there's mail and a telegram for you in your clinic, ma'am."

"Thank you."

"Did you get married while we were gone?" Barbara asked her, dragging off her shawl and bonnet and dropping them into Addie's outstretched hands.

Owen chuckled, and Addie shot him a scowl.

"I'd nae go and get wed without the two of you. A daft question, Miss Barbara." She collected Celia's things. "There's tea waiting in the dining room for you. I'll heat the kettle for more hot water."

Tea, as ever, being the solution to all of life's ills.

"What are you doing here, Owen?" Celia asked, rolling her shoulders to ease the stiffness that had taken hold of them . . . well, days ago, truth be told. She collected her mail and returned to the entryway. "It's late. Don't you need to get up early tomorrow for work?" He'd lost several jobs in the time that Celia had known him. On one occasion, it had been her fault that he'd been let go.

"I do, but I had to tell you what I found out," he said. "From Mr. Weaver's servants."

Barbara exhaled loudly. "Can't this wait until the morning? I'm exhausted and I have a headache."

"Look in my cabinet and see if I have some powdered angelica root. That might help," Celia said. "I'll tell you tomorrow what Owen has discovered."

"Good night, Owen." She yawned and trudged off.

"I'll go and help her, ma'am. Bring her some hot water for a quick sponge bath," Addie said. "She looks pure done in, poor lass."

Owen scampered after Celia like an excited puppy as she crossed the parlor, bound for the dining room. She sat and lifted the teapot, hot beneath its cozy.

"None for me, ma'am," Owen said, taking a chair opposite her.

She poured herself a cup and set aside the strainer. Her hands shook from fatigue. "So, tell me what you learned from the Weavers' servants."

"I learned that a woman named Mrs. Gannon came looking for Mrs. Merrill not that long ago. And, according to Mary—she's the servant that answers the door—Mrs. Gannon was mad that Mrs. Merrill hadn't responded to some letters she'd sent her," he said. "I was told that Mrs. Gannon thought that if she mentioned she wanted to talk to Mrs. Merrill about her stepson, Mrs. Merrill might be more interested in letting her into the house."

Dennis Merrill again. How intriguing.

"And was she more interested? Did she speak with this woman?" Celia asked, glancing at the post she'd placed on the table. How could she have amassed so much correspondence in the short time she was gone?

"Yep," he replied. "Finally."

"And what was in those letters?"

"Don't know, ma'am."

"This is all very curious, Owen, but I'm not certain that the woman and her letters have anything to do with Mrs. Merrill's suspicious death," she said, reaching for the telegram and breaking open the seal on the envelope.

"Well, Mrs. Davies, there's one way we could find out. Isn't there?"

She smiled at him. "Are you proposing a small adventure to the Weavers' house, Owen?"

"I might be."

"Then how does tomorrow morning sound? Say, at half six?" she asked, sparing a glance at the contents of the telegram. *Gad.*

"What is it, ma'am? Have you decided we shouldn't go after all?"

She must have been frowning without realizing it. "No, Owen, it is merely this telegram I have received. From a 'Friend.'"

He leaned over the table to try to read it. "What's it say?"

"'Mind your own business.'" Received earlier that day at San Francisco's main telegraph office. The telegram did not reveal, however, who had sent it or where it had come from. Another anonymous author.

"Somebody doesn't want you to investigate, ma'am," Owen said, sounding concerned.

"Which means they're worried that I might uncover the truth. So I must continue." She stuffed the telegram back into the envelope. "But do not tell Barbara or Addie about this. And we must proceed carefully during our visit to the Weavers' house tomorrow."

Very carefully.

ॐ CHAPTER 12 ॐ

"Heard you got back last night, sir. Glad you're here, because Captain Eagan was starting to ask questions," Taylor said, stepping through the half-open door of the detectives' office. He took his usual chair against the wall. "We got the news about what happened to Mrs. Merrill and the fellow suspected in her death. Sounds terrible."

"It was." Nick hadn't seen the body. He hadn't needed to; he could easily picture how horrible her injuries would've been.

"I decided to look into Mr. Parker Young, see if he happens to be a resident of San Francisco or hereabouts," his assistant said. "I figured if he killed Mrs. Merrill, they might've known each other already."

"Everybody states that they didn't. It's possible Young is simply a deranged individual who likes to toss women into boiling hot mineral pools," he said. "Mrs. Davies doesn't think he's guilty, though." And Nick had learned to trust her intuition.

Taylor's brow furrowed. "Then why'd he run off?"

"Two options, Taylor," Nick said. "He actually *is* guilty, or he saw the person responsible and got scared."

"Could be, sir," he said, nodding in agreement. "I did happen to find a fellow in San Francisco named P. Young, though."

"Interesting."

"If he is the same fellow, it's an awful strange coincidence that he was visiting the geysers when the Weavers and Merrills were. Right, sir?"

Unless it wasn't a coincidence. "Plenty of folks travel there, Taylor."

"Suppose so."

"Mrs. Merrill's death might be connected to a blackmail note Mrs. Davies found in one of the woman's pockets," Nick said. "Somebody staying at the hotel had written it, because the author had used a hotel menu card. Maybe Young. He was spotted trying to talk with her and other members of the traveling party before she died. The sense I get is they had no interest in talking to him, though."

"But why target her? She wasn't involved in that bribery scheme."

"Maybe the blackmailer—let's presume it is Young—thought that Mrs. Merrill would be more willing to shell out money than Hiram Weaver," Nick said.

"Why not try to meet with Mrs. Merrill here in the city, though?" he asked. "Rather than go all the way to the geysers."

Maybe he had tried, like Celia had suggested.

"Taylor, find out if Young had ever been turned away at Weaver's house. And see if you can uncover a connection between Young and any of the folks who'd traveled to the geysers."

"Yes, sir." He dragged out his notebook and jotted a memo to himself.

"Also, look into Dennis Merrill, the dead woman's stepson," he said. "Mrs. Davies overheard him arguing with his stepmother. Also, we might have a witness placing him in the vicinity when Mrs. Merrill died." Two witnesses, if he included Gabriella's implication that she'd noticed him on the trail.

"Maybe the argument had to do with his business going belly-up recently," Taylor said. "When I was out . . . um, doing some police work, I came across a store he used to own. Mr. Merrill was a fur dealer, but workers were busy scraping his name off the window glass when I went past."

"Recent financial difficulties, eh?"

"Looks like it," he replied. "Wonder if he'll inherit money from Mrs. Merrill."

Stepchildren didn't automatically. "Try to find out the details of Dennis Merrill's father's will, too."

Taylor scribbled more notes to himself.

Nick stretched out his legs, stiff and aching from yesterday's long ride. More stiff and sore than last night. He'd barely been able to descend the steps into the station this morning without grimacing. "Mullahey finally got one of Weaver's employees to admit that he was the person who'd deposited those funds into Julius Thompson's bank account."

"I've been thinking about that, sir. What if it was just a loan?" Taylor asked. "Mr. Thompson could claim that, couldn't he?"

And likely would. "In addition to the blackmail note Mrs. Merrill had, Mrs. Davies found one in Thompson's room at the hotel."

"So, you've got the Merrills, the Weavers, and Thaddeus Thompson all up at the Geyser Hotel together," Taylor said. "And two of them received blackmail notes."

"I don't think we can get to the bottom of this, Taylor, until either

Thompson or Weaver admits to their little bribery scheme. Giving us a chance to learn who all might've known about it." Nick got to his feet and collected his hat from the top of his desk. "So let's go see if we can get one of them to fess up."

• • •

"You're not worried about that telegram, are you, ma'am?" Owen asked, striding alongside Celia.

"No, Owen," she lied. She'd hardly slept from speculating about who could have sent it. It was not impossible that one of the Weavers or Mr. Merrill had done; their stop in Calistoga had been long enough to allow someone to go to the local telegraph office and dispatch a message.

"That's good. So, what's our story?" he asked. "I told Mary I was bringing condolences from you. Don't know how to explain why I'm back this morning and you're with me. You already offered the Weavers your sympathy when Mrs. Merrill died."

"I am going to tell them that I'd lent Mrs. Merrill a shawl while we were up at the geysers. In the aftermath of her death, however, I neglected to retrieve it, since the family was so upset," she said, pausing at the curb to wait for a buggy to pass. "I've come to collect it because I need the shawl for an event this evening, and it is probably packed among her belongings."

"Think they'll believe you, ma'am?"

"I shall attempt to be most persuasive."

He chuckled in response. "Any idea where Mrs. Gannon's letters might be?"

"If Mrs. Merrill was like most people, she would have stored them in the most secure location she could find." Celia dodged a fellow calling out "Strawberries! Strawberries!" at the top of his lungs, a flat box loaded with red berries atop his head and a pair of scales by which to weigh them hanging from the waist of his pants. He looked hopefully at them, letting them pass when he realized he wasn't getting a sale. "Namely, a lockable case or drawer somewhere in her bedchamber at the Weavers' house."

"I can pick the lock for you, if you'd like, ma'am," Owen offered.

She looked over at him. "I did not realize you knew how to pick locks, Owen." His abilities were likely superior to hers.

"Mr. Taylor taught me, and I've been practicing."

"Well, hopefully your skills will not be required, because it would be most awkward to justify why you're hunting for my shawl in Mrs. Merrill's bedchamber."

"What should I be doing while you're up in her room, ma'am?"

"Distracting Mary." She stopped halfway up the road and eyed the house across the street. "This is the Weavers', correct?"

"Yes, ma'am."

She drew in a long breath. "Then let us proceed and discover how charming we both can be."

• • •

Julius Thompson had an office on Montgomery not far from the bank he used, situated along the stretch of the road where the fashionable set enjoyed promenading on a nice afternoon. As far as Nick and Taylor could make out, Julius Thompson's primary occupation, in addition to being a city supervisor, was sitting on the boards of various corporations. And possibly taking bribes on the side to fatten his bank accounts.

The office was located above a jeweler's. A whip-thin fellow with a massive mustache all out of proportion to his narrow face was seated at a large roll-top desk when Nick and Taylor arrived. He stood and identified himself as Julius Thompson's secretary. He also brusquely informed them that Mr. Thompson was not in the office at present, indicating the closed door at his back. Which was fine by Nick; he often got more out of an employee than he ever did out of the person he wanted to question.

The secretary appeared to think his response would prompt Taylor and Nick to immediately turn around and leave. The downward movement of his mustache indicated that he'd realized they weren't going to and was frowning.

"Mind if we come inside?" Nick asked, revealing his badge and pushing past him.

Nick strolled around the outer office, examining the certificates and documents and a very patriotic picture of President Johnson hanging on the walls. Thompson had a license to practice law—interesting that he didn't appear to be using it—and wanted everybody to know that he was a member of the Independent Order of Odd Fellows. In fact, according to another document in a fancy gilt frame, he was a Vice Grand of a local lodge. Or had been at one time. The document was dated to almost five years ago.

His secretary cleared his throat. "What is it you gentleman want, if I might ask?"

Taylor chuckled over being referred to as "gentlemen." Not many folks would agree with the description.

"Will your employer be back soon?" Nick asked. "We'd like to speak with him."

"His next appointment is not until noon, so I'm not expecting him to come into the office until then, Detective."

"In that case, maybe you can answer some questions."

"Is that necessary? I'm quite busy."

"I wouldn't bother if it wasn't necessary."

Taylor reached into his inner coat pocket and pulled out his notebook and pencil.

"Is his appointment with Hiram Weaver, by any chance?" Nick asked. "Maybe to discuss the money Mr. Weaver recently had one of his employees deposit into Mr. Thompson's bank account?"

The secretary blinked a few times. "I don't know what you're talking about, Detective."

Nick picked up a bronze inkwell sitting atop one of the unoccupied desks. The inkwell had an inscription on its square base—*To J. Thompson. In thanks for your service*—and the name of an IOOF lodge beneath. He might've left the Odd Fellows, but at one time they'd clearly appreciated him.

"You mean, in your capacity as secretary, your boss didn't inform you of an infusion of cash in exchange for, oh, favors?" Nick asked.

"Favors?" His gaze darted between Nick and Taylor, whose note-taking was agitating him. Funny how that always happened with folks. At least with those folks who might have something to hide. "I don't know anything about supposed favors."

Nick leaned his hips back against the desk edge. "The police have been approached by an individual wanting to lodge a complaint against Mr. Thompson. The complaint being that your employer is favoring certain businessmen for city contracts in exchange for . . . gifts, let's call them."

"That is false! A slanderous lie. Mr. Thompson's reputation is pristine."

What man could claim to have a "pristine" reputation? Not many, in Nick's experience.

"I'll keep that in mind," Nick said. "What has Mr. Thompson said about plans for his son to marry Mr. Weaver's daughter?"

"Mr. Thaddeus?" he stuttered, the abrupt change of topic catching him off guard.

"Is there more than one son?" Taylor asked.

"Yes, but the other one, the youngest, lives in Cincinnati," he said. "Mr. Thompson has not shared any such plans with me."

"Because he wouldn't? Or because the arrangement has come about so quickly that he hasn't had the chance to?" Nick asked. "I guess I presumed that you, as his secretary, would be informed about any changes to his calendar to accommodate an engagement announcement, for instance."

"Mr. Thompson hasn't told me about wedding plans, and I can't explain why, Detective," he said. "I am very pleased for Mr. Thaddeus, though. That is very good news."

"You sound like you're surprised," Nick said. "Is Thaddeus Thompson not the type to go and get married?"

"It's just a blessing, that's all. Mr. Thompson will be relieved to see his eldest son settled at last, and with the daughter of a good friend."

"Never thought it would happen, I take it."

"Well, Mr. Thaddeus *is* forty, Detective," he said. "Too many years spent sowing his wild oats."

"Has he struggled to find a young woman who'd want to take him on as a husband?" he asked. "After all, a lot of men sow their wild oats. Doesn't usually stop them from getting a wife, especially if they're related to someone like Mr. Julius Thompson. Unless his father's reputation isn't as pristine as you'd like us to think. Some folks might find that off-putting." Or maybe it was Thaddeus Thompson's reputation Nick should be questioning.

The secretary's face turned an alarming shade of red. "I will be sure to inform Mr. Thompson of your crass accusation that he is accepting bribes, Detective, and he will take the proper steps." He stomped over to the office door and threw it open. "Now, good day to you both."

Great.

• • •

"You're here again?" the young woman who answered the door asked Owen. Mary, Celia assumed.

Owen shot Celia a look as if to say, "I told you so."

"Sorry, ma'am, about being rude. We've been on pins and needles here, we have, ever since we heard about Mrs. Merrill," Mary said. At her back, the entry hall and the rooms to either side of it were heavy with shadows, the curtains having been drawn to reflect a family in mourning. Plunging the house into darkness as though it was blasphemous to allow a wink of sunshine to penetrate the somber gloom. "But Mr. Weaver was confused, too. Said he didn't understand why you sent somebody to extend condolences when you'd been at the geysers with them when Mrs. Merrill died."

"When Owen here heard about Mrs. Merrill's death, he took it upon himself to extend condolences from our household. He can be impulsive," Celia said, shaking her head over his spontaneous gesture. "However, we have returned because I have a small request."

"And what's that?"

"I lent a shawl to Mrs. Merrill while we were at the geysers and, as you might imagine under the circumstances, I forgot to reclaim it." She smiled apologetically. "I can quickly retrieve the shawl from her luggage rather than disturb Mr. Weaver or Miss Weaver. I'd not intrude were it not for the fact that I'd planned to wear it to an occasion I am attending this evening. It matches my gown." *Please, please, please let me in.*

"Mr. Weaver isn't here, and Miss Weaver is resting."

"I have no wish to disturb Miss Weaver, nor do I wish to encumber you with a silly request. Not when the household staff is undoubtedly busy with the numerous tasks involved in preparing for Mrs. Merrill's funeral, God rest her," Celia said. "I promise I shall be quick as a wink."

Her persistence weakened Mary's resolve, and she sighed. "Mr. Weaver won't like it if he finds out I let you inside the house."

"Thank you so much."

"*You* have to stay right here, though," Mary said to Owen, indicating the rectangular Turkish carpet in the entryway where she expected him to wait.

"Sure, but . . ." He began to sway a little, reaching for Celia's arm. "Sorry, ma'am. I'm not feeling so . . ."

"Owen, are you having one of your spells?" Celia wrapped an arm around his shoulder. *Quick thinking, Owen. Excellent.*

Mary's eyes widened with alarm. "What's wrong with him?"

"The excitement, you see. He gets faint sometimes," she answered. "Perhaps you can take him to the kitchen and give him some cool water. If that's not too great an inconvenience."

"Do you need me to get the gardener to help you walk to the kitchen?" Mary asked Owen.

"No, I think I should be able to follow you."

"First door on the right at the top of the steps, ma'am. Door's not locked," she said. "And be quick."

Mary strode off. Owen turned and winked at Celia before trailing after her, moaning every so often for effect.

Celia hiked her skirts, grabbed the banister, and climbed the stairs as rapidly as she could.

She located the bedchamber and went in, the brocade curtains drawn against the morning sunlight. It was even darker inside the chamber than in the rest of the house, and Celia used a few precious seconds to allow her eyes to adjust. Her room held the usual assortment of furnishings, all of good quality, but lacked any paintings or pictures to personalize the space. Perhaps Elnora had not foreseen that she would be living here as long as she had done. What would have happened to her once Cassandra married and Elnora no longer held the position of being her chaperone and companion? A position that had included a room in this house.

"I cannot imagine Dennis Merrill taking her in," she whispered.

Elnora's bags sat at the foot of her four-poster bed. They'd been opened and the contents returned to the various drawers and hooks in the room, leaving behind only a receipt from a shop in Healdsburg for the purchase of a fan. The haste to store her things seemed unnecessary; Elnora wouldn't ever be wearing the items again. Unless Cassandra had requested an inventory in case she might want a particular piece of clothing.

Or she'd been searching for Mrs. Gannon's letters among her aunt's belongings. She or her father.

Unfortunately, the chest of drawers in the bedchamber was securely locked, and she was running out of time to test her lock-picking abilities or to retrieve Owen from the kitchen. Celia turned to Elnora's dressing table. She had greater luck there.

She rummaged through the contents: fine linen handkerchiefs, embroidered with an *E* in sapphire-colored thread, tortoiseshell combs and brushes, pins and ribbons for tying up her hair at night, a nearly empty jar of facial cream. Another drawer held a tray of jewelry. There were lovely filigreed-silver brooches and jet earrings and a coral necklace, along with a pair of diamond-and-emerald earrings. Dennis Merrill had claimed that his stepmother was a spendthrift. Perhaps the jewels were proof, although they did not seem excessive.

She finished searching the dressing table, throwing open every drawer, reaching inside and feeling around for secret compartments or paper affixed to surfaces. Nothing. And a hasty inspection of the fire grate in the room indicated that it hadn't been used in months and certainly didn't hold any guilty evidence of letters having been burned there.

Sighing, she slid shut the dressing table drawers. The center one caught as she tried to close it. Was it damaged? Celia crouched down and examined the wood where the top of the drawer met the frame. There were gouge marks immediately above the keyhole, as though someone had used a metal implement to pry open the drawer.

"Mrs. Davies?" Mary called from the top of the steps. "Have you found your shawl?"

Bloody . . .

She stood and spun to face the door just as Mary stepped inside the bedchamber.

"Mrs. Davies? What are you doing?" She peered over Celia's shoulder at the dressing table. "Were you looking through Mrs. Merrill's personal things?"

"What? No," she said, wondering if Mary could hear her heart thudding, as fiercely as it was beating. "Actually, I should confess that I was hoping to find smelling salts in one of her dressing table's drawers. Being inside her bedchamber raised anew the horror of seeing her inert body on the rocky trail, and I became lightheaded. But the drawers were all locked."

"She locked them before she left."

But someone had broken the lock. Who?

"I should also confess my ridiculous silliness," she continued. "My shawl was not among Mrs. Merrill's belongings, because I forgot that I'd not lent it to her. She changed her mind about needing it."

"You did not give Mrs. Merrill your shawl?"

"No. Where has my head been? I did not realize how greatly Mrs. Merrill's death has distressed me. Such a shock to all of us. One moment she was hale and hearty, vibrantly alive, and the next . . ." Celia shook her head. "How quickly everything can change, and how little we can control matters. 'What fates impose, that men must needs abide.'"

"What?"

"Shakespeare." She exited the room and descended to where Owen stood in the entryway. "We came all this way for no reason, Owen."

"You didn't find your shawl, ma'am?"

"I now remember that I never lent it to Mrs. Merrill," she said. "My deepest apologies for disturbing you, Mary. Come, Owen."

He followed her out onto the street, looking back at the house and nearly tripping over a break in the pavement. "You should've asked me how I was doing, ma'am," he said. "Mary'll realize that I was faking and wasn't really feeling sick."

"I believe Mary already suspects that we were not there to retrieve my shawl and that my pretext was a ruse," she said, rushing along in her haste to get away from the house. "I do apologize if you're concerned about her opinion of you, though."

He blushed. Ah, he'd been hoping to interest Mary.

"Doesn't matter, Mrs. Davies," he said. "Did you find any letters?"

"No," she replied, breathing easier as they turned the corner and moved out of sight of the occupants of the Weavers' home. "Someone may have retrieved them before I attempted to. One of the drawers in Mrs. Merrill's dressing table had been pried open. There was a visible gouge in the wood above the lock, and the lock itself has been damaged."

"The damage might've been there for a while, ma'am."

"Except that, according to Mary, Mrs. Merrill wanted the dressing table locked while she was gone. If the lock was already broken, she would have requested that it be repaired."

"Maybe somebody jimmied the lock to steal Mrs. Merrill's jewelry when they learned she'd died," he suggested.

"Unless Mrs. Merrill owned a more valuable piece than a pair of diamond-and-emerald earrings, jewel thievery was not what the pilferer was interested in."

"The letters, then."

"That is what I am assuming, Owen," she said. "And there are only a handful of individuals who would have had the opportunity to pilfer them since we all returned last evening. Namely, the occupants of the house."

"Or one of the servants while the family was away, ma'am," he said. "Or somebody snuck into the house and took them."

"Both are possibilities," she said. "We should have asked if anyone has been to the house recently. I suppose we'd be pressing our luck to go back there to question Mary again. Or Cassandra."

"Miss Weaver isn't home."

"What do you mean?"

"While the cook was getting me a glass of water, I asked how Miss Weaver was doing, just to make conversation," he said. "She told me that Miss Weaver got up early and left about a half hour after her father went out this morning."

"But Mary claimed she was resting."

"Guess she wasn't," he said. "The cook was worried, because Miss Weaver refused to let any of the staff go with her and she wasn't back yet."

"She could not have gone to visit with Mr. Thompson," Celia said. "He's not scheduled to return to San Francisco until later today at the earliest, according to Mr. Weaver."

"The cook thought her leaving the house in such a rush had to do with a note that was delivered this morning. Sun had just come up when the messenger knocked on the door," he said. "Guess it upset Mr. Weaver, and he dashed off about fifteen or twenty minutes later."

Owen had the most amazing ability to discover information. "Was the note for him or for her? And did the cook mention who'd sent it?"

"She didn't say. Sorry, ma'am."

"Perfectly all right, Owen. You have learned information we might not have obtained otherwise."

"It's sorta curious, don't you think, Mrs. Davies?" he asked. "Them both running off so early this morning."

"Curious indeed."

✂ CHAPTER 13 ✎

"Sorry to bother you, Miss Ferguson," Nick said, removing his hat as she ushered him into the hallway. "I was hoping to speak with Celia. Is she around this morning?"

"She's gone off with Owen. To the Weavers'," she said.

Damn. Off investigating. "She just got back last night from a trip to the geysers with them."

"Och, you know her, Mr. Greaves," she said. "Would you care to come in and wait?"

As she turned to gesture toward the parlor, light glinted off the new ring on her hand. So, Taylor had found one and given it to her while Nick was away. A feeling like guilt twisted. He owed Celia a ring, owed her a promise to be at her side for the rest of their lives. But he always hesitated, too chicken-hearted to commit.

"Congratulations, Miss Ferguson, on your engagement."

Her eyes glistened with what could only be described as pure, serene joy. Taylor had done that for her. Made Addie Ferguson happy.

"Thank you, Mr. Greaves." She smiled. "And you may call me Addie."

"If it's okay with you, I'll stick with Miss Ferguson for now," he said, uncomfortable with the closeness that was going to come with her being married to Taylor. "Did Celia explain what she wants with the Weavers?"

She frowned. "'Tis a rare day when she explains to me what she's aboot, sir. I'm sprouting gray hairs from the fretting."

"Good morning, Mr. Greaves." Barbara, yawning, walked into the parlor. "Or is it afternoon already?"

"There's tea and toast waiting for you in the dining room, Miss Barbara," Addie said.

"Wait. Are you wearing an engagement ring?" She caught hold of Addie's hand. "You are. Why didn't you tell us last night that you'd accepted Mr. Taylor?"

"I wasna about to go and prattle on about it at the late hour you and Mrs. Davies returned."

"I think you should have."

"And I should be going," Nick said, wanting to escape the argument brewing between them. "Tell Celia I was here, Miss Ferguson."

"Has she gone off someplace?" Barbara asked. "To investigate, I presume."

"To the Weavers'," Addie replied stiffly.

"Probably because Owen uncovered some information from one of their servants, Mr. Greaves," Barbara said. "About letters Mrs. Merrill recently received. The woman who sent them also visited her, wanting to speak with her about Mr. Merrill. I think that's what Owen said."

"Were you listening to their conversation through the floor grate in your bedchamber, Miss Barbara?" Addie chastised.

Barbara perked her chin. She looked like her cousin when she did that. "Sometimes my listening comes in handy, Addie. Like now, for example."

"Hmph."

"Did you learn anything else, Miss Barbara?" Nick asked.

"The woman's name was Gannon, I think."

"Thank you," he said. "Miss Ferguson, please tell Celia that I'd like her to come to the station as soon as possible."

He left them to squabble over Barbara's snooping and returned to the station. A woman with the last name of Gannon looking to talk to Mrs. Merrill about her stepson. Based on Nick's impression of Dennis Merrill, she was probably a spurned lover looking for him to make good on broken promises.

Nick reached Portsmouth Square just as Taylor came jogging out from the basement police station and onto Kearny.

He hailed him. "There's been a body found, sir. Mr. Greaves. A murdered man."

"Where?"

"At the address I'd found for P. Young." He trailed after Nick as he headed inside the building and downstairs into the station. "According to the officer I spoke with, it was a Mr. Young, but he didn't know the fellow's first name."

"Maybe it's a different P. Young and not Parker Young." *How likely is that, Greaves?*

"Maybe, sir," Taylor answered, looking as skeptical as Nick felt. "The fellow was strangled, according to the officer. The coroner's there now, examining the body."

"Well, if it is our P. Young, what was he doing in San Francisco, Taylor? Why wasn't he thousands of miles away?"

"Don't know, sir."

"Wasn't expecting you to."

They strode into the detectives' office. Celia was perched on the chair in front of Nick's desk, her hands clasped in her lap.

"Ah, there you are, Mr. Greaves. Mr. Taylor."

"Been waiting long?" Nick asked, taking a seat at his desk and contemplating the pile of papers strewn across it. Had it grown since last night? Sure looked that way. A recently added one mentioned a fellow who'd been brought in for operating a hand organ without a license. *Great.*

"Not at all. I just arrived from the Weavers'," she said. "By the way, congratulations on your engagement, Mr. Taylor. Addie showed me the ring you gave her. Very lovely."

Nick's assistant grinned. Blushed, too. "Thank you, ma'am."

"You are most welcome," she said. "But I sense that you and Mr. Greaves were having an important discussion."

"A dead body's been found, ma'am," Taylor said. "This morning. At a boardinghouse."

"You might find it interesting to learn that the dead man's name is Young, Mrs. Davies," Nick said. "Murdered."

Her forehead puckered. "Is it Parker Young, Mr. Greaves? Here, in the city?"

"Could be," he said. "And I can't comprehend why he was in San Francisco, either."

The puckering of her forehead didn't ease. "I wonder, Mr. Greaves, if the arrival of an upsetting note at the Weavers' early this morning is in any way connected to his death," she said. "The timing is suspicious."

"An upsetting note?" Nick asked.

"Yes. It arrived around five o'clock this morning and resulted in both Mr. Weaver and Miss Weaver departing within a half hour or so of its appearance," she said. "Where is the body, Mr. Taylor? I would like to have a look at our murder victim."

"He'll probably be at the undertaker's, ma'am, by the time you get there," Taylor answered. "Or soon after."

Nick's assistant meant the basement of Massey's Coffin Warerooms, where the coroner's bodies were stored while they awaited autopsies or for somebody to claim them. Or both.

"While we walk there, Mr. Greaves, I can tell you what Owen and I have learned."

• • •

"You and Cassidy went to the Weavers' to see what you could uncover about the Gannon woman and the letters she sent to Mrs. Merrill, didn't you, Celia?" Nicholas asked.

Barbara must have been eavesdropping and told him about them.

"To search for the letters, actually," Celia replied, strolling alongside him. Would these walks, which they'd so often taken, feel different if they were no longer colleagues but wed to each other? Would she even continue to be involved in his cases and take these walks? Assuming he ever asked her to marry him.

"And?"

"We did not find them, Mr. Greaves," she said. "I assumed Elnora would have stored them in her bedchamber. I searched the room, but there weren't any letters from Mrs. Gannon. That is why I came to the station; I wanted to let you know."

"Somebody let you inside to search her bedroom?"

"Apparently I am very persuasive."

He took her elbow and guided her across the street once the Omnibus Railroad horsecar passed. "And you say Weaver wasn't at home when you were hunting around."

"No, he was not. Neither he nor Cassandra," she said. "They'd not returned from their early morning jaunts."

"Interesting."

Or highly suspicious, if the murdered man did indeed turn out to be Mr. Parker Young. Found dead early this morning, when Cassandra and Hiram Weaver were out . . . doing whatever it was they were doing.

"Remember the argument I told you I overheard in Healdsburg between Elnora and Dennis Merrill, Nicholas?" she asked. "It was about a woman who'd informed Elnora of something distressing. The timing of when Mrs. Gannon visited the Weavers' house and that heated discussion occurring shortly afterward makes me think they were arguing about her."

"Probably."

"Her letters and her visit might also explain Elnora's agitation before we departed for the geysers," she said. "Mrs. Gannon was apparently extremely angry, according to one of the Weavers' servants. I only wish Elnora had explained better what was bothering her. I may have been able to—"

"Prevent her death? You can't blame yourself, Celia," Nicholas gently chided. "She had plenty of opportunities to tell you if she was afraid of Mrs. Gannon, or of somebody else, and didn't. You're not a mind reader."

"Sadly, no, I am not." But she still blamed herself.

"Maybe Mrs. Merrill disposed of those letters, Celia," Nicholas said, sidestepping the supplies that a fellow—occupied with replacing several missing street bricks that had most likely been stolen—had stacked on the pavement.

"I did consider that, Nicholas, and inspected the bedchamber fire grate for any evidence of burned papers. However, it does not appear to have been used in ages."

"There are some officers at the station who should take lessons from you, Mrs. Davies."

"Few men who would endure taking advice from a woman, Mr. Greaves."

"Isn't that the truth."

"Curiously, one of the drawers in her dressing table had been pried open." Jimmied, as Owen had referred to it. "Someone else may have retrieved Mrs. Gannon's letters before I had the chance to."

They arrived at Sacramento Street, where the building housing Massey's Coffin Warerooms was located, and entered the establishment. The display of coffins, alongside ebony black feathers and drapery destined to adorn wagons and horses, always caused her to shiver. Nicholas showed his badge to Mr. Massey's assistant and explained why they were there. The fellow directed them to the basement.

"I may never get used to going down here, Nicholas," she said as they descended into the cool, damp room, the sickening smell of embalming fluid becoming stronger with each step taken.

"If it makes you feel any better, I don't think I ever will, either." He squeezed her hand and indicated a table at the far end of the room. It held a body draped in a dark cloth. "I believe that's our man, Celia."

She hated the way she recoiled, the way her stomach clenched. It should be easier to examine the wounds found on a deceased person's body than to tend to the cuts and bruises and burns of the living.

Patients who moaned and writhed beneath her touch, in such pain that they resisted her attempts to help, to heal. But it was not easier.

She squared her shoulders and crossed to the table. "All right. Let us see who it is."

Nicholas peeled back the edge of the cloth that concealed the man's head.

"Yes. It is Mr. Parker Young." A contusion marred his right temple, but it was not enough damage to make him unrecognizable.

"Well, well."

"I hope the coroner will not object to a brief examination on my part." She turned Mr. Young's head to get a better view of the injury it had suffered. The greasy basement windows only allowed a meager amount of light to enter the room, and she and Nicholas had not bothered to take the time to light any lamps.

"Does the coroner believe the blow to his temple is what killed him, Nicholas?" she asked. "It does not look to be sufficient."

"Haven't heard his conclusions, but the officer called to the scene reported that the man died from strangulation."

"Ah." Celia removed the cloth covering Mr. Young's body. He was down to his shirtsleeves and stockinged feet. He must have been in bed when he was attacked. It was most unfortunate that he didn't have his shoes on; she would have liked to inspect them.

She ran a finger around the edge of his collar, tugging it down. "Here, Nicholas. Hiding beneath his shirt collar. An inch-wide purple bruise encircling his neck."

"I see it. Thank you, Celia."

She considered Mr. Young's body. Stiffening and cold on the morgue table, he had been a small man. Small and easy to subdue. She felt a surge of pity for him. "I suppose his weak left arm made him more vulnerable to being attacked. He may have found it difficult to defend himself with only a single strong one."

She felt more than observed Nicholas's flinch. His old wound pained him in moments like this, when memories of the war would surface.

Celia replaced the cloth that had covered Mr. Young's body and stepped back. "He was such an energetic man. It is odd to see him like—" A memory struck. "Nicholas, I just recalled his waistcoat."

"What about it?"

"It was a very eye-catching scarlet plaid. I saw him with it on not long before Mrs. Merrill died," she said, looking over at him. "He should have been easy to notice on that hillside, as bright as a bullfinch on a barren twig. It seems he truly could *not* have been the fellow Mr. Fletcher spotted."

"Then who did Fletcher see? Merrill?"

"No. He was climbing the trail with me," she answered. "Mr. Thompson, perhaps. Or Mr. Fletcher has a flawed imagination."

"Hmm." His attention returned to Mr. Young's cloth-draped body. "I'll make sure the coroner learns that we've identified him as the man wanted in connection to Mrs. Merrill's death."

"Why go all the way to the Geyser Hotel, Nicholas?" she asked. "If he was from San Francisco, he could have more readily approached the Merrills or Mr. Weaver here."

"Maybe it was simply easier to get near them at a public hotel."

Where no one might prevent him from approaching any of them, Celia thought. And he'd learned of their trip to the geysers from an advertisement Mr. Shafer had placed in the newspapers, bragging about prominent guests.

"I suppose now we must ask ourselves who wished to kill Mr. Young," she said. "The individual actually responsible for Elnora's death or another person entirely?"

Nicholas was watching her. "Celia, you need to be careful," he said. "There's a murderer out there and you could be in danger."

I should tell him about the telegram. The warning. But either from stubbornness or sheer foolishness, she did not. Instead, she said what she always said.

"I shall of course be careful, Nicholas."

To which he, like always, responded with a scowl.

• • •

Damnable woman. Celia Walford Davies had absolutely no intention of being careful. She could be so blasted infuriating.

Nick descended the steps into the station and strode over to Taylor's desk. His assistant was bent over some paperwork, a curl of cigar smoke rising over his head.

"Glad you're still here, Taylor. It's definitely Parker Young," Nick informed him. "Have one of the men notify the coroner that he's the man wanted in the death of Elnora Merrill."

"Yes, Mr. Greaves." He got to his feet. "I've heard that the coroner has concluded that Mr. Young died no more than three or four hours before he examined the body around eight this morning. Also, Mr. Mullahey wants you to know that he's gone to question any witnesses at Mr. Young's place. A rented room off O'Farrell near Market Street."

"Rough part of town." Narrow side streets mostly occupied by women offering up their services to men willing to pay for them—and there were always plenty willing—and sailors looking for someplace cheap to stay while they were ashore. Not the sort of folks who enjoyed talking to cops. Although, a lot of people never wanted to speak to the cops, unless they were looking to complain. "Let's head over there and see what Mullahey has learned so far, Taylor."

"Yes, sir," Taylor said, pausing to puff on his cigar. "You know, it seems to me that Mr. Merrill might want to kill Mr. Young. Revenge for his stepmother's death."

"I didn't get the feeling that Dennis Merrill was all that heartbroken about her dying, Taylor."

"Mr. Thompson, then?" his assistant asked. "Wanting to stop the man behind the blackmail note he'd received?"

"Not sure Thompson is back in town yet. And even if he is, I don't think he or Merrill would've expected Young to be in the city." But Weaver might've known that Young was here, if the early morning message he'd received *had* come from him. "Besides, he could've had any number of enemies. Maybe one of the other boarders didn't care for him. It's easier to imagine one of them killing Young than an outsider sneaking into his boardinghouse to strangle him."

Taylor took a few more puffs on his cigar. "Gotta say, sir, it is mighty strange how close Mr. Young's place is to the Weavers' house."

"Exactly how close?"

"An easy walk," he said. "They live on Mason near those nice homes on Sutter and Bush Street. Probably have a nice house, too."

Where the streets did not stink of urine and decay like they did near the cribs. Instead, houses along those roads climbed the side of one of the city's many hills, benefiting from breezes and fresher air.

"Definitely an easy walk, Taylor. Ten or fifteen minutes at the most," Nick said. "Not much effort at all for Mr. Weaver to get there and quickly."

• • •

"Who's come to the Weavers' house in the past few days?" Owen asked the housemaid scrubbing the front steps of a house across the street.

He'd gone to the docks to unload ships but hadn't been able to stop thinking about who could've taken those letters out of Mrs. Merrill's dressing table. Aside from Mr. Weaver, Miss Weaver, or one of the servants, that was. If an outsider *was* responsible, somebody who lived on the Weavers' street might've noticed them. Unless the person had climbed over their back fence or something. Owen's thoughts had gone round and round, distracting him so much that he'd dropped a crate and it had split open, spilling onions everywhere. After that, his boss had demanded that Owen leave for lunch. It wasn't totally clear if he'd be allowed to return that afternoon.

"Have you seen anybody at all?" he asked.

"I'm too busy to be noticing what's happening over at the Weavers'," the housemaid said over the scritch-scritch of her brush.

"But they only live right there." The street wasn't even that wide.

She sighed and dropped her scrub brush into the bucket of soapy water at her feet. "There was a coal delivery," she said. "And a painter came by to do some work in their parlor."

"And nobody else?"

"It's not like they had company while they were gone."

"What about last night?" he asked. "Did Mrs. Merrill's stepson come by, for instance? Or maybe Miss Weaver's fiancé?"

"Is that stony-faced fellow her fiancé? Well, I'll be." She shook her head. "Don't like his looks at all."

"Is that a yes or a no?"

She scowled. "That's a no."

"What about the person who delivered a note this morning? Shortly after sunrise." Maybe that note had been a ruse to get the Weavers out of the house so that the sender could sneak inside and take those letters. Heck, he and Mrs. Davies had managed to get inside pretty easily.

She eyed him. "Remind me again why you're asking all these questions. Are you a cop or something? You look too young to be a cop, though. Too skinny, too."

Did he? Shoot.

"I do help the police sometimes," he said, jutting his chin. "And before I send an officer here to question you, why don't you talk to me? Did you or did you not see the person who brought a message to them this morning? I'll bet you were up early enough to have noticed. Having to work for folks who own a house like this one."

"Ain't that the truth. I have to be up at five to set the fire in the kitchen range to boil the water for tea and coffee." She wiped her hands across her apron. "Not in bed until after the dishes are all cleaned and the master's had his brandy in the parlor and the missus has had her tea and her bedroom's ready for her to retire. Which is always late. After ten, most evenings. A waste of lamp oil, it is, the hours they keep. Criminal."

Owen wouldn't complain about working at the docks anymore. At least he could go to bed at a reasonable time. Assuming the fellows who occupied the room next to his in the boardinghouse weren't up late drinking—even though their landlady had rules that nobody was supposed to be drinking in their rooms—and arguing loud enough for Owen to hear through the paper-thin wall.

"Did you see anybody or not?" he asked the maid. "A person came by and dropped off a note for one of them."

She eyed him again and shook her head. "I was probably in the morning room, dusting the furniture."

Well, dang.

"But I did notice Miss Cassandra this morning, running up the road. My ma would say it's not ladylike to run." She tutted over the behavior of her betters who didn't act like they were better at all. "I was shaking out the entryway rug before taking coffee up to the missus. She likes to have a cup at eight on the dot before she comes down for breakfast, you know. Anyway, there she was, Miss Cassandra, her skirts lifted so high you could see her ankles, all out of breath and running hard. Pale as ashes, she was. Like she'd seen a ghost."

"Running up the road." Owen looked down the incline of Mason then at the maid again. "You mean, from that direction. Back to her house."

"Of course that's what I mean," she said, exasperated. "Wasn't I plain?"

"I wonder what that was all about."

"Whatever it was, it wasn't right."

CHAPTER 14

"Mr. Young's body has been found, Barbara," Celia said to her cousin, who was yawning over the newspaper she'd been attempting to read at the dining room table. "Here. In San Francisco."

"Oh, don't tell me. He's been murdered."

Indeed. Celia sat down and took up one of the pages her cousin had finished and discarded. She did not feel like reading it, though.

Addie brought a tray of toast, cold beef, and the tea things. "You didna take your breakfast this morning before you ran off with wee Owen, ma'am." She slapped the food on the table next to Celia.

"I believe I did, Addie." *Didn't I?*

"You can always have more. Along with some lunch," she stated and returned to the kitchen.

"Well? Was he murdered?" Barbara asked. "I'd guess he was, or else you wouldn't be acting like you are."

"And how am I acting?" she asked, setting aside the newspaper. And was her behavior different from "that look"?

"Totally preoccupied," her cousin answered. "How was the murder carried out this time? Gunshot? Knife wound? Poisoning? Cracked head?"

"Actually, someone strangled him," she said. "He had a contusion on his forehead, but not enough to kill him. I do wish I'd had more time to inspect his body for any additional wounds. None were immediately obvious."

Barbara poured herself a fresh cup of tea. "I never would've expected that Mr. Young would turn up in San Francisco. He was a wanted man."

"Neither would I, if I'd not seen his body myself," she said. "Something odd happened early this morning, Barbara. Mr. Weaver received a note at his house, after which he hastily left. I wonder if Mr. Young sent it. A summons to meet, if you will."

Her cousin leaned forward. "But Mr. Weaver would've handed him over to the police for killing Mrs. Merrill, wouldn't he?"

"I would think so," she said. "Interestingly, Mr. Weaver was not the only one who dashed out of the house. Cassandra did, as well. Not long after her father."

"If you're suggesting that Cassandra had a hand in Mr. Young's death . . . it wouldn't be possible."

"Never say never, Barbara."

Her cousin got up from her chair. "You can be so maddening," she said and stormed from the room.

"And whate'er was that about, ma'am?" Addie asked from the doorway to the kitchen.

Me being maddening and unnecessarily provocative.

"How plausible do *you* think it is that a young woman could strangle a grown man, Addie?"

"Weel, I've watched our neighbor's wee daughter back in Scotland kill a chicken often enough. Given the proper reason, I'd think the lass could kill anything," she replied. "Aye, remorseless, she was. And fierce."

"A chicken and an adult male are not the same thing, Addie." Even one with a damaged arm.

"That may be so, ma'am, but you didna see the gleam in the lass's eye."

• • •

"I don't know nothin'," replied a fellow lounging on the front steps of the two-story wood-shingled boardinghouse where Young had been found. "Not a durned thing."

Despite the ruckus of having police and a coroner tromp through the house, the place was quiet, even though it was noontime. The narrow street it was located on was also quiet and mostly empty, aside from one industrious lady out on her stoop hunting for customers, her colorful petticoats hiked above her ankles. She'd winked when Nick and Taylor had walked by.

"A man was murdered in this building, but you didn't hear anything or see anything?" Nick asked.

The man took a long drag on the cigar tucked in his mouth. Out of the corner of Nick's eye, he noticed Taylor itching for a smoke. "I had a long night."

That was obvious from the stubble on his chin, his red-rimmed eyes, and the rank smell rising off his body.

"Did you know the victim?" Nick asked.

"Him? I stayed away from him," he said, spitting out a flake of tobacco that had gotten caught in his teeth. "He was always listening in on folks' conversations in a way that was downright rude. He'd smooth-talk until you admitted stuff you wouldn't want even your confessor to know."

"What about your landlord? What does he know about Mr. Young?"

"Landlady, you mean. You can talk to her, but the other cop already did that."

The man had left the front door open, and he jabbed his thumb in the direction of a woman wielding a broom in the hallway. She'd been sweeping as if it was a normal day and a dead body hadn't been found in one of her rented rooms. Could be a normal day for her.

Nick and Taylor skirted the fellow on the steps and went inside. The open door wasn't helping the smell inside the house, which stank of damp and sweat and sewer gas.

The woman noticed them and frowned over Taylor's uniform.

"I'm Detective Greaves, and this is Officer Taylor," Nick said.

"An officer has already been here," the landlady said. "And I'll tell you two what I told him—nobody around here heard anything, saw anything, or knows anything. So you can stop bothering us."

"We'd greatly appreciate it if you could share whatever you know about Mr. Parker Young, ma'am," Taylor said in his most soothing tone.

"I ain't got time for this," she grumbled.

"The sooner you speak with us, the sooner we'll be able to leave," Nick pressed. "Why not speed that process by telling us what you know about Young."

She sighed and leaned on her broom. "He rented a room on the second floor. My smallest one. He didn't seem to mind the size."

"How long has he boarded with you?"

"It's been several months," she said. "Lucky I had a space available when he first turned up. Don't usually. Like I told the other officer."

"A while, then," Nick said.

"Yep. Mr. Young got my name from a friend of his. Said he was good for the daily amount I charge. Didn't give me the name of his friend, but since I had a room empty, I took him at his word," the landlady said. "Looked decent enough, unlike some of the sailors who rent from me."

Looking decent being sufficient to recommend him. "He was wanted for a homicide up at the geysers."

Her eyes widened. "I'll be hanged! The other officer didn't mention that," she said. "Never would've thought that he'd be a killer. Seemed all right. Paid his rent on time, but I couldn't ever figure out how he was earning a living."

Nick could suggest an explanation, and it involved all that eavesdropping Young had enjoyed doing.

"I'd like to see his room," he said.

"Sure." She set aside the broom and headed for the stairs.

"Did Mr. Young give you a reason for why he was heading to the geysers?" Taylor asked as they followed her, the treads creaking beneath their feet. One of them was loose.

"It was all very abrupt, I'll say that. Told me his arm was bothering him bad. Not that he'd complained about it paining him before," she said. "Asked me to hold his room because he'd be back in a few days."

Arriving at the man's room, she opened the door.

It wasn't the worst rented space Nick had ever been in, but it shared characteristics with the others. Places that always had stains on a wall where rain had leaked in, worn rugs, and narrow cots with mattresses that could use a fresh refill of straw. Scuffed pieces of furniture. Young's room additionally came with a mostly empty whiskey bottle, which was overturned on the floor, and a vest in a bright red plaid tossed atop a chest of drawers. Nick understood what Celia meant about the color. There was also a scattering of personal items, including a cheap print of a winter scene he must've liked and had tacked to the wall. As for the cot, its bedding was in disarray, and the stool next to it had been knocked over. Signs of a scuffle.

"The fellow outside told us that Mr. Young liked to pry," Nick said to the landlady. "I'd guess his fellow boarders weren't all that fond of him."

"This is a house full of men, Detective. There's always fights and misunderstandings going on between folks," she said. "But none of those fights have ever led to anybody getting killed here."

There was always a first time.

"Who found his body?" Taylor asked, pencil raised to jot down her answer.

"One of my other boarders. He was headed outside to the privy," she explained. "He's got a room on this floor too, and he went past Mr. Young's. The door was ajar. Who leaves a door open?"

Not anybody living in a crumbling boardinghouse in a neighborhood populated by transients. "What time was that?"

"A couple of hours after sunrise," she answered. "Glad he noticed when he did, because I don't know when Mr. Young might've been found otherwise. I like to respect the men's privacy, you see. Don't come wandering around upstairs until necessary."

"Of course," Taylor said.

"I didn't even realize Mr. Young was back in town," she said. "Not until this morning. He must've come in late last night without my hearing him."

"So, your boarder's curiosity aroused, he decided to take a minor detour from his trip to the outhouse and peeked inside this room." Around seven or a bit later that morning.

"Wouldn't you?" she asked, taking them both in with a quick look. Taylor obliged by nodding. "Anyway, there poor Mr. Young was, all crumpled on the floor. Dead as a doornail."

She pointed at the very spot. There weren't any evident bloodstains, but then strangulation didn't leave behind much of a mess.

"Taylor, see if you can find any samples of the fellow's handwriting." He'd like to know whether Young could've been the author of the note Celia had found in Elnora Merrill's pocket.

"Yes, sir." Taylor squeezed past the landlady and began to search the room.

"How easy is it to get inside your boardinghouse?" Nick asked her. "Any indication that one of the exterior doors had been forced, for example?"

She sighed again. "Some of the fellows forget to lock up when they get back from wherever they've been all night," she said. "Normally there'd be more folks around to spot an intruder, but the sailors who rent rooms on this floor are still out at sea."

Fewer eyes and ears, Nick supposed. Fortunately, for the killer. "And you don't bother to be sure that the doors are locked?"

"At the hours some of them keep?" she asked, scoffing. "I'd be up all night. I do remind them about locking up, but they don't always listen."

"You're not worried about being robbed?"

"Most people know not to bother me or take any of my stuff. Some of the men who live here are downright protective of me and my place,

Detective. This is often the only boardinghouse that'll take them in, and they appreciate it," she said with a touch of pride. Misplaced pride, possibly. "I suppose I should say folks *used* to know not to bother me. But after today . . ." She frowned at the cot.

Taylor finished searching. Since there wasn't anything in it besides the chest, the stool, and the cot, the search hadn't taken long.

"No luck, sir," he said. "Just some socks with holes in them, a nickel, and the clothes he must've taken off before going to bed." He'd pulled out a pair of thick-soled shoes from underneath the cot and set them aside.

"Taylor, are there any yellow stains on those shoes?"

He examined them quickly. "Not that I can see, Mr. Greaves," he replied. "But what do you think about these?" He held up a pair of suspenders.

Nick took them from him. They weren't made of twill or gum, like many suspenders were. Materials that stretched. These were made of leather. He wrapped one of the straps around his hand and pulled. Strong enough to strangle somebody with.

"Take these to the station, Taylor," he said, handing them back.

"Yes, sir."

"Mr. Young didn't appear to own much," Nick said to the landlady.

"No, he didn't," the landlady, who'd been watching Nick's handling of the suspenders with wide-eyed horror, said. "Most of what he owned could be packed in that saddlebag of his, and it was a small one at that."

"But there's no saddlebag here," Taylor said.

"Maybe Mullahey took it back to the station." Young hadn't left the bag behind at his room at the Geyser Hotel; Nick had searched it.

"The officer didn't have the bag with him when he left. I'd have noticed if he had," the landlady said. "Don't know if Mr. Young brought it back with him. Since I didn't see him come in last night."

"Maybe the fellow who found his body took the bag," Taylor suggested.

"Him?" She shook her head. "Never seen a person go so white. He was plum scared to take a step inside. Was standing out in the hall pointing, his arm shaking like a leaf on a tree. Wouldn't have had the nerve to come in here and snatch a saddlebag."

"Thank you, ma'am," Nick said. "You've been very helpful."

They left, Taylor carrying Young's suspenders. Outside, the fellow who'd been smoking a cigar was gone. As was the woman with the bright-colored petticoats who'd been sitting on the stoop across the road. Maybe the two absences were linked.

Taylor used his unoccupied hand to fish around in his coat pockets for a cigar. "If Mr. Mullahey didn't take Mr. Young's saddlebag, who did? The coroner?"

"No, he'd have left collecting any evidence to the police." Nick exhaled and glanced up and down the street. Still quiet. Eerily so. "I'm going to stop by Weaver's office. See if he has an alibi for when Young was murdered."

"What about Mr. Julius Thompson, sir?"

"What about him?"

"He hadn't been to his office yet this morning when we went to question him," Taylor reminded Nick. "We might want to ask where he was, also."

"Get those suspenders to the coroner, Taylor, and tell him they could be the murder weapon. And track down Mullahey and find out what he might've uncovered. Once you're finished, meet me at Thompson's office again," Nick said. "Maybe he has a simple explanation for where he was this morning while a man was being strangled to death."

• • •

"You sure they'll be back soon?" Owen asked the booking sergeant, who was always standing at the desk by the door to the lockup and was doing the same right then.

"Did I say I was sure they'd be back soon?" The fellow crossed his arms and frowned. "And how many times are you going to come in here and ask that question?"

Too many, Owen supposed.

"Hey, look at that. Mr. Taylor is here now," the sergeant announced. "Thank the good Lord," he added under his breath.

"Have you been waiting for me, Owen?" Mr. Taylor asked, striding across the station.

"I've got some important information to tell you. About the case," he said. "What do you got there, Mr. Taylor?"

"Mr. Young's suspenders."

"What?" Had he heard right? Mr. Young?

"Just a minute, Owen. Has Mr. Mullahey been back to the station?" he asked the sergeant.

"Left you a note." The officer nodded in the direction of Mr. Taylor's desk.

He went to retrieve it then headed for the detectives' office, where he set the suspenders he'd been carrying on Mr. Greaves's desk.

"What is it, Owen?" Mr. Taylor asked. He got out his notebook, which made Owen feel useful.

"Mrs. Davies and I went to the Weavers' place this morning to search for letters that a woman named Mrs. Gannon sent to Mrs. Merrill. Something to do with Mr. Merrill, apparently."

"She didn't mention that when she was in the station earlier."

He liked being the first to inform Mr. Taylor. "Well, we didn't find them. But did she tell you that a message came to the Weavers' house around sunrise, and that both Mr. Weaver and Miss Cassandra ran off after it arrived?"

He wasn't taking any notes, and Owen was starting to wonder why he'd risked his job by coming here instead of staying at the docks.

"She did," Mr. Taylor said. "But I'll bet you haven't heard that Mr. Young was found dead a few hours ago. And these here suspenders might've been used to strangle him." He tapped the innocent-looking items, coiled atop a pile of Mr. Greaves's papers.

Owen felt his mouth drop open. "Shoot. Shoot! Maybe that's why Cassandra Weaver looked like she'd seen a ghost when she came running back home this morning."

"What's that?"

Finally. Something important enough that Mr. Taylor licked the tip of his pencil and set it on a blank page in his notebook.

"The maid across the street from the Weavers' saw Miss Cassandra running up the road to her house around seven thirty or maybe a bit later," he said. "Pale as if she'd seen a ghost. Scared."

"Mr. Young was found dead not long after seven. Sun rises around quarter till five . . ." Mr. Taylor said, looking up at the ceiling as he estimated times. "Let's say Mr. Weaver got that message between five and five thirty. Both he and his daughter left soon after, right?"

"Right," Owen agreed. "You know, I don't think I've ever met rich folks who get up that early, Mr. Taylor." Not that Owen had a vast experience of rich folks.

Mr. Taylor lost interest in the ceiling. "And then she came back around seven thirty or so." He wrote that down. "Which means she was gone for a good two hours."

"She was off killing Mr. Young?"

Mr. Taylor considered the possibility. "How big is Cassandra Weaver?"

"She's a little thing, based on the one time I saw her at Miss Barbara's house." A pretty little thing, Owen didn't add because his observation wasn't pertinent.

"Small, huh? Too small, maybe," he said. "Or maybe she discovered that somebody else had killed him."

Mr. Taylor remembered the note from Mr. Mullahey that he'd stuck in his trouser pocket. He retrieved it, read quickly, and looked over at Mr. Greaves's desk.

"Mr. Mullahey found an item in Mr. Young's room that we might think is interesting," he said. "A heavy inkwell. Not the saddlebag. Durn it."

"You mean this inkwell here?" Owen asked, trying to ignore the suspenders on Mr. Greaves's desk. He didn't want to look at them. Not when they'd been used to take somebody's life. "It's not Mr. Greaves's, right?"

Owen had only ever noticed a glass one, which usually got buried under all the paper stacked on the desk. The bronze inkwell had been tucked behind one of the stacks and wasn't easy to spot from the office doorway. Heavy, it had a thick square base that was topped with a well shaped like an urn and covered all over with a leaf pattern.

Mr. Taylor set down his notebook to take it from Owen. "Has to be." He stared at the object for a while. "It's from the IOOF."

"Mr. Young was a member of the Odd Fellows?" Owen asked.

"Along with Mr. Weaver and both Thompsons, Owen. Heck, I wouldn't be surprised if Mr. Merrill is a member, too," he said. "All of which sounds mighty suspicious to me."

CHAPTER 15

"Mr. Weaver is not in," the clerk replied to Nick's question.

"Has Mr. Weaver been in at all today?" Nick asked, looking around the office. It was small and cramped, a section of the room partitioned off to provide a more private spot for Weaver to conduct business. The clerk was one of two currently at work. The one Nick wasn't speaking to was hunched over a ledger and making as if he wasn't listening in.

"Briefly," the clerk replied. "He left again because of numerous appointments he had around town today with prospective clients."

"He'd scheduled appointments even though he wasn't expected to get back from his vacation for another couple of days?"

"Mr. Weaver is not somebody who wastes an opportunity, Detective, and Fridays are good days for meeting with clients."

Well, Nick was not going to chase all over San Francisco trying to hunt him down. "Tell Mr. Weaver he needs to come to the central police station. Immediately."

The fellow glanced at the other clerk and leaned toward Nick. "I already spoke with one of the other officers, Detective," he whispered. "About the . . . you know."

The deposit. "And I appreciate what you told him," Nick said. "But I still need Mr. Weaver to come into the station. If he isn't inclined to cooperate, I can always send somebody to force him."

"Yes, Detective."

Nick slapped his hat back onto his head. "Oh, before I go. Has a fellow with the last name of Young ever come here looking for Mr. Weaver?"

He shook his head. "Not that I'm aware of."

Interesting. "Tell your boss to come to the station. Or else."

Nick stomped out. Thompson's office was only a few blocks away from Weaver's and a short walk. Taylor was waiting for Nick outside the building.

"Mr. Mullahey found an item that might show that Mr. Young knew the Thompsons and Mr. Weaver, sir."

Nick glanced up at Thompson's second-floor office, its window open to the afternoon breeze, and pulled Taylor down the road. Far enough so that anybody in the office couldn't overhear. "What?"

"An inkwell. A heavy bronze one, sir. Mr. Greaves, sir," he said. "I'm pretty sure it's identical to the one on the desk in Mr. Thompson's office. You were looking at it this morning."

"Was a name inscribed on the base along with a message of thanks from a local Odd Fellows lodge?"

"There wasn't a name, but there was an inscription from one of the lodges, sir," he said. "Do you think the inkwell belonged to Mr. Young?"

"Doubt that his killer brought it along to drop it off in his room."

"They did all know each other, didn't they, sir?" his assistant asked. "From before going to the geysers."

"The chance they were previously acquainted is looking more like a probability, Taylor," Nick said. Up at the hotel, Fletcher had noticed Young's interest in Thaddeus Thompson. Maybe his interest had begun when he'd learned something damaging about the man, or his father, at an Odd Fellows lodge. "None of them are likely to admit it, though."

"What did Mr. Weaver have to say?"

"He wasn't at his office. We'll track him down eventually," Nick said. "Did Mullahey find anything else?"

"Not according to the note he left for me."

"No saddlebag, then."

"No, sir."

Damn. Maybe it wasn't important to the case that the saddlebag was missing. Maybe Young had misplaced it on his trip back from the geysers.

"Let's find out what Julius Thompson has to say for himself," Nick said.

The secretary looked up from his desk when Nick and Taylor barged into the outer office. He frowned, his immense mustache sinking, and got to his feet.

"Officers. Mr. Thompson is far too busy to speak with you, I'm afraid."

The door behind the man's desk was closed. Again. But this time, Nick could see movement through the frosted glass set into the wood. "Who's he with?"

"He is in a meeting to discuss important business, and I believe I answered all of your questions earlier," he replied. "So, if you please . . ." He swept his arm in front of him, gesturing toward the hallway.

Nick dropped onto one of the hard wood chairs against the wall and took off his hat, setting it on his lap. "Officer Taylor and I are both happy to wait," he said. "Although I expect that anybody else coming into this office might not be so happy to see two policemen inside. I gotta say, it might even look really bad for Mr. Thompson, don't you agree? Since he's already the subject of some pretty interesting rumors."

"I . . ." he stuttered. "Really, Detective Greaves. This is not the right time."

"Would it be better if I had Mr. Thompson brought into the station for questioning?" he asked. "Thought it might be more private to conduct my interrogation here."

The man relented. "I'll see if Mr. Thompson can see you."

"That'd be perfect," Nick said. "Oh, wait a second. I've got another question for you."

The fellow paused. "Yes?"

"Has a man named Parker Young ever come here wanting to speak to Mr. Thompson? Either of the Thompsons," he said. A man who might've learned about a bribery scheme through mutual friends at an Odd Fellows lodge.

The secretary cleared his throat. "Umm . . ."

"Yes or no?" Nick asked. "That's all."

"Yes," he said. "A man calling himself Mr. Young did attempt to meet with Mr. Thompson. Mr. Julius, that is. One time. I told him to leave."

"Thank you so much." He glanced over at Taylor, who was scrambling for his notebook to jot down the information. "Now, please tell Mr. Thompson we're waiting out here."

After a brief consultation with the occupants of the office, the secretary showed Nick and Taylor inside.

Julius Thompson slowly got to his feet, in no hurry to welcome police officers. He was a barrel of a man, broad and thick and tall. The man standing alongside his tufted-leather chair had to be his son. They looked too much alike to not be closely related. Thaddeus Thompson was equally tall and also had his father's intense brown eyes. But there was more to Thaddeus Thompson, a characteristic Nick couldn't exactly pin down. Recklessness, maybe.

"Back already, Mr. Thompson?" Nick asked. "I was told you

wouldn't show up in the city until later today."

Thaddeus Thompson frowned. "You're the detective who came to the Geyser Hotel, aren't you?"

"Sorry we didn't get a chance to meet there, Mr. Thompson."

"I hope you're here to tell us that the Young fellow has been apprehended," the senior Thompson said.

"Do you mind if we sit, Mr. Thompson?" Nick went ahead and took the nearest chair. Which was far more comfortable than any of the ones in Nick's office, including his own. "Speaking of Mr. Young, you two gentlemen are members of the Odd Fellows, right?"

"I still am, but my father has joined other fraternal organizations," Thaddeus Thompson replied for the both of them.

"Ever see Mr. Young at a lodge meeting?" Nick asked. "He was a local member, too. Fancy that."

"There are nearly twenty encampments and lodges in this area, Detective. Too many members to ever meet them all," Julius Thompson said. "Had you ever encountered him before your stay at the Geyser Hotel, Thaddeus?"

"No, Father," he said. "And I'm glad for that. He was obviously a mean sort. Miss Weaver was afraid of him."

"She was? That's the first I've heard," Nick said.

"She's been reluctant to talk about the events surrounding her aunt's passing, Detective," he said. "You understand."

Julius Thompson's heavy brows beetled. "How did you come to be involved in the investigation of Mrs. Merrill's death, Detective? The crime occurred in Sonoma County. That is not your jurisdiction."

It seemed like everybody enjoyed pointing that out.

"Mrs. Davies, who was traveling with the Merrills, sent for him," his son said.

"My question stands."

"Maybe you'll figure out the reason I'm involved once you answer a question of mine, Mr. Thompson. A question for the both of you," Nick said. "Where were you early this morning? Between four and seven o'clock. According to your secretary, Mr. Thompson, you weren't here in your office, and you weren't at home, either." He didn't actually know if the latter was true; he hadn't had time to ask at Thompson's house.

"I don't know where you got the information that I was not at home, because I was," Julius Thompson said curtly. "An associate of mine came for breakfast to discuss business."

Nick would have Taylor confirm his story. "Over breakfast at your house. Before seven. That seems early to be conducting business, Mr. Thompson."

"'Early to bed, and early to rise, will make a man healthy, wealthy, and wise,' as the adage goes, Detective," he said. "Thaddeus?"

"I concluded my affairs in Calistoga early, Detective, and was waiting to board the morning ferry from Suscol at that time," he replied. "Just got into town, in fact."

"You don't happen to have your ticket with you, do you?" Nick asked.

"I . . . I discarded the stub. Why would I keep it?"

As confirmation?

"You have your answers, Detective," his father said. "Now kindly tell me what our responses have to do with finding the man responsible for Mrs. Merrill's death."

"Well, we have found Young. Unfortunately, he's dead. Killed in a rented room near Market Street. He was strangled," he said. "And his murder *is* within my jurisdiction."

Only the briefest flicker of disquiet crossed either of the men's faces.

"We have provided alibis for you, Detective," Julius Thompson said. "We're finished here."

No, they weren't. "Did Young ever attempt to blackmail either of you gentlemen?"

"Why would he?" Julius Thompson asked impatiently.

"Because of those rumors, Father," his son answered. "The lies implying that you're accepting bribes."

"Lies, Mr. Thompson?" Nick asked. "I have received credible information that Mr. Weaver has recently deposited funds into your father's bank account. Looks suspicious, I have to admit."

The cords in Julius Thompson's neck stood out like lengths of twine. "I'd like to know who told you that, Detective."

I'm sure you would. "You mean it's not true?"

"It was not a bribe. It was a business transaction. Furthermore, Mr. Young never attempted to blackmail me," Julius Thompson stated. "Now, please leave."

150

"And what about you?" Nick asked Thaddeus. "Did he attempt to blackmail you over that 'lie'?"

He blinked. "Yes, he did try," he admitted. "In response, I firmly told him off and that was the end of the matter."

His father was staring at him. "What do you mean, Thaddeus?"

"When was this?" Nick asked at the same time.

"Late the evening before Mrs. Merrill died," he replied. "He'd had too much to drink and was quite obnoxious. In fact, I witnessed him arguing with Mr. Weaver that same evening."

"Why didn't you inform the authorities about this argument earlier, Mr. Thompson?"

"I didn't think it had anything to do with Mrs. Merrill's death," he replied. "I suppose it would be best for you to ask Mr. Weaver about it."

Now he was getting advice on how to do his job from suspects. *Great.* "Why, thank you, Mr. Thompson," Nick said dryly. "I will keep that recommendation in mind."

• • •

"Mrs. Davies, why are you back again?" the Weavers' servant, Mary, asked. "You said that you remembered you hadn't lent your shawl to Mrs. Merrill. Or did you re-remember differently?"

"I've returned for another reason. I must speak with Miss Weaver. It is most important. The man suspected of causing Mrs. Merrill's death has been murdered. Here in the city," she hurriedly told the young woman, hoping the news would keep Mary from shutting the door on her. "I wanted to be the one who tells her. Is she at home?"

"Yes, she is." Mary's eyes widened. "Is that why an officer was here earlier, looking to talk to Mr. Weaver? He didn't mention a murder, though. I told him Mr. Weaver wasn't home and he left. Thank goodness he didn't try to talk to Miss Cassandra. She's been beside herself upset."

"I will be brief."

Mary opened the door all the way. "I'll tell Miss Cassandra you're waiting for her in the parlor."

"After I leave, Miss Weaver might find a warm infusion of horehound calming," Celia said to her.

"Cook was going to get out the laudanum."

"I'm sure she was."

Mary showed Celia into an elegantly appointed room off to the left, all rose silk and plush imported Brussels carpets. Mary did not take Celia's bonnet or lace shawl, though; she'd not be allowed to stay long.

While she waited, Celia strolled the room, anxiously drumming her curled fingers against her waist. The parlor appeared to be infrequently used and somewhat neglected; no one had yet cleared old ashes from the hearth. A book had been left atop a table next to a wingback chair, however. Celia examined the title. A romantic novel. Was it Cassandra's, or had it belonged to Elnora? It was morose to consider the book awaiting the woman's return, a narrow blue ribbon marking her place.

Celia absently thumbed through the book, turning to the point where Elnora had left off. A scrap of paper, folded tight, had been tucked inside. It fluttered to the floor.

I love you. I won't let anybody interfere. Ever. I promise.
—T.

"Well." Not Elnora's, but Cassandra's. And the scrap of paper concealed within its pages was rather damning, a motive to remove one especially interfering individual spelled out in eleven words.

"Mrs. Davies?" Cassandra asked from the doorway. "What are you doing here? What are you looking at there?"

Celia startled, stuffed the note into her bodice, and turned to face the young woman.

"My apologies, Miss Weaver," she said, trying to slow the mad racing of her heart. *Breathe evenly, Celia. Calm. Down.* "I allowed my inquisitiveness to get the better of me and was perusing your book to see if it was one I might enjoy."

She held out the book.

"That was where I left it." Cassandra marched across the parlor and snatched it from Celia's grip. She tucked the book under her arm. "Mary informed me that there's news about Mr. Young."

"He was found dead this morning, Cassandra. Here in the city," she said. "Murdered."

She recoiled. "Oh."

"Where were you this morning? I came here to search for a shawl I thought I'd lent to your aunt." She may as well continue the falsehood, as it did serve a purpose. "I learned that you'd gone out early. Very early. Around the time that Mr. Young was murdered, as it turns out."

"You think *I* murdered Mr. Young to . . . to revenge my aunt's death?" she asked. "How could you think that?"

It was easy.

"Would you prefer to speak to the police? In your father's presence, I might add," she said. "They did not question you earlier when they were here, but they shall eventually."

She drew in a breath. "I went out for a walk."

"Not long past sunrise when you'd just returned from an arduous trip to the geysers?" Celia asked. "A very long walk, I might add."

"I needed to think. I couldn't sleep," she said. "I haven't been able to at all since my aunt died."

"So you did not head out in response to a message that arrived here shortly after sunrise."

She protectively tightened her arm around the book, or, rather, the slip of paper that was no longer inside. "A message?"

"Tell me who the intended recipient of that note was, Cassandra. Please," Celia said. "Was it your father or you? As well as who sent it."

"I didn't see the note. Mary told me about it and that my father had gone out afterward."

"Did he say where he was going?"

"No."

"What about you? Where *did* you go, Miss Weaver?" Celia pressed. "Not for a walk, I assume."

She rolled her lips between her teeth. "To Thaddeus's. I thought he might've sent the note to my father. Begging him to reconsider delaying our engagement," she said. "Thaddeus is desperate to marry me, Mrs. Davies. Because of how much he loves me. Because he cannot imagine life without me, and because no other woman has made him feel like this. He doesn't want any delay."

"You thought Mr. Thompson had returned to San Francisco already?" Celia asked. "That's not what I recall of his plans."

"It was silly of me."

Silly, or an outright lie.

Footsteps sounded out in the hallway as Mary scurried to answer the front door; Celia was not the only person to ignore the black crêpe that had finally been wrapped around the knocker.

"What happened when you arrived at his house?" Celia asked.

"Nothing. He wasn't there," she replied. "Nobody was, because he wasn't back yet. Like you said."

"What did you do afterward?"

"I took my time coming back home. That's all," she replied. "Everything that's happened has been so upsetting."

"Another question, if you will," Celia said. "During our stop in Calistoga, did you notice if anyone from our party sent a telegram from the office there?"

Her brows twitched together. "No," she stated. "A telegram?"

"What's this about a telegram, Cassandra?" Dennis Merrill asked, striding into the parlor before Mary, scurrying into the room behind him, could make an announcement.

Blast.

"Nothing, Denny," Cassandra hastily said. "Just some talk between women."

"Ah." His gaze, full of speculation, slid from her face to Celia's. "What brings you to this house of mourning, Mrs. Davies?"

"I thought I would stop by to ask Miss Weaver if there was anything I could do for her."

"Is that why you're here too, Denny?" she asked coolly. "To see if there was anything you could do for me? I'm surprised you haven't come by earlier."

A comment that might exonerate him from having purloined Mrs. Gannon's letters.

"I did not want to disturb you, Cassandra," he said, a thinly veiled dig aimed at Celia. "I know how distraught you are about Elnora's death. Are you doing all right?"

"Yes. Everything is fine, Denny," Cassandra replied. Even though she did not look as though everything was fine.

"I am glad you've come by, Mr. Merrill, because I have a question for you," Celia said.

He smiled his Cheshire cat smile, curious and smug simultaneously. "Ask away."

"Did your stepmother ever tell you about letters she received from a woman named Mrs. Gannon?"

It was impossible to decide which of them blinked first upon hearing the name, Cassandra or Dennis Merrill.

"Who?" he asked.

"A Mrs. Gannon," she repeated. "Have either of you ever heard the name?"

"No, I haven't," Cassandra said. "Who is she?"

"That is what I would like to know, Miss Weaver," Celia replied.

"How strange. She sent letters to Elnora? Odd," Dennis Merrill said.

"Yes, it is." Cassandra made a movement toward the door. "Well, I thank you both for coming by, but I'm very tired. I must ask you to leave."

"Certainly, Cassandra. Let me escort you out, Mrs. Davies," Denny Merrill said, taking Celia's arm. "Perhaps you'd like to accompany me to the police station? I need to report that I've spotted Gabriella in the city."

Cassandra gasped. "She's here? She must have—"

"The police will be most interested to hear your news, Mr. Merrill," Celia interrupted before Cassandra could finish her sentence, which likely was going to conclude with "killed Mr. Young."

That smile danced on his lips again. "Maybe I should speak to . . . What was that detective's name, Mrs. Davies? The one who came to see you? Griffs? Green?"

"Greaves," Celia stated. "Thank you for seeing me, Miss Weaver."

She extracted her arm from Mr. Merrill's clasp and headed for the front door, where Mary stood waiting. Thankfully, Dennis Merrill accompanied Celia out onto the street rather than stay behind to interrogate Cassandra about their conversation.

"You went out of your way to visit with Miss Weaver, Mr. Merrill," she said. "Her house does not lie between your residence and the police station." Not even close.

"You know where I live," he said, amused.

"I am an inquisitive lady detective, after all," she answered. "And my inquisitiveness forces me to ask if you are positive that Elnora never mentioned Mrs. Gannon's name to you. It's my understanding that the correspondence she'd had with your stepmother concerned you."

"Concerned me?" He scoffed. "Probably the friend of one of Elnora's acquaintances hoping to introduce her daughter to me. She's been approached before."

"Of course."

"So do you intend to accompany me to the station?"

"No, I need to return to my clinic," she replied.

"Then I bid you a good day."

He tipped his hat and strode off. Celia waited until he had turned the corner at the bottom of the hill before she made to follow him.

• • •

Dr. Harris was in Nick's office when he returned to the station. Nick hadn't seen him in weeks. Since he wasn't the coroner any longer, excuses to drop by were getting scarce.

"Don't you have patients to tend to, Doctor?" Nick dropped his hat on his desk and took a seat.

"You know how much I miss you, Detective," he answered, chuckling.

"What you actually miss is your old job, Harris," Nick said. "Run for the office when the current coroner's time is up. Maybe you'll get reelected."

"Wouldn't mind the extra income again, but I think my wife is happy for me to stick with my practice," he said. "Heard you've got another murder victim on your hands. Is that why you're scowling?"

"I'm scowling because interviewing suspects is so enjoyable," Nick said. "What have you heard about the victim that you're itching to share with me?"

"Dr. Letterman completed his full autopsy about an hour ago, Greaves," Harris said, leaning forward. "Strangulation, eh? And a minor contusion on his forehead. Probably caused during the struggle with his attacker. Given the amount of alcohol found in the man's stomach, he'd probably been too drunk to fend off the person. Having a damaged left arm also put him at a disadvantage."

"He might've been strangled with a pair of leather suspenders we found in his room," Nick said. "The victim, Mr. Young, is the fellow wanted in the death of Mrs. Merrill up at the Geyser Hotel. You probably saw an article about it in the newspaper. Doesn't make a whole lot of sense for him to have come back to town, though. He was risking arrest, after all."

"Maybe he had nowhere else to go." Harris leaned back and crossed his legs. He was the only person who ever looked comfortable sitting in that chair. The only person aside from Celia. Witnesses and suspects never looked comfortable. "Dr. Letterman is confident that he was murdered no earlier than five this morning, if that helps you, Greaves. Rigor mortis hadn't set in yet when he got to the boardinghouse to examine the body."

"Which narrows the time he was killed to between five and a little after seven, when he was found."

"Is his murder related to Mrs. Merrill's death?"

"If it's not, Harris, I might never figure out who killed him."

• • •

"Are you truly heading for the police station, Mr. Merrill?" Celia whispered, drawing an alarmed look from a passing matron. The woman increased her speed to put distance between her and Celia. A typical reaction when Celia muttered aloud in public.

Perhaps Mr. Merrill never had intended to go to the police station. Perhaps his claim that he'd spotted Gabriella in San Francisco was also false. One thing was certain—where Dennis Merrill *should* have continued on until he'd reached Kearny, the street upon which the station was located, he instead turned left onto Dupont.

Where are *you going?* To visit someone, perhaps, who might be interested to learn that Celia had been at the Weavers', poking around. Asking about a Mrs. Gannon.

Celia followed him as closely as she could. She didn't want Mr. Merrill to catch sight of her and change his course. She also didn't want to lose him.

They arrived at Pine, the congestion of a busy street making it nearly impossible to see ten feet ahead of her, let alone the distance between her and Dennis Merrill. *Blast.* Had he ducked into that shop? No, there he was. Crossing the road, looking around as he ran.

She hurried along, dodging crates being unloaded from of a wagon. *Mind your own business.* It would be safest for her to follow that tersely worded instruction, but then she'd not learn what Mr. Merrill was up to, and she badly wanted to learn that. A gaggle of men spilled out of an oyster shop and onto the pavement, their boisterous laughter mingling with the din of traffic, their bodies blocking her view. She swerved around them, scanning the street. *Blast, blast, blast!* Where *had* he gone?

Hiking her skirts, she sprinted along the road, searching every doorway, peering behind every stack of goods on display. An alleyway led off of Pine, and she ventured down it, heading for the street visible at its end. If she did not spot him there, she'd have to admit that she'd lost him.

She reached the end of the alley and stopped.

"Blast," she cursed. Just as she heard movement behind her. Followed by a heavy object colliding with her upper back, pain jolting through her body and sending her lurching into the street.

Right into the path of an oncoming Central Railroad horsecar.

That was idiotic of you, Celia.

Especially considering that she'd been warned. *I should have paid more attention to that telegram.*

"Ma'am! Are you all right?" A woman, worry pinching her face, bent over her. She had a spray of freckles across her cheeks and an Irish lilt to her voice to go with them. "You almost got run over there, you did. Thank all the saints I pulled you out of the way before the worst."

Celia tried to sit up. The freckled woman gave her a hand and helped her lean against the wall of the lamp dealer's shop behind her. She winced as her shoulder contacted the bricks.

"I am fine," Celia said. "Thanks to you."

All she apparently suffered from was a ripped skirt and torn gloves, the scrapes on her palms bleeding through the fabric, and a badly bruised shoulder. Fortunately, she was taller than the typical female; her height meant that the implement her assailant had wielded had missed her head and landed on her upper back instead. She still hurt, though.

"'T'was nothing, ma'am."

"Someone hit me from behind," Celia said. "Did you see them?"

The woman shook her head. "No. No, I didn't. A fellow hit you?"

"Why'd you step in front of that horsecar?" asked an aproned boy, pushing forward through the crowd that had gathered. "You almost got squashed flat as a biffin."

Why had she followed Dennis Merrill down a shadowy alleyway was a better question.

"Did you happen to notice a man heading this way? I was attempting to flag him down. He's the brother of a friend I've not seen in ages," Celia said, her lower back throbbing. She must have wrenched it when she'd fallen. "He had on a tan linen coat."

What other features might describe Dennis Merrill? She couldn't think of any in particular, especially since her hands were starting to hurt nearly as much as her back, distracting her.

"No, ma'am, didn't see him," the aproned boy said.

"Hey, what's all this about?" A policeman shouldered his way through the crowd. "Everybody needs to move on. You're blocking the sidewalk. Don't make me arrest you."

Celia looked up him. "Hello, Officer." She didn't know his name but did recognize him from the station.

And he recognized her as well. For a reason she did not care to contemplate, he didn't appear surprised to find her propped against a wall, her clothing mangled and her hands bleeding, with a throng of people surrounding her. "Ah, Mrs. Davies."

She extended her less-wounded hand toward him, and he helped her to her feet. "Thank you."

"Are these folks bothering you, ma'am?"

"Quite the opposite. Thank you all," she said, dusting off her skirt and frowning at the rip near the hem. Addie would tut ferociously over the tear.

The crowd dispersed. The freckled woman collected a carpetbag she'd left by the curb before looking back at Celia and walking off.

"Do you need an escort home?" the policeman asked.

"No, I can return home under my own power," she replied, straightening her bonnet, which had been knocked askew. "But, if you would, please get a message to Detective Greaves that I need to speak with him. Urgently."

"Detective Greaves, eh?" he asked, stifling a grin.

Gad. Who in the station house had *not* heard about their relationship? Nicholas must suffer endless teasing about it.

"You did not happen to observe a man in a tan coat running along the street, did you, Officer?" she asked.

"I might have."

"Might have, or did?"

"I *did*, Mrs. Davies," he answered curtly. "He went into a building. On the corner there." He pointed to the intersection he meant.

Thank heavens he'd noticed. "Which of the buildings? The bank? The hotel? The saloon? Or the estate agents' office?"

Annoyed by being peppered with questions, he gave her a black look. "The hotel, ma'am."

"Thank you. I shall inform Detective Greaves how very helpful you were."

She headed for the hotel before the officer thought to stop her. Attempting to make herself more presentable, she tore off her bloodied gloves, stuffed them into her reticule, and went inside. If the reception clerk noticed the rip in her skirt, he'd likely toss her out for violating the standards of a decent establishment. The hotel was very handsome. The lobby's dark wood floors gleamed from a recent polish, and ornate gas lamps cast their pleasing glow over a collection of comfortably padded chairs. Under different circumstances, she'd not mind staying here.

Shoulders squared and her chin raised confidently, she strode up to the clerk's desk.

He narrowed his eyes suspiciously, nonetheless. "Yes, miss?"

"Ma'am," she corrected, tucking her left hand beneath her right and wishing she'd not stopped wearing the wedding ring that Patrick had given her. "A relation of mine, a Mr. Merrill, arranged to meet me here. In your lobby, of course. Not anywhere private that might be scandalous. I do not see him, however, and was wondering if he arrived. A fellow in a tan coat."

"Him? He went straight upstairs."

"Mr. Dennis Merrill, correct?"

The man reached for the hotel register without taking his eyes off her, smoothly sliding the book across the surface of the desk toward him. He gave it a quick perusal. "There is no one named Merrill staying here, ma'am. And I do not know the name of the gentleman in the tan coat."

"Oh, I know!" She smiled giddily and pressed her hands together. "He has devised the most wonderful surprise for me. His sister, Mrs. Gannon, must have arrived in San Francisco for a family rendezvous. What is her room number? I'd like to join them upstairs, if I might."

The clerk conducted another hasty perusal, in case a moment's inattention encouraged Celia to dash up the broad staircase to his left and commit some form of criminal atrocity upon one of the guests. She attempted to read the entries upside-down. One of the names might have been Gannon. In fact, she was quite certain it was. *Excellent guess, Celia.*

"This establishment is not in the habit of providing information about our guests to people . . ." He cast Celia a disdainful look. "People who wander in off the street."

"Does your reply mean that she *is* registered at this hotel? Because I believe that is her name right there." Celia pointed at the signature.

He snatched the register away before she could grab it. "If a Mrs. Gannon does arrive, I shall inform her that you inquired after her," he said. "I presume she knows how to reach you?"

"Most certainly she does," Celia replied. "Tell her that Mrs. Smith came by."

She thanked him and went out onto the street, the sun falling warmly on her face.

Well, Mr. Merrill, you've never heard of Mrs. Gannon, have you?

She smiled and headed home, the stiff ache in her back miraculously feeling so much better. The warning in a telegram completely forgotten.

• • •

"You payin' attention there, Cassidy?" asked the fellow working with him. They were unloading a newly arrived steamer carrying a shipment of beef and pork packed in barrels. One of the last ships of the day. "You're gonna get run over by one of these here barrels if you don't stop your daydreamin'."

The barrel the fellow referred to thudded as he rolled it off the edge of the ramp and onto the pier.

"I am not daydreaming," Owen said. *I'm busy thinking about how I can help Mr. Greaves and Mr. Taylor.*

"Sure looks like you are to me." He maneuvered the barrel past Owen and indicated with a shrug of one thick shoulder the others waiting on the boat.

Owen trotted up the plank. Mr. Taylor hadn't left him with the impression that the police were going to hunt for Mrs. Gannon, so he'd had the idea of trying to find her himself. He'd snuck into his boss's office in the warehouse to have a peek at the city directory. There were only three Gannons in the book and just one of them was female, but she was listed as a "Miss." Which left Owen with two possibilities—that Mrs. Gannon was a married lady, and not mentioned in the directory as a result, or she was visiting the city temporarily. He could stop by the addresses of the other two Gannons and ask about their wives. He grabbed the nearest barrel and rolled it toward the plank. But if she was only visiting, there were an awful lot of hotels in town. There was one, though, that welcomed ladies and wasn't far from where the Weavers lived. If Mrs. Gannon was in town to talk to Mrs. Merrill, she'd most likely stay there. Well, that's what he would've done, at least.

"Barrels, Cassidy!" his coworker shouted up from the pier. "Are you tryin' to get fired? Get on it!"

Owen hurried the barrel down the plank, nearly tipping it over the edge in his haste. He wouldn't get a chance to do any investigating if he didn't get finished here. But then the next boat would dock, and—

"Hey, you two!" A bowlegged fellow, striding along the pier, called out to them. "Our last ship's been delayed until tomorrow."

Hallelujah, thought Owen, rushing to get the remainder of the barrels to the warehouse. Now to find Mrs. Gannon.

• • •

"You think this scrap of paper is proof Thaddeus Thompson killed Elnora Merrill?" Nicholas—who'd responded quickly to Celia's request that he visit—dropped the note she'd found in Cassandra's book onto her examining room desk.

She folded her arms. "All I am suggesting is that it is evidence of a motive."

"Evidence of a motive isn't evidence of a murder, Celia."

She inhaled slowly; she was not going to allow his frustration about having two murders on his hands infect her. "All right. So the note is not proof that he acted on wanting Elnora out of the way."

"Thank you," he said. "I presume you went back to the Weavers' to ask about the early morning message they received."

"I did," she said. "Cassandra told me she thought it had come from Thaddeus. A request for a meeting to beg her father to reconsider delaying their engagement. Worried, she went to his residence, but he wasn't home. She wanted me to believe she'd forgotten his travel plans."

"According to him, he was in Suscol getting ready to board the morning ferry," he said. "Taylor and I found him at his father's office this afternoon. He apparently returned earlier than planned from Calistoga."

But not early enough to have killed Mr. Young. "I also questioned her about Mrs. Gannon. Both she and Mr. Merrill—he turned up at the Weavers' house not long after I did—denied ever having heard of her. However, I am certain he was lying to me." She explained about his visit to the hotel and the name she'd read in the register.

"Are you sure the name you read—upside-down—was actually Gannon, Celia? It could've been Cannon."

"As certain as I can be," she said. "I should also inform you that Mr. Merrill wanted me to know that he saw Gabriella in the city today. He pretended that he was going to the station to tell you, but obviously he did not."

"He spotted Gabriella?" he asked. "How convenient."

"Has he provided an alibi for when Mr. Young was murdered?"

"Not yet. I'll have Merrill brought into the station and find out what he has to say for himself."

"What about the others, Nicholas?" she asked. "What have you learned?"

"We've found a connection potentially linking Weaver and the Thompsons to Young. They were all members of the Odd Fellows. Young might've learned about their bribery scheme through mutual acquaintances," he replied. "We haven't found any samples of Young's handwriting, though, to prove he wrote the note you found in Mrs. Merrill's pocket."

"Nonetheless, he may have been the author and a threat to them."

"Maybe, but Julius Thompson was with a business associate while Young was being murdered," he said. "I'm having Taylor confirm that, though."

"Both of the Thompsons have an alibi." Very disappointing. "What about Mr. Weaver?"

"He's been evading all of our efforts to question him so far," he replied. "The boardinghouse where Young was found isn't far from Weaver's house, by the way."

"Close enough for Mr. Weaver to speedily get there and return?" Mr. Weaver or Cassandra.

"I'd say so."

"Ah." She reached up to massage her forehead. "I do wish I could see my way through to the answer, Nicholas."

He eyed her hands. "When were you planning on telling me why your hands are bandaged, Celia? Or were you thinking I wouldn't notice?"

"I had a fall and scraped my palms." Barbara had done an excellent job tending to her wounds. After making clear that she was still upset over Celia's suggestion that Cassandra might be a murderer.

"How exactly did you end up falling?" Nicholas asked. "Because you're not prone to clumsiness."

"You mean the officer who gave you my message did not provide the details?"

"No, he spent too much time chuckling to himself," he said. "What happened?"

"Someone struck me with a sturdy object. A piece of wood, probably." She might not be prone to clumsiness, but she *was* prone to assailants hitting her from behind. "The impact propelled me into the path of a Central Railroad horsecar. I was rescued from being squashed flat as a biffin by a woman. Sadly, the incident delayed me from more closely following Mr. Merrill and discovering precisely who he was visiting at the hotel. My money is on Mrs. Gannon, obviously."

"That's how you knew that Merrill had gone to that hotel. You were trailing him." He rolled his eyes. "I should've figured you wouldn't be careful."

His admonitions and a telegram had not been sufficient to stop her from being reckless.

"I am sorry, Nicholas."

Her apology softened the tension in his shoulders. "I worry about you, Celia."

"I know," she replied.

He released a long breath. "All right, Mrs. Davies. I'll send Mullahey to the hotel to question Mrs. Gannon, if she *is* registered there. And if she hasn't legged it already."

"I do wonder who she is."

"Somebody whose existence needs to be kept quiet, apparently."

"Kept quiet from whom? The Weavers' servants know about her." About her existence, but not much else, it was true. "Furthermore, Elnora received several letters from her. Their contents must have explained who she was and what she wanted."

He somberly considered her. "And now Elnora Merrill is dead, those letters are missing, and Young's been murdered," he said. "Who's next?"

• • •

"For a second, I thought you was gonna tell me you're her brother," the hotel domestic said. She was missing a front tooth, which made her *s*'s whistle. "All those freckles and everything."

He didn't have that many freckles, did he?

"Is Mrs. Gannon still here?" Owen asked.

Last night, he'd eliminated the two Gannons listed in the city directory. They'd both been bachelor men. One of them had been downright mean about Owen asking if he had womenfolk in his house. He'd been forced to run before the situation turned ugly. After that encounter, he'd decided to start over this morning with the hotels. There'd actually been two near the Weavers' house that allowed unaccompanied women to stay. He'd gotten kicked out of the first place when he started asking questions. He hadn't needed to venture inside the second hotel and risk getting kicked out again, though, because he'd found one of the staff dumping soapy water into the street when he'd arrived.

"Her? Nope, she skedaddled yesterday," she said, hooking the empty bucket over her forearm.

"Any idea where she went?"

"No idea," she said. "Sometimes guests leave forwarding addresses, but not her. She wasn't here long enough to be collecting mail."

"How long is not long enough?"

"Two weeks? Three?" She shrugged. "She didn't have much with her. I clean the rooms on the floor she was staying on. Thought for sure she'd only be with us for a few days, based on how small her bag was."

"She didn't leave any letters or other identifying information laying around, did she?" he asked.

"You implying that I might root around in a guest's belongings?"

Well, that was what he was suggesting, but it was best not to say so out loud.

"Just thought you might've noticed something that could help me find her," he said.

She peered at him. "Why you asking all these questions?"

"I, um . . . I'm helping a debt collector track her down." Telling folks he assisted the police didn't always work well, as he'd learned yesterday.

"Why am I not surprised to hear a debt collector is after her?" She looked around and leaned in close to Owen. "The proprietor was getting worried she was gonna skip out on her bill. She kept saying she was expecting funds any day now. Enough to pay for weeks of bills! Gotta wonder where she was gonna get that sort of money. Although I have an idea, and it's not a Christian one. If you know what I mean." She nodded for added emphasis.

He did know what she meant, and he didn't want to think about it, because then he might blush. "Did she ever mention a man with the last name of Merrill?"

"Never heard that name, but I was sweeping the hall yesterday afternoon when some fellow came charging along it and barged right into her room. Good-looking fellow in a nice tan duster. She must've already skedaddled and left the door unlocked," she said. "Without paying her bill."

Now that was interesting.

"He stormed back out soon after with a mighty thunderous look on his face." She shook her head over the recollection. "Wouldn't want to cross him. Not at all."

• • •

"Weel, ma'am, I see the fellow who owns that hotel at the geysers hasna stopped advertising the place, even though a murder was committed there," Addie announced, wandering into the entryway as she read the Saturday morning newspaper. "Some honorable judge and his family are due to be his guests next week. A judge. One would think he'd know better. Wait," she said, finally looking up. "Care to tell me where you are going?"

"I have a patient to visit," Celia said, her shoulder aching as she reached up to adjust her bonnet.

Addie pointedly looked at the floor near Celia's feet. "Then where is your medical bag, ma'am?"

Not with her, obviously. "Ah."

"You're nae going anywhere," Addie stated, barring the front door with her outstretched arms, the newspaper dangling from her hand. "You've had enough excitement lately."

"I am perfectly recovered from yesterday's minor accident, Addie," Celia insisted. "And I must make inquiries at Mr. Merrill's residence about the mysterious Mrs. Gannon. See what I can learn about the woman from someone who might be willing to tell me." Someone other than Dennis Merrill, who hopefully was preoccupied elsewhere—such as the police station—when she arrived.

"Mrs. Gannon?" Barbara asked, leaning over the staircase railing. Listening in on conversations, again. "The woman who sent letters to Mrs. Merrill?"

"Barbara, didn't your tutor supply you with reading assignments to complete over the summer? Should you not be doing them?"

"I've finished them all." She descended the stairs. "You can't go to his residence alone, Cousin. Not after what happened yesterday. Somebody's trying to hurt you. Warn you off."

In more ways than one.

"Aye, ma'am. 'Tis dangerous," Addie said. "I'll send for Jer . . . Mr. Taylor. He can do your investigating for you."

"Or you can take me," Celia's cousin suggested.

"Absolutely not, Barbara. I will be perfectly fine." *Should I bring a weapon, though?*

"I'm getting my things anyway." Barbara turned and pounded up the stairs. "And we can take Angelo with us, just to be safe," she called down from the upstairs landing.

"I am not taking our neighbor's eight-year-old boy with us," Celia shouted back to her. Although he had gotten involved in other investigations before. Unfortunately. "Barbara! Do you hear me?" *Blast.*

A knock sounded on the front door. Addie answered it.

Owen stepped into the entry hall. "You'll never guess what I discovered, Mrs. Davies!"

"Please say you've discovered the identity of Mr. Young's murderer."

He frowned. "Sorry, ma'am. Can't do that."

"Och, I've forgotten the potatoes I set to boiling on the cooking stove," Addie exclaimed and hurried back to the kitchen.

"Then what did you discover?" Celia asked him.

He straightened to his full height. "I've found out that Mrs. Gannon has been staying at a hotel near the Weavers' place."

"A hotel off of Dupont?"

He squinted at her. "Have you been there?"

"Yesterday afternoon, I followed Mr. Merrill to that very hotel," Celia said. "However, when I questioned the clerk about Mr. Merrill and Mrs. Gannon, whose name I noticed in the register, he refused to admit that she was a guest."

"Well, I didn't talk to any clerk, ma'am. I spoke with one of the hotel domestics," he said. "Mrs. Gannon was definitely at the hotel but skedaddled yesterday afternoon. Right after a handsome fellow in a tan duster, who was angry as all get out, visited."

Ah, Mr. Merrill. "Did anyone know where she went?"

"No. Sorry, ma'am," he said. "Guess my information isn't much help if we don't know where to find her."

"It is of help, Owen. You have proven that Mr. Merrill did indeed lie to me." The clerk, too. She tiptoed over to the bottom of the staircase and scanned what she could see of the landing. No Barbara in sight. "If you are not needed at the docks yet, come with me to Mr. Merrill's house. And quickly, before Barbara finds out that we're leaving and demands to accompany us."

CHAPTER 17

Dennis Merrill lived in a two-story brick home of modest proportions, not too dissimilar from the house Celia occupied with Barbara and Addie. His was located in a newer part of the city, a respectable neighborhood suitable for the families of businessmen.

"This is a nice place," Owen said, examining the building as they climbed the short flight of front steps.

"My thoughts precisely," she agreed, twisting the brass doorbell handle.

A woman, a scarf wrapped around her hair and a broom in her hand, answered the door.

"Yes?" Her gaze took in first Celia and then Owen, standing at her side. "If it's Mr. Merrill you're looking for, he ain't home. He went to the . . . he ain't home. And you shouldn't be disturbing us, as we're in mourning here." She stepped to one side to indicate the mirror just inside the front door, draped in black.

"My deepest sympathies for your loss."

"Not my loss," she said. "But you should be going, 'cause I've got cleaning to finish."

"It appears we will have to delay our search for your aunt," she said to Owen before turning back to the domestic. "You see, I agreed to help him find the woman. He works for my father, in his office, and has been such an excellent assistant. We both feel quite sorry for him." Celia smiled gently at him, and Owen assumed a suitably forlorn expression. "We were told Mr. Merrill might know of her whereabouts. Apparently they are acquainted with each other, although we've not quite reasoned out the connection."

"Mr. Merrill?" she asked.

"Her name is Mrs. Gannon," Owen said. "That's my aunt. I haven't heard from her in months, and I'm awful worried."

The domestic's eyes widened. "That thing? You mean the woman who came by here claiming to be the sister of Mr. Merrill's wife?"

Celia gasped; she could not help herself.

"That's her!" Owen exclaimed, recovering from the revelation more quickly than Celia.

"I can see the resemblance." The domestic squinted at him.

"You've got her freckles. She didn't look old enough to be your aunt, though."

Freckles? "Did she leave an address where she could be contacted?" Such as the address of a hotel off Dupont? Not that confirming she had been staying there helped them find her now.

"There might've been one on the message she left for Mr. Merrill, but I don't know where that went to," she said, gripping the door with every intention of closing it, and quickly.

"Has anyone else attempted to contact Mr. Merrill recently?" Celia asked. "A Mr. Young, perhaps?"

"What's he got to do with Mrs. Gannon?" she asked, growing wary.

"He's looking for her, too," Owen answered. "He's my . . . my brother."

"I'm not sure I believe you two," the woman said. "So you need to get outta here before I find a cop and tell him that you're vagrants going up to folks' houses to beg for money."

"Just tell me if Mr. Young has ever come here to speak with Mr. Merrill, and we'll cease bothering you," Celia said.

"He might've, but I don't live here, so I don't know what happens at all hours," she said. "I get here around six thirty, leave around five, after I've made dinner for Mr. Merrill. If anybody visits before or after then, I wouldn't know."

Celia had a thought. "Was Mr. Merrill here yesterday morning when you arrived for work?"

The woman's gaze narrowed. "Why are you asking?"

"That's probably when my brother, Mr. Young, came to see him," Owen answered for Celia. "He likes to take care of stuff real early. Don't get it, but he's always been an early riser."

"Mr. Merrill was here, but I didn't start work at my usual time," she said. "He told me not to get here until about an hour later than normal."

"You mean seven thirty." *This woman's account is causing a definite problem for an alibi, Mr. Merrill.*

"An hour later. That's what I said." She scowled. "You're done now. Right?"

"Yes. Thank—"

She slammed the door before Celia could finish thanking her.

Owen trotted down the steps behind her. "Mr. Merrill has a wife?"

"I am equally startled by the news." But the existence of a wife explained so much, including the cause of an argument in Healdsburg.

"Folks had to know, didn't they, Mrs. Davies?"

"Perhaps it was a brief relationship, a marriage hastily contracted several years ago and likewise rapidly abandoned," she said, pausing at the corner. "Perhaps his father was not even aware, if Dennis Merrill and his wife had lived elsewhere."

"The Mrs. Gannon who came here has to be the same one who'd been staying at that hotel," he said. "The maid at the hotel also mentioned that Mrs. Gannon had freckles."

"Strangely enough, I may have encountered her, Owen," Celia said. "When I had my accident, which might not have been accidental. She saved me from being run over by a horsecar."

"Well, if Mr. Merrill *is* married to somebody else, he won't be able to marry Miss Weaver, will he?"

"Only if people find out about his wife, Owen," she said. "To what lengths, I wonder, might Dennis Merrill be willing to go in order to keep her existence a secret?"

• • •

"I have been meaning to stop by the station, Detective," Dennis Merrill said, lowering onto the chair in front of Nick's desk. "To tell you that I spotted Gabriella in San Francisco. Yesterday, if you can believe it."

"I wouldn't have needed to send an officer to bring you in if you'd stopped by earlier, Mr. Merrill," Nick said, leaning back. "Mighty embarrassing, having the cops visit you at your house."

"It was."

The brief smile he gave was certainly fake. A lot about Dennis Merrill was fake. Nick disliked him, the smoothness of his demeanor, the overconfident way he lounged in the chair. Disliked Merrill so much that he risked not treating him fairly.

Taylor slipped into the room, took his usual chair, and opened his notebook. "He was at home, sir. All morning. Multiple witnesses." Confirming Julius Thompson's alibi. One less suspect.

Merrill perked his eyebrows as though he hoped Nick would elaborate on who Taylor meant.

"Thank you, Taylor," Nick said. "Why should we care that you'd spotted Gabriella in San Francisco, Mr. Merrill?"

Young's name hadn't been publicly linked to the man found murdered in a boardinghouse—not yet—and Merrill shouldn't be aware that Gabriella could be a suspect.

"Because, Detective, I assumed that if she's in town, then Young is probably in town, too. She was seen leaving his room at the Geyser Hotel, right? Clearly they have some sort of a relationship," he said. "I thought you might want to know. Was I wrong?"

"Where did you see her?" Nick asked.

"Not far from the Weavers' house," he answered.

"Near the Weavers'." And Young's place, for that matter.

"I find that location suspicious, don't you, Detective? What was she planning to do?" he asked. "I should've tried to confront her, but I lost her in the crowd. Apologies."

"You didn't rush into the station to tell us. Why not?"

"I had other matters to attend to first. Business that I'd neglected while I was up at the geysers."

Right. "Heard about your fur dealer venture going under. Sorry to hear that."

"Businesses fail all the time, Detective. I'm determined to eventually succeed."

Nick leaned forward and rested his elbows on his desk, tenting his fingers beneath his chin. "You know, it's funny you mentioning Gabriella, Mr. Merrill," Nick said. "She told me that you'd asked her to hunt for a telegram in Mrs. Davies's room. What was that about?"

"She said what? Why would I have her do that?" he asked, sounding genuinely bewildered. "I honestly have no idea what she's talking about, Detective."

Knuckles rapped on the office door, and one of the officers poked his head through the opening. "Sorry about interrupting, Detective, but—"

"Thank you, Officer," Celia said, sweeping past him and into the room. "Ah, Mr. Merrill. I am so glad to find you here at the station. At last."

She sounded cheerful; she'd learned something important.

Taylor stood, and she took his chair, her deep blue skirts spilling over the seat edge. "Have you been explaining to Mr. Greaves how you cannot possibly know Mrs. Gannon?" she asked Merrill.

"No, because the good detective hasn't questioned me about her," Merrill replied. "But I will repeat that I've never heard of the woman."

"Oh, you mean she is not your wife's sister?" she asked.

Damn.

Dennis Merrill looked as though he might choke.

"The woman who cleans and cooks for you informed me that Mrs. Gannon paid you a call at your house. Left you a message, as well," Celia continued. Taylor scribbled as fast as he could push a pencil. "Did she hope you might provide for your abandoned wife? Return to your connubial bliss, perhaps?"

"This is utter nonsense, Mrs. Davies."

"Is it?" she asked. "It's true that I have no proof of the existence of a wife. Aside from the word of a charwoman, who has no motive to lie. And the letters Mrs. Gannon sent to Elnora, which one of the Weavers' servants told me about, have conveniently vanished. Perhaps you have removed them, Mr. Merrill. It was easy enough for me to go upstairs and search for the letters in Mrs. Merrill's bedchamber. The staff is not so plentiful nor so attentive as to have stopped me."

"You're admitting, in front of the police, that you searched my stepmother's bedroom for some letters," Merrill said. "Did you have a warrant to do that, Mrs. Davies?"

Ah, the old warrant question.

"After her attempts to speak with you got her nowhere, was Mrs. Gannon then forced to approach the only other Merrill she could find in San Francisco?" Celia asked. "Namely, Elnora."

Nick leaned back again and folded his arms. He may as well get comfortable.

Merrill shot Nick a look. "Detective, do you always allow citizens to conduct searches and interrogations without the proper authority?"

"Not always." Just Celia. But maybe it *was* time for her to stop. "Meanwhile, I'd like to hear what else Mrs. Davies has to say and how you might respond."

He frowned. "I'm being interrogated about some deranged woman while Gabriella is roaming free in the city."

"Please continue, Mrs. Davies," Nick said.

"Thank you, I shall," she replied, smiling. "I overheard you arguing with your stepmother at the hotel in Healdsburg, Mr. Merrill. It strikes me, now that I think back on what I heard, that Elnora was upset about what she'd learned from Mrs. Gannon. That you have a wife already. A woman you abandoned, I gather. You duped both Elnora and the Weavers and cannot possibly extend an offer of marriage to Cassandra Weaver. You wish you could, don't you? 'May the best man win,' Mr. Merrill. That is what you said to me."

"Mrs. Gannon is lying about my having a wife."

An admission that Mrs. Gannon exists, thought Nick.

"Is that why you went to the hotel yesterday where she was staying?" Nick asked. "To confront her about her lies? Or to buy her silence?" Or worse?

Merrill turned to Celia. "It *was* you following me."

"You ought to know," she said. "You pushed me in front of an oncoming horsecar."

He sighed. "No, Mrs. Davies, that was not me. You have other enemies, apparently."

"Mr. Merrill, where were you yesterday morning between five and seven?" Nick asked.

"Sleeping," he said. "Why? Oh, wait. I saw the paper this morning. A man was murdered at his boardinghouse. Who was it?"

"Mr. Young."

Merrill reacted with a low chuckle. "No surprise. But I wasn't out murdering him," Merrill said. "Although maybe I should've been. He killed my stepmother for no reason. Anybody who could do that is a vicious animal."

"Had Mr. Young discovered your secret about your wife, Mr. Merrill?" Celia asked. "Perhaps he heard more of your argument with Elnora than I did, enabling him to piece together the puzzle of what it meant."

"I did *not* kill him."

"Did he attempt to blackmail you about your wife?" she asked. "Were *you* the intended recipient of the note I found in Elnora's skirt pocket? A message written in haste on a menu card from the Geyser Hotel. Up at the hotel, you'd let slip that the blackmail attempt had been delivered via a note. You knew of it."

"Detective, this is damned ridiculous. Letting a woman conduct an interrogation for you," he said. "I won't tolerate it any longer."

Merrill jumped up from his chair. Taylor, always quick on his feet, intercepted him before he could leave the office.

"Please sit back down, Mr. Merrill," Nick said.

Merrill resumed sitting and folded his arms.

"Your charwoman told me that, per your request, she did not arrive at your house yesterday at her usual time," Celia continued. "Why did you ask her to delay?"

"I told you. I wanted to sleep," he answered. "We had a very arduous journey back from the geysers. Can't speak for either of you, but I was exhausted. Wanted the extra rest. So I sent her a message telling her to come in an hour later."

"Strange that the woman was convinced that you'd been awake for some time," Celia said. "Had possibly even left the house."

"Can't fathom why she thought that."

She considered Merrill for long enough that Taylor looked up from his notebook to see what had caused the break in her questioning.

"Your shoes, Mr. Merrill," Celia said. "They weren't where you usually leave them when you retire at night, and where she always finds them in the morning."

"What?" He chuckled mirthlessly and shook his head. "Okay, okay. I did get up when I normally do yesterday. But I wasn't out killing Young. I didn't even know he was in town. How would I?"

"Because he'd contacted you?" Nick suggested.

"He didn't."

"If you weren't with Young yesterday morning, where had you gone, then?"

Merrill's cheek protruded where the tip of his tongue prodded the inside of his mouth. Weighing the consequences of what he was about to say, or whether Nick would even believe him.

"I didn't go anywhere, but I had gotten dressed because of an unexpected visitor," Merrill said. "A woman whose reputation I'd rather not sully by mentioning her name."

"If she can provide you an alibi confirming where you were at the time Mr. Young was murdered, then you might want to give us her precious name, Mr. Merrill," Nick said.

"She's not going to appreciate my telling you, Detective, but if you insist." He glanced at Celia before giving the woman's name. "My visitor was Cassandra Weaver."

• • •

"All right, Nicholas. I admit that Mr. Merrill's charwoman did not discover that his shoes were out of place and conclude that he'd gone out yesterday morning," Celia confessed. "But you cannot let him go. You must arrest him and throw him in jail. He had a motive to kill Mr. Young. And Barbara smelled his cigarillo smoke near where Elnora died. He has to be our murderer."

"I thought you liked Dennis Merrill, Celia," he said, his strides lengthening as they strode up Kearny. He was escorting her home because, as he'd put it, she needed to stay there and "keep out of police affairs." "Wasn't that why you asked me about everyone else's alibis yesterday?"

Her cheeks warmed. "Whatever gave you such an idea?"

"Oh, just a feeling."

"I do *not* like Dennis Merrill, Nicholas," she stated.

"Got it. Well, to be frank, I can't decide if Dennis Merrill is our murderer," he said. "He's annoying, it's true, but I also think he's far too clever to resort to violence simply to keep the existence of a wife quiet. And we don't have any proof Young knew about the woman."

Celia looked over at him. "You don't honestly believe Mr. Merrill's alibi that he was having a liaison with Cassandra Weaver, do you?"

"Why not?"

She stopped at the peak of the incline where Kearny intersected Vallejo. "From what I've observed of Cassandra Weaver's interactions with Dennis Merrill, she can barely tolerate him."

"I don't have to tell you that folks can be good at concealing their true feelings," he said. "She might've taken advantage of her father's abrupt absence to go to him."

Gad. Had she been blind to the possibility?

Celia considered the road ahead of them, which stretched toward her house. One of her neighbor's children was playing out on the curb. Another neighbor sat on her porch, hemming a dress. A sedate-seeming late morning, but they were not all like that. Because even on her street, people erected façades behind which they hid any number of secrets. Hid all types of pain and misery. Secret longings.

"Unfortunately for us both, Nicholas, Cassandra will likely deny that she was with Dennis Merrill, even if she was," she said. "But Mr. Merrill *could* have killed Mr. Young, couldn't he have done? Possibly because Mr. Young had obtained Mrs. Gannon's letters. She had to have mentioned her sister in them."

"He'd have to have learned they existed and where they were hidden. Then somehow manage to steal them."

"Perhaps, during that argument in Healdsburg, Elnora mentioned the letters and that they were in safekeeping inside her dressing table." She was only speculating, but it sounded reasonable to her.

Nicholas stopped. "Young's saddlebag is missing. What if Mrs. Gannon's letters were in it?" he asked. "When could he have gotten ahold of them, though? He was up at the geysers the entire time."

"Not the entire time. He departed a good twenty-four hours before we did," she explained. "He may have headed straight for the Weavers' house when he arrived back in San Francisco. Which would have been Wednesday evening, giving him most of Thursday to break in."

"Maybe Young found it just as easy to get inside Mrs. Merrill's bedroom as you did."

She could imagine the situation, the servants lax and incautious because the master and his family were away from home.

"Mr. Merrill invented the story of Gabriella being in San Francisco, didn't he?" she asked. "To protect himself."

"Possibly. But I still don't think you strangle somebody over some letters revealing that you have a secret wife. Strangling seems like such a personal, emotional method of killing." He shook his head. "I just can't see Merrill working up that much of a lather. Pay Young off, destroy the letters, and be done with it."

"Perhaps you're right, Nicholas," she replied. "But what if his motive to kill Mr. Young was something else? Such as the man having seen him push Elnora?"

"Now there's an idea, Mrs. Davies." He took her arm and helped her over a puddle of dirty water that had been tossed onto the street. "Incidentally, when I questioned Thaddeus Thompson at his father's office, he admitted that Young had attempted to blackmail him. Told me that right before informing me about a disagreement between Young and Weaver he'd witnessed. The night before Mrs. Merrill died."

"Mr. Young *was* the author of the note I found in his hotel sleeping room," Celia said, feeling vindicated.

"Thompson mentioned a confrontation, not receiving a note."

"I doubt Mr. Thompson was being blackmailed by two different individuals, Nicholas."

"Interestingly, Young never attempted to approach Weaver prior to their quarrel at the Geyser Hotel. Not at his house or at his office," Nicholas said. "However, he did try to contact Thompson at *his* office but got turned away."

"A professional blackmailer," she said. "He had to have been attempting to obtain money from Mr. Merrill as well. I truly believe that."

Nicholas inclined his head. "Yes, yes, Celia. I give in," he said, smiling. "Maybe now we can answer why Young came back to San Francisco. He'd discovered a potential source of funds in Merrill and the Thompsons, and he wasn't going to let it go."

"Unfortunately, Mr. Young underestimated how difficult it might be to get every victim of his blackmail attempts to cooperate." Maybe one of them *had* worked up enough of a "lather" to strangle him.

Nicholas rubbed the old wound in his arm that ached whenever he became uneasy. "I'll have an officer get a statement from Miss Weaver. If she refuses to provide an alibi for Merrill, I'll arrest him. For murder."

• • •

"There's a young lady in your office, Greaves." The booking sergeant waggled his eyebrows, which meant she was pretty. "Why don't they ever ask for Briggs?"

Because Detective Briggs wasn't competent? "I'm just so appealing to the ladies, Sergeant."

He winked. "I won't tell Mrs. Davies."

"Very funny."

Mullahey stood up from his desk in the main room and signaled for Nick to come over. "We've located Mr. Weaver, Mr. Greaves. He's at his office waiting for you, and I encouraged him to not leave. He agreed. Or he will, when he notices the man I've stationed outside on the street." He winked.

Weaver must have finally finished with all those appointments that had lasted well into the evening, according to a message Taylor had left on Nick's desk. His assistant had spent much of yesterday trying to track the man down and failing.

"Thank you, Mullahey," he said. "Oh, I also need you to get a statement from Cassandra Weaver. Ask if she was with Dennis Merrill yesterday morning. Between when she was last seen at her house around five thirty and seven. He claims she was."

Mullahey whistled.

"Very gentlemanly of him, wasn't it?" Nick asked.

"I'll not be saying what I'm thinking, Mr. Greaves," he said.

The woman in the detectives' office turned out to be quite the surprise.

"Well, Mr. Merrill wasn't lying when he said he'd spotted you in town," Nick said to Gabriella, removing his hat and taking his chair.

"Mr. Merrill?" She'd been sitting with her back ramrod straight, but on speaking his name, her shoulders twitched. "What did he say about me?"

"Not much beyond stating that he'd seen you, and thought you might lead us to Mr. Young," Nick answered. "Is Young why you've come into the station, Miss . . ."

"Raas. Gabriella Raas," she said.

"Tell me why you've come into the station, Miss Raas." His brain was already concocting all sorts of reasons.

"I wanted to tell you that I went to see him, yesterday morning, once I learned where he lived."

"You mean Parker Young."

"I do," she said. "It is his fault I lost my job with Mr. Shafer. He owes me."

And she'd just given Nick a reason why she might've wanted Young dead—vengeance. "He owes you money?"

"He promised me he would give me help, if I ever wanted it. I have family here, but they do not want to support me," she said bitterly. "They told me I can't stay for long."

Had Young made that promise before or after she'd agreed to meet him in his hotel room? "You didn't have to go to his room and lose your position with Shafer, Gabriella."

"I was stupid," she admitted. "And now I have no job and only a few dollars after paying one of Mr. Foss's riders to take me all the way to the Petaluma ferry."

"How did you know to look for Young in San Francisco?"

She stared down at her hands. They were bare, her knuckles chapped from hours spent in soapy water, and strong-looking. "He told me his plans. To get the money he was promised, was what he said. And then he was going to Oregon."

"Money from who? Promised for what?" For keeping quiet about secrets was the plausible answer. Or in exchange for a mysterious item.

"He did not tell me who or why."

He paused, letting the silence stretch. "When I questioned you at the Geyser Hotel, you said Young had gone to the trail that heads up to the geysers the morning Mrs. Merrill died."

She nodded. "To meet with someone. He did not give me their name."

To meet with someone. She hadn't divulged that before. "You have previously claimed that he couldn't have killed her, Miss Raas. Do you want to continue to state that?"

"Yes. He did not," she stated. "All he wanted was to get away. To Oregon. Killing someone would have made that more difficult. He had no reason to harm Mrs. Merrill."

"But you don't know who might've killed her."

"No. How could I?"

Nick reached for the burning ache in his arm. "So, you went to visit Mr. Young yesterday morning at his boardinghouse. Bet he was startled to see you."

Her brow creased. "He was not alive, Mr. Greaves."

"You went inside the building?"

"The front door, it was open," she explained. "Also, the door to his room. It was . . . I've never seen a dead man before, Detective. I pray I never do again. It was horrible."

Could he trust her? Or was she playing games in order to appear innocent? "Thank you for sharing this information, Miss Raas, but the police already know about Mr. Young's murder."

"That is not all, Mr. Greaves." She reached across his desk with one of her raw-knuckled hands. "I am here to tell you that I saw him."

"Who?"

"The man who killed Parker Young."

෨ CHAPTER 18 ෨

"I put a notice in the newspaper requesting that Mrs. Gannon contact the police, sir. Mr. Greaves, sir," Taylor said between puffs on his cigar, the smoke trailing off in the breeze slicing up the road. "If she's still in town, that is."

"Not sure we need her to contact us any longer, Taylor."

"But isn't it important to prove that Mr. Merrill is already married?" he asked, a quizzical look on his face. "Because if he's lying about his wife, he could be lying about all sorts of stuff."

"Oh, I definitely think he's lying about all sorts of stuff, Taylor," Nick said. "But he wasn't lying about one particular thing. While you were at the newspaper office, I got a visit from Gabriella Raas."

Taylor plucked the cigar out of his mouth. "The woman from the Geyser Hotel is in San Francisco, too?"

"She has family here. And Young had promised to help her out," Nick said, rounding the corner. "She doesn't have a job any longer and is dead broke."

"Did she go to Mr. Young's place, but he refused to help her?" he asked. "If she was desperate, she might've been pretty upset."

"She did go there yesterday morning," Nick said. "But she claims he was already dead when she arrived. She also told me she saw the man who killed Young leaving the boardinghouse right as she was coming up the road. Between six and six thirty, by her reckoning."

"Did she recognize him?"

"She said it was Dennis Merrill."

Taylor halted and released a long whistle. "Shoot."

His assistant had been hanging around Cassidy too much.

"Why'd Mr. Merrill come into the station and tell you he saw her if he's guilty of killing Mr. Young?"

"Maybe he was hoping we'd blame her," Nick said. "Not realizing she'd seen *him* outside Young's boardinghouse."

Taylor resumed puffing on his cigar. "Should we believe that the young lady saw Mr. Merrill, though, Mr. Greaves?" he asked, shifting his cigar in his mouth to get the words out. "What if she's just making up a story because *she* killed Mr. Young? And thought Mr. Merrill was somebody worth accusing."

"If Cassandra Weaver refuses to give Merrill an alibi, then he *is* somebody worth accusing."

"Are we still going to question Mr. Weaver, though?"

"Yes, because that message that arrived at his house around sunrise yesterday is still bothering me," he replied. "And we should keep walking."

Nick gestured for them to move. People passing on the road kept glancing at the store they'd stopped in front of, probably wondering if the proprietor was suddenly in trouble with the police. The store owner had taken to glaring at them through the window. Cops hanging around outside his establishment would not help business.

"Maybe Mr. Young had finally gotten around to trying to blackmail Mr. Weaver, too," Taylor asked, falling into step next to Nick. "And that's what that message was about."

"It might've been exactly that, Taylor."

"Who wasn't Mr. Young attempting to blackmail, sir?"

"Good question."

"They can't all have killed him."

"They all might've wanted to, though."

• • •

Celia retrieved the notes she'd composed at the Geyser Hotel, her list of suspects in Mrs. Merrill's death. She closed the door to her clinic behind her, sat at her desk, and unfolded the piece of paper. Mr. Young, Cassandra, Mr. Thompson, Mr. Merrill, Mr. Weaver, Gabriella. All those she'd considered worth suspecting. How did the list now change when considering those who might also have wanted to kill Mr. Young? Apart from the removal of his own name.

She should probably add Unknown Individual to her list. If the man was fond of collecting gossip and making money off it, Mr. Young may have had any number of enemies.

"I cannot question every one of the man's associates, however," she murmured.

She simply had to limit her suspects to her previously composed list. Among them must be his killer. Because why else had Mr. Young made a last-minute trip to the geysers, his stay at the hotel miraculously coinciding with theirs?

The one person she kept returning to repeatedly was Dennis Merrill. A man she already suspected in his stepmother's death. Barbara having smelled his cigarillo smoke when he'd walked past her bathing hut was an important clue. Had he sought to get rid of Mr. Young for the same reason he had murdered Elnora, the need to keep his wife's existence quiet?

"To use Cassandra Weaver as your alibi was boorish, though, Mr. Merrill." Celia refused to give credence to his statement. Cassandra had frequently proclaimed her love for Thaddeus Thompson. She couldn't be such an accomplished liar that she'd fooled everyone with her pretense.

Nicholas had said that he thought it required an emotional reason to strangle someone. Would Mr. Merrill be sufficiently upset about the revelation contained in Mrs. Gannon's letters? Nicholas thought not. He may have been sufficiently upset if Mr. Young had witnessed him push his stepmother into that mineral pool, however. Why return to San Francisco and risk encountering Mr. Merrill again, though?

Unless he'd not originally planned to stay long enough to have that encounter.

She considered Hiram Weaver's name, written below Mr. Merrill's. He'd hurried off in response to yesterday's message, which Cassandra had mistakenly thought was from Thaddeus Thompson but could have been from Mr. Young. A request, perhaps, for a meeting to discuss a bribery allegation that Mr. Young, a fellow member of the Odd Fellows, had learned of.

Celia wondered if Mr. Weaver had produced an alibi yet. And to murder a man because he'd discovered that you'd bribed a city official seemed just as extreme as killing someone for knowing of the existence of a wife. However, in her brief time as a "lady detective," she had encountered blackmail as a motive to kill someone before.

She massaged the ache in her low back. The bruise from where she'd been struck hurt, too.

If that urgent, sunrise message *had* come from Mr. Young, there was another individual in the Weaver household who would have learned that he'd returned to the city.

Celia sat back and tapped the end of her pencil against her chin. "Ah, Cassandra."

What would be her motive? Perhaps to conceal her part in Elnora's death, if she had—accidentally or otherwise—pushed her aunt into that mineral pool. However, Mr. Young had been assumed guilty, leaving her in the clear. Unless he'd returned to San Francisco hoping to blackmail *her* because he'd witnessed Elnora's death and Cassandra's part in it.

Celia truthfully couldn't imagine her strangling Mr. Young, though. That would require a strength Celia didn't see in the young woman's slight frame and elegant hands. Even if Addie had witnessed a neighbor girl back in Scotland kill chickens often enough.

Might someone else have committed the crime for her? To protect her from scrutiny in her aunt's killing? A man who could not imagine life without her. A man who'd vowed to . . .

"What had his words been?" Celia opened the drawer in her desk and retrieved the note she'd found tucked inside a romantic novel.

I love you. I won't let anybody interfere. Ever. I promise.

"Indeed."

She put the note away, her gaze moving to Thaddeus Thompson's name, further up the page. If Cassandra had caused her aunt's death, even accidentally, the ensuing scandal would have ended their relationship. A bigger scandal than the bribery scheme. He couldn't have killed Mr. Young, though. He'd been in Suscol awaiting the morning ferry to San Francisco, according to Nicholas.

"Which makes it appear that I cannot include you in my list of suspects, Mr. Thompson."

And why do I feel so disappointed in that fact? Or so uncertain that his alibi is factual?

The door opened, and Barbara stepped through. "Are you busy?"

"No. Come in." Celia set down her pencil and pushed her notes aside. "I've finished with my appointments for the day and was working on my suspects. Which has to include Gabriella, it appears. Mr. Merrill told me that he spotted her in the city."

She shut the door behind her. "Really?"

"I have my doubts about his information, as well, Barbara," she replied. "Especially when you consider that he has been concealing a very important fact. Namely, that he has a wife, and that Mrs. Gannon is her sister."

Barbara's eyes widened. "A wife!" she exclaimed. "That means he'll never be able to marry Cassandra, even if he did convince her to give up Mr. Thompson."

The "best man" unable to win.

"The existence of a wife did not prevent him from using Cassandra Weaver as an alibi," Celia said. "He dared to suggest they were together while Mr. Young was being murdered."

"The cad."

Indeed. "I was just sitting here contemplating Thaddeus Thompson, Barbara. What is it about him that I find so perplexing? Or rather, what it is about his relationship with Cassandra that I find so perplexing?" she asked. "He's so much older than her. Does a young, beautiful girl like Cassandra Weaver truly love a man like him?"

A fellow Mr. Merrill had referred to as a fraud, and not what he appeared to be. *I've yet to puzzle out what you meant by your comment, Mr. Merrill.*

"Well, he's not unattractive. And their marriage would please Mr. Weaver, not just because of some business advantage he might gain," Barbara said, taking a seat on one of the chairs in the room. "I think that is really important to Cassandra, making her father happy. Especially since her mother died."

"I'd not considered that," she said, glancing at her notes. Perhaps she had misjudged Cassandra Weaver. "And Mr. Thompson, by all accounts, is deeply in love with her. I discovered a note he'd written to Cassandra when I was at the Weavers' house yesterday. A message promising her that he would remove any obstacles to their being together."

"Maybe he pushed Mrs. Merrill to a terrible death."

"I wonder if Elnora had spotted him with Cassandra," Celia said. "In a romantic embrace, shall we say. An embrace that upset Elnora and may have prompted an argument."

"A romantic interlude up by the hot springs? I would've gone down the path that follows the river," Barbara countered. "It was leafy and cool, and far more secluded than rocky outcroppings with only manzanita for cover."

"Several men had gone to the river to fish at sunrise. Cassandra and Mr. Thompson would not have been alone on that path," Celia said. "However, no one was expected to head up to the mineral pools for another hour. Except Elnora Merrill, for some reason, had had other ideas. Cassandra's story about following her aunt and hearing her speaking with someone could have been a lie."

Barbara peered at her. "Does this all make sense, Cousin?"

"Let us examine the pieces of information we have," Celia replied. "Elnora had started onto the geyser trail long before anyone else. Mr. Young was briefly out in the yard. Mr. Weaver exited his sleeping room, spoke with me, and went downstairs to the dining room shortly after you did. Around that same time, Mr. Merrill wandered off toward the ravine. You went to the bathing hut before climbing the hill. We know you smelled Mr. Merrill's cigarillo smoke. Mr. Thompson denies that he'd gone up there that morning, which could be false. I never observed his whereabouts that morning to definitively say what he was doing. We know Cassandra climbed the trail, but not precisely when or why. We know she ended up standing over her aunt's dead body. Mr. Young was observed running away around the time that Cassandra began to scream. Mr. Fletcher claimed to have noticed an individual fleeing through the brush shortly before I arrived on the scene. The timing suggests that person could not have been Mr. Young, however."

"Mr. Merrill?" Barbara questioned.

"No, because he was with me," she said. "More likely Mr. Thompson. Or someone else entirely."

"I can imagine Mr. Thompson arguing with Mrs. Merrill and pushing her, Cousin. She clearly disliked him and was very protective of Cassandra. And he'd vowed to not let anybody stand in their way," Barbara said. "He might not have meant it to be a fatal push. Or even if he had, it's easy to believe that Cassandra might lie to protect him. To protect the man her father had chosen for her."

Perhaps Cassandra Weaver was not the complete innocent Celia had presumed her to be. Had wished her to be.

"Mr. Thompson killed Mr. Young, too. Because of that bribery scheme," her cousin asserted. "Or because Mr. Young had witnessed him pushing Elnora." Barbara scowled for a moment. "How did he know Mr. Young was in the city, though?"

"He did not need to know, Barbara," Celia said. "Because Thaddeus Thompson was purportedly in Suscol at the time Mr. Young died."

She tucked her brows together. "But what if he'd taken the Thursday evening ferry from Petaluma? Maybe he lied to Mr. Weaver about heading to Calistoga. Took the Petaluma ferry, avoiding us on the Thursday evening Suscol ferry, and arrived in San Francisco that night.

Making it possible for him to kill Mr. Young. Presuming he was aware the man was here."

"I suppose I shall simply have to ask him," Celia responded. "And even if he can provide proof that he'd taken the Suscol ferry yesterday morning and couldn't have strangled Mr. Young, Barbara, it does not mean he didn't push Elnora Merrill to her death."

• • •

"Kind of a cramped space you've got here, Mr. Weaver. Stuck in the corner like this." Nick looked around him. The office that had been carved out of the larger room barely accommodated Weaver's mahogany desk and bookcase. Barely accommodated him. A haze of pipe smoke hung in the air, the aroma overwhelmingly sweet. Weaver should open a window, except that then he'd have to smell the outside air, which was not overwhelmingly sweet. "Way smaller than Julius Thompson's."

"Your officer, the one who threatened me, already informed me that Mr. Young was murdered yesterday morning, Detective," Weaver said flatly, not offering Nick one of the leather-upholstered chairs he'd crammed into the office. Nick was content to stand. "And it wasn't necessary to station a policeman outside my office."

"Just wanted to make sure you didn't wander off again, Mr. Weaver, before I had a chance to talk to you," he said. "And it's interesting that Young was found dead not far from your house."

"I was not aware the man was in San Francisco, Detective," he said. "But if I *had* learned that he'd stupidly come here, I would've notified the police to arrest him for murdering my sister-in-law. May she rest in peace."

"She was a good woman. A good companion for your daughter," Nick said, watching him for any sign that he didn't agree.

"She was my wife's sister, and a living reminder of a woman I loved."

Not exactly a resounding confirmation of Nick's statement. Nick had never met Elnora Merrill, but from Celia's brief description of her, she sounded as though she'd been strong-willed and opinionated. A lot of men didn't like those characteristics in females.

"I hear that you and Mr. Young had an argument while you were both staying at the Geyser Hotel," he said. "What was it about?"

Weaver laughed. A thick, heavy sound. "That? The man was a leech."

"He'd found out about that contract with the city, didn't he?" he asked. "The one you didn't want to talk about when I questioned you at the Geyser Hotel. Tried to blackmail you over it."

"Why might Mr. Young attempt to blackmail me over a fairly and cleanly obtained contract, Detective?"

"'Cleanly,' Mr. Weaver? You mean the money you had one of your employees deposit into Mr. Thompson's bank account was not a bribe?" Nick asked. "That's good to hear."

Weaver flushed an astonishing shade of crimson. "That is—"

"A lie? Don't bother to finish your sentence, Mr. Weaver. We know you did," Nick interrupted. "Julius Thompson admitted you gave him money."

"It was *not* a bribe."

Nick waited for him to claim it was merely a business transaction, like Julius Thompson had said, but he never did.

"Nonetheless, Young tried to blackmail you over that innocent money transfer," he said.

"That was *not* what our argument was about, Detective Greaves," he spat. "And I'm not obliged to tell you what it did concern."

"Now you're making me think you're guilty of killing him, Mr. Weaver." Even if he hadn't been the man Gabriella Raas had spotted outside Young's place.

"I repeat that I was not aware he was in San Francisco."

Nick ran the brim of his hat through his fingers. "You know, Mr. Weaver, I think you *were* aware that Mr. Young was in San Francisco," he said. "You received a message at your house early yesterday morning. And I'm told that, not long after it was delivered, you hurried off in response."

"It wasn't from Young."

"Who *was* it from?"

"I am not free to answer that question, Detective."

"You might want to, Mr. Weaver," Nick said. "Especially since we haven't yet identified a firm suspect in the man's murder, and you were suspiciously absent from your house at the time that he was killed."

Weaver's jaw clenched. "Do you have a witness placing me in the vicinity of his boardinghouse, Detective?" he asked. "Or are you trying to get me to confess to a crime I did not commit?"

I wish you would confess, frankly. You or Merrill. Nick wasn't about to be choosy.

"I'm sure my men will be finished questioning Young's neighbors soon and find a witness." Nick eyed him. "In the meantime, Mr. Weaver, tell me who sent you that message and what was in it. I'll get out of your office sooner if you do."

Weaver, maybe looking for the comfort of a smoke, reached for his pipe. It was crafted from dark brown briarwood and not made of cheap clay like the pipes most of Nick's fellow soldiers had used during the war. Weaver's fancier pipe had gone cold, though, and he set it back down.

"This is harassment, Detective," he declared. "Between you and Mrs. Davies, repeatedly showing up at my house to nose around and upsetting Cassandra, I don't know whose behavior is more outrageous. I've had quite enough of this, frankly."

No doubt he had. "Again, how about telling me who sent you that message and what was in it."

He drew in a breath and tugged on his vest to straighten it. "All right. The message *was* from Young."

"Thank you, Mr. Weaver." And now Nick wished he'd brought Taylor along to take notes. "Why didn't you inform the police that Young had contacted you?"

"I was angry and not thinking. The gall of the man to contact me," he huffed. "The man who killed my sister-in-law."

"What did he want?" Nick asked. "Cash in exchange for keeping quiet about that innocent money transfer?"

"No. His message said he had information he thought I might find interesting," he said. "I have no idea what that information was, though. Because when I went to where he'd told me to meet him, he wasn't there."

"Oh, he was definitely at his boardinghouse, Mr. Weaver," Nick said. "Which is where you strangled him with a pair of his suspenders."

"No, Detective, I did not kill him," he stated. "And Young didn't ask to meet at his boardinghouse. He requested that we meet at a coffeehouse a block south of my home."

"I'll need the name of the place, Mr. Weaver."

He exhaled angrily and gave it to Nick, who repeated the name multiple times in his head so he wouldn't forget.

"I waited for a while, and when Young didn't turn up, I left," Weaver continued. "I briefly came here to take care of some paperwork before heading out for the numerous meetings I had scheduled yesterday."

"And that was it?" Nick asked. "You didn't sneak into his boarding-house and kill him?"

"I did not," he said, emphasizing every word. "Although if I *had* ever spotted Mr. Young in San Francisco, I might've killed him myself. If someone else hadn't beaten me to it."

⌘ CHAPTER 19 ⌘

"Heard you got engaged, Taylor," Briggs said on his way out of the detectives' office, patting Nick's assistant on the shoulder as he passed him. "Congratulations."

How had he heard about Taylor's engagement to Miss Ferguson? Was Briggs friends with Taylor? Didn't seem possible. Nick thought everybody in the station disliked Briggs as much as he did.

"Thank you, Mr. Briggs," Taylor called after him, smiling. He stopped smiling when he noticed the look on Nick's face. "I told some of the fellows, Mr. Greaves. Guess they told Mr. Briggs."

"Guess they did," Nick said. "What have you learned?"

"Confirmed that Mr. Weaver was at that coffeehouse, sir," Taylor said. "He was there as soon as the place opened, which was why the fellow at the place remembered him so well."

"Did you ask him if a man matching Young's description ever showed up?"

"I did, Mr. Greaves. And the owner says no."

Because Young was dead.

"What about a statement from Cassandra Weaver?" Nick asked.

"I spoke with her, Mr. Greaves. She absolutely denies being with Mr. Merrill yesterday morning," he replied. "Looks like I need to bring him in, doesn't it?"

"Yes, Taylor. It does. Bring him in and book him for murder." Nick rubbed the ache in his arm. "Once you've done that, head home. It's a Saturday, it's late, and we're finished here."

• • •

The next morning, once Celia had returned from Sunday services and had quickly perused the city directory, she went to Thaddeus Thompson's residence. He had questions to answer.

His house was situated not far from where her friend Jane Hutchinson lived. A splendid neighborhood that Cassandra should feel comfortable living in. Once she was wed to a man Elnora Merrill had never liked. A husband who would please her father.

The female servant who answered Celia's knock had on a walking dress and appeared annoyed that her leisure plans for the day were being disrupted.

"Is Mr. Thompson in?" Celia asked.

"No," she said, securing the straw bonnet she'd been carrying over her hair.

"Where might I find him?" she asked. "It is most urgent that I speak with him on a delicate matter concerning his fiancée. Miss Weaver."

The servant's hands, which had been occupied with tying her bonnet ribbons, stilled. "Mr. Thompson got engaged?" she asked, her eyes goggling. "Never thought I'd hear that!"

"I believe the announcement is imminent," Celia said, even though it likely was not. "Miss Weaver is a dear friend of my ward's, and I am quite worried about her. I am seeking his counsel on how to proceed. Especially now that her companion, Mrs. Merrill, has passed away and I can no longer turn to her for advice."

She gaped at Celia, still attempting to absorb the news about an engagement.

"Can you help me?" Celia asked.

"Oh. Yes." The servant gave Celia the name of a nearby restaurant where she'd find Mr. Thompson. Fortunately for Celia, he'd not retired to some men's club where she would be refused admittance.

"Another question, and then I shall let you get on with your plans for the day," Celia said. "Can you tell me when Mr. Thompson returned from his trip to the geysers?"

"Umm, Friday sometime, I think."

"Ah. Thank you." Perhaps his story about being in Suscol was true, and she could not consider him a suspect in Mr. Young's murder. Or he'd simply not returned to his house until later, hoping to conceal his movements.

She departed and easily located the restaurant. One of the few establishments permitted to operate on a Sunday, it had a striking exterior, its large windows overhung by eye-catching striped awnings that shaded the dining room furnishings from California sunlight. She'd never been inside this particular restaurant, but it was a comfortable enough space with a tasteful display of cut-glass lamps, clean white tablecloths, and tidily aproned waiters. Quite comfortable, truth be told.

Several of the diners noticed her arrival and frowned as she crossed the room. Unaccompanied females strolling through a restaurant, even if it advertised itself as being a "Ladies' and Gents'" establishment, were always suspect.

"Ah, Mr. Thompson, I do hope I am not disturbing your breakfast," Celia said, gliding over to the table he occupied.

He looked up from his contemplation of the menu, a flash of irritation dancing across his face. But only momentarily. "How did you find me, Mrs. Davies?"

"Were you not intending to be found, Mr. Thompson?" she asked. "If so, you should have chosen a more private location than a public restaurant."

"I'm expecting company, Mrs. Davies," he said. "My apologies, but whatever you have to say needs to be brief."

She pulled out the chair opposite his—for him to offer the courtesy would imply that she was welcome to join him—and sat, rather than hover like a bee waiting to land.

"I shall attempt to be brief, then, Mr. Thompson." *Although I am most curious who your company will turn out to be.* "I have been looking into the death of your fiancée's aunt—"

"Miss Weaver and I are not yet engaged, Mrs. Davies," he stated. "Furthermore, the man responsible for Mrs. Merrill's death has been found murdered. As is only fair for a person like him." He tapped the newspaper folded alongside his plate. "There's nothing left to look into. So, if you don't mind . . ."

"I have been mulling over a comment one of the guests at the Geyser Hotel made to me, Mr. Thompson," she continued as if she'd not heard him. She'd rehearsed her bluff on the walk to the restaurant, and she needed to proceed quickly before she botched what she'd planned to say. "This individual—whom I will not name since they made their remark in confidence—told me they'd noticed you on the hillside path leading to the mineral springs before Cassandra found her aunt's body. Isn't that astonishing? But then you are very tall and easy to observe. I initially dismissed this person's statement, but I cannot seem to forget it."

She paused, waiting for a rejoinder, which he did not offer. Instead, he reached into his coat pocket and pulled out a cigarillo. A waiter darted over to light it.

"I did not realize you smoked cigarillos, Mr. Thompson," she said.

"I don't usually," he said between puffs. "But Mr. Merrill lent me some of his and they're good."

Ah, Barbara. It may have been Mr. Merrill's cigarillo you'd smelled. However, he may not have been the one smoking it.

"You climbed the hillside to rendezvous with Miss Weaver, did you not, Mr. Thompson?" she asked with growing certainty. "Some precious time together with your beloved. It must have been startling to encounter Mrs. Merrill, already enjoying the geysers and mineral pools ahead of the scheduled tour."

He stared at her in silence. His brown eyes were much like Nicholas's, although nowhere near as warm. Had Cassandra found Mr. Thompson's to be warm and captivating, or had her affection for Thaddeus Thompson bloomed solely out of a desire to please her father? And were the demands of filial duty enough to cause Cassandra to lie for the man seated opposite Celia?

"Well, Mr. Thompson?" Celia asked when so much time had elapsed that one of the restaurant's waiters strolled by their table, perhaps to assess if they were still breathing or had frozen in place.

"You appear to already know, so, yes," he said. "I did go to meet Cassandra. I didn't want to previously admit that out of respect for her good name."

An admission that placed Cassandra on the hillside for a reason other than the one she'd provided to Celia.

"I presume Mrs. Merrill happened upon you two together," Celia said. "I can picture the terrible argument that must have ensued."

"Actually, I didn't come across Mrs. Merrill," he replied, his gaze flicking in the direction of the restaurant's front entrance, which he'd been stealing glances at for the past few minutes. Worried about the imminent arrival of his dining companion, she surmised, an individual he seemed reluctant to allow Celia to encounter. "I must have missed her somehow."

"You mean you did not pass her on your way back down the hill?" she asked. "She had to have been climbing the trail at that time." Perhaps he'd run off to seek cover in the scant undergrowth around the mineral pools and was indeed the person Mr. Fletcher had noticed on the hillside.

"I truly don't understand why you're asking me questions, Mrs. Davies. The coroner's jury reviewed the available evidence, and it became obvious that Mr. Young was the person to suspect in her death," he said. "Not me, which is what I believe your intrusive questions are implying."

They were. "Has Miss Weaver told you about a note she received Friday morning, the morning of Mr. Young's death? Very early in the day."

"I haven't been to see her since I returned from Calistoga," he replied. "Her family is in mourning, and I am honoring their grief by keeping my distance."

"Then the note did not come from you."

"How could I have sent her a note the morning of Mr. Young's death, Mrs. Davies?" he asked. "I was in Suscol at that time. Waiting for the ferry home."

"Oh? I must be mistaken, then, about what your maid told me," she said, casting her proverbial dice and hoping it landed in her favor. "That you'd returned home on Thursday evening. The night before his murder."

He scowled. "She couldn't have said that to you, Mrs. Davies, because I didn't return home on Thursday."

"I see. My error."

He sharply exhaled a stream of smoke. "Listen, I know you believe you're helping the police, but my father and I have spoken to the authorities," he said. "Furthermore, my lunch companion should be here any minute. So, if you would."

He signaled for one of the waiters, who hurried over. She was to be shown out, with force, if necessary; the man was rather robust and strong-shouldered.

She stood and strolled through the restaurant ahead of the waiter, who herded her like a dog managing a wayward sheep. A snicker, issued by one of the customers observing her passage, added to her humiliation.

Outside, Celia waited for the traffic to clear and crossed the street. The waiter watched her from the doorway to ensure that she was not going to return. Once he was satisfied, he went back to his work. Celia retraced her steps until she reached a spot on the pavement where she could see the interior of the restaurant, and Mr. Thompson's table, but not be readily visible to those inside.

A few moments of waiting were rewarded when a woman strode up the road and turned into the restaurant. A woman Celia recognized.

"Well, well, Gabriella," she murmured. "Welcome to San Francisco."

Gabriella headed straight for Mr. Thompson and sat at his table. After some urgent whispers were exchanged, she handed him a small envelope, which he hastily concealed inside his coat.

"Ma'am?"

The voice at her side startled her. It belonged to a police officer.

Gad. "Ah, Officer," she said, smiling. Knowing what was coming next. "I was—"

"You are loitering, ma'am, and need to move along." He was *not* smiling. "Now."

"Certainly," she said, casting one final look at the occupants inside the restaurant. "You need not arrest me, Officer. I intend to go to the police station all on my own."

• • •

Knuckles tapped on the office doorframe, and Taylor leaned through the opening. "Busy, sir?"

"Didn't expect to see you in the station on a Sunday, Taylor," Nick said.

"Just wanted to let you know that Mr. Merrill has taken up residence in one of our cells, sir," Taylor said. "Brought him in last night after you'd gone home."

"What did he say when you arrested him?"

"Only that he wanted the most comfortable cell we had."

"Don't think we've got one of those," Nick replied. "Thanks for letting me know. Go enjoy the rest of your day."

He beamed. "I will. I'm going walking with Miss Ferguson."

A stroll with a woman you loved sounded so good to Nick that he nearly rethought his intention to talk to Merrill. But he didn't.

"Give her my regards, Taylor."

"I'll do that, Mr. Greaves," he said and hurried off.

Nick strode out into the station, waited for the booking sergeant to unlock the heavy jail door, and went inside. They were surprisingly light on prisoners for a Sunday, when they usually had Saturday night revelers in the lockup. The vacancies meant Mr. Merrill could enjoy more peace and quiet than was typical. The smell, though . . . that never improved.

"Mr. Merrill," Nick said to him.

He'd been resting on the cell's cot—Nick should suggest he limit doing that if he preferred to not get infested with bugs—and sat up. "Ah, Detective. To what do I owe the pleasure of your visit this fair morning?"

"The matter of your alibi. I'm sure Mr. Taylor informed you that Miss Weaver denies being with you when Young was killed, Mr. Merrill," he said. "Which means you don't have one any longer."

"I didn't kill Young," he said. "And you don't have any evidence that I did, Detective."

"Maybe I do, Mr. Merrill. You were spotted outside Young's boardinghouse about an hour before his body was found."

He shot to his feet. "Who told you that?" He narrowed his gaze. "Wait. Did Gabriella tell you that?"

"She is our witness."

He snorted a laugh. "You've got the story backward if you're believing her over me," he said. "I didn't realize that she'd noticed me, though."

"You're admitting that you were there. That you killed him."

"All I'm saying is that she did see me, but not outside Young's place," he said. "At least I don't think I was anywhere near it. Did he live near the Weavers?"

"Yes."

"Damn." Merrill dropped back onto the cot, the impact releasing a puff of dust from the straw mattress. "What rotten luck to be on that road right then."

"You *had* gone out," Nick said. "Which is why you asked your housekeeper to arrive later than usual."

He stared up at Nick. "I can't be the only person in all of San Francisco you think had a reason to kill Parker Young, Detective."

"Maybe not the only person who had a reason, Mr. Merrill, but you are the only person whose alibi isn't holding together."

"How would I have possibly learned he was in San Francisco soon enough to have alerted my chore-girl to alter her plans for the morning?"

"Gabriella knew Young was returning to San Francisco," Nick said. "Maybe he'd told you, too."

He sighed. "I simply just wanted another hour of sleep before the cacophony of buckets banging against the floors and rug beaters slapping got underway."

"You weren't enjoying a rendezvous with Miss Weaver."

"My additional hour of sleep was interrupted when she rang the bell, Detective. Turning up unexpectedly, as I've already told you, and not for any romantic reasons. Sadly, I might add," he said. "You probably won't believe me, but I do care for her."

"Even though you're already married."

He didn't keep denying that he had a wife, and instead gave a wry laugh. "It does happen, you know. Falling in love when you shouldn't."

Nick did know very well how you could fall in love when you shouldn't. Celia had saved him, though, from repeating that mistake.

"Did you kill Young to get those letters from Mrs. Gannon back? Or was the reason because he'd seen you push Elnora?" he asked Merrill. "Maybe you hadn't planned to. It just happened."

"I think I just explained that I was with Cassandra Weaver, Detective Greaves. Which is why Gabriella saw me on the road," he said. "I'd escorted Miss Weaver back home. At least part of the way."

"Such a gentleman."

Merrill cocked an eyebrow. "I'm rather astonished you haven't asked my next-door neighbor if she noticed Miss Weaver at my house, Detective. She seems to notice everything."

"I might do that, Mr. Merrill."

"Tell her Miss Weaver is a small, blond-haired young woman who was wearing a . . . green dress on Friday, I think," he said. "Furthermore, Detective, I wouldn't bother to kill Young for those letters because I'm pretty sure he hadn't gotten ahold of them."

"What makes you think that?"

"Well, Detective, the lovely little blackmail note he tried to pass to me at the hotel didn't mention them," he said. "He *had* found out about my wife, it's true, but I'm not sure how. Oh, wait. I remember. I believe I drank a bit too much in Healdsburg. Mr. Young was in the saloon at the same time. I must have blabbed about her. Hell, Denny, that was stupid."

Nick rubbed the ache in his arm. He was starting to believe Dennis Merrill, and he didn't particularly like it. Right about now, he'd usually be hearing the remembered voice of his Uncle Asa offering advice on how to be a good cop, a good detective. But Asa had turned out to be the worst sort of cop, and his voice didn't make an appearance.

"Her name's Thea. My wife, that is," Merrill continued. "She is kind, Detective. Caring. Rather pretty, in her own way."

"She sounds like a fine woman." *And you're a cad.*

"She is. She deserves better than me," he said, sounding remorseful.

"Did you kill your stepmother because an argument about Thea got too heated, Mr. Merrill?" Nick asked. "Maybe you'd had enough of her."

"I won't deny that we argued occasionally. Our latest argument *was* about Thea," he said. "But I didn't dislike her enough to kill her, Detective. Not Elnora. Not Young."

"You'd inherit the money your father had left her, wouldn't you?"

"Cassandra gets that money as Elnora's closest blood kin."

"Which gives you a good reason to want to marry Miss Weaver, what with your business failing and all."

"Which gives me a good reason to try to kill Thaddeus Thompson, Detective. Which I didn't do, by the way." He shook his head, his shoulders slumping. "Why am I bothering to talk, though, when you seem to have all the answers? The wrong answers, I might add."

Was he wrong? About everything? He could really use some words of wisdom right then.

"Did you pay off Young's demands?" Nick asked.

"I didn't have the money," he answered. "Of course I didn't want Cassandra to learn that I already have a wife, that I'd misled her. But I wouldn't kill Young to keep my secret from her. What would be the point? She's set on marrying Thaddeus Thompson." He couldn't conceal his contempt for the man.

"You don't like the fellow. Why?"

"He's not what he pretends to be," he replied. "Let's leave it at that, Detective."

Interesting. "We have evidence that Mr. Weaver bribed Julius Thompson in exchange for favoring his business for a city contract," Nick said. "Thaddeus Thompson may be complicit."

"Well, I'll be. I hadn't heard about that." Merrill scoffed. "He's even worse than I thought he was."

Nick considered him through the iron grating that stood between them. "If you care for Miss Weaver so much—and if I believe she *was* with you, despite what she says—why drag her name into this mess?

Why not come up with a better alibi?" he asked. "Because if you use her as your defense, Merrill, it'll be reported in every newspaper in this city. Her reputation will be destroyed."

"Better to destroy her reputation than . . ." Merrill stopped himself before he went any further.

"Than what?"

"I'm not going to answer that."

Nick peered at him. "Maybe I should finish your sentence for you, Mr. Merrill. Better to destroy her reputation than see her accused of murdering Parker Young," Nick said. "Is that it?"

"I'm not going to respond to that, either."

"Mr. Young was strangled, Merrill. Is she seriously strong enough to murder a man that way?" Nick asked. "And why would she have a reason to kill Young? He wasn't trying to blackmail *her*. Also, you two were together the entire time. Right?"

Merrill closed his eyes and dropped his chin to his chest. Valiantly protecting a woman he loved. *Protecting . . .*

"You think Miss Weaver had a motive to kill Young because you also think she caused your stepmother's death," Nick said. "Did you see her do it? Maybe they'd been arguing and she pushed Elnora into a mineral pool. And if you saw it happen, Young might've seen it, too."

Merrill looked over at him with blank, sad eyes.

Nick might not be able to picture Miss Weaver strangling Young. Even if the man had been drunk and only had the use of one good arm. But Merrill must. Must believe she had the composure and the strength to commit the crime. Or had the fierce passion and the strength. He must believe that, or else he wouldn't be so damned tight-lipped.

Nick leaned into the iron grating. "You'd rather rot in jail, possibly hang for killing a man, rather than risk having her accused of killing Young."

"I'll take my chances with the justice system, Detective," he said.

Nick pushed away from the cell door. "Good luck, Merrill. Because I think you're going to need it."

CHAPTER 20

"She's young and blond, and was wearing a green dress, I'm told," Nick said to Dennis Merrill's neighbor. The woman who purportedly noticed everything. "Did you see her? Very early on Friday."

Her eyes, almost as pale as Celia's, shone with a bright spark of intelligence. She was whip-smart, he could tell. And possibly used to people dismissing her because of her age.

"You believe I might have observed her because Mr. Merrill thinks I am an annoying busybody, Detective," she said.

"The police don't find busybodies to be annoying, ma'am."

She smiled, her eyes twinkling. "I do remember her, Detective. She's been to visit Mr. Merrill before. Usually in the company of Mrs. Merrill. Elnora used to live next door with Mr. Merrill and his father before he passed away. It had been the senior Mr. Merrill's house, you see. Very sad, his passing," she said. "Anyway, on Friday, I'd taken Pop out for a walk and a bit of a sniff around. He likes his morning strolls about an hour after sunrise, you see. It was then that I saw her on Mr. Merrill's stoop. Talking urgently with him. He let her in—scandalous— and she must have been inside his house for at least an hour."

Did her information mean that Cassandra Weaver couldn't have killed Young before turning up at Merrill's place? The timing would have been tight.

"Did you see her leave?" he asked.

"I did. Mr. Merrill escorted her out and up the street. He came back not too long after," she said. In the depths of the house, a small dog yapped for attention. "I'll be with you soon, Pop. Anyway, Mr. Merrill noticed me looking through my window and waved rather jauntily. He's a rascal, that one."

A rascal? Maybe she'd change her opinion of Dennis Merrill if Nick told her about the wife he'd abandoned. Unless she was so charmed by him that she wouldn't care. Celia had certainly found Merrill charming, he thought with a surge of jealousy.

"And what time was this, do you think?" he asked, happy to take his mind off Celia being charmed by other men. "When you saw him return to his house."

"Seven fifteen? Thereabouts."

"Might I look at your city directory, ma'am?" he asked. "I need the address for a young woman I have to speak to. Given what you've told me."

He didn't have with him the information Gabriella had provided on where she was staying. But he'd remember her relatives' address if he saw it again.

"Step inside, Detective, and I'll fetch it for you."

He removed his hat and waited inside the woman's comfortable entry hall. If Nick pressed Gabriella, would she admit that she'd stretched the truth about where she'd spotted Merrill? She might. Unless *she* was a killer and had no interest in being honest.

• • •

"Mr. Greaves is not here?" Celia asked the booking sergeant, who, since it was a Sunday, was not the usual officer.

"I'm going to tell you what I told that Irish kid," he replied. "Mr. Greaves left a few minutes ago. After he finished speaking with one of our prisoners."

"Owen Cassidy was here?" She shouldn't be surprised; Owen was often at the station.

"Is that his name?" he asked. "I found Mr. Cassidy poking around in Taylor's desk and tossed him out."

Hopefully figuratively and not literally. "Might I ask the name of the prisoner Mr. Greaves was questioning, Sergeant?"

He frowned. "That is police business, ma'am."

"Mr. Greaves will not mind you telling me," she said. "I am Mrs. Davies."

"Are you, then," he said, cocking an eyebrow. "Mr. Merrill is our prisoner, Mrs. Davies."

"Ah." *Oh, dear, Mr. Merrill. You have been accused.* Of a murder she was no longer certain he'd committed. However, if she wished to learn more about Gabriella, he might be the perfect person to ask. "I would like to speak with Mr. Merrill. As a friend. A Christian visit on a Sunday."

The officer sighed so loudly that anyone else might think he'd suffered an acute attack of angina.

"This way."

He unlocked the heavy door. At the far end of the aisle, the warden had fallen asleep on his stool. The sergeant indicated a cell a few feet down.

Celia drew in a breath through her mouth, to avoid choking on the stink, and walked up to it. "Mr. Merrill."

Stretched out on the ratty cot, he propped open an eyelid. "Ah, Mrs. Davies. I thought it sounded like you." He sat up. He was wrinkled and tired-looking. "To what do I owe the pleasure?"

"Tell me about Gabriella, Mr. Merrill," she said. "I have observed her in the city, by the way."

"See, Mrs. Davies? I am as honest as the day is long," he said and winked. "Unfortunately, the good detective is prone to believing her story over mine. She informed him that she spotted me at Young's place on Friday morning, which is why I'm a resident here. A lie."

Intriguing. "Why might she have given a small envelope to Thaddeus Thompson, Mr. Merrill?"

"Beats me altogether, Mrs. Davies," he said. However, the expression on his face shifted, as though he'd comprehended why. Unfortunately, he did not share his comprehension with her.

"All I can conclude is that it held the item he'd attempted to blackmail Mr. Thompson over," she said, recalling the contents of a note hidden in Thaddeus Thompson's room. "Something that he was desperate to retrieve."

"Sounds reasonable."

"How Gabriella obtained it from Mr. Young is unclear, although one can imagine the scenario," Celia continued. A rendezvous in a hotel room. A theft from a boardinghouse. "I have also been wondering if Mr. Young purloined Mrs. Gannon's letters. Although you are, obviously, a more likely candidate."

"Well, I can assure you that neither I nor Mr. Young got ahold of the letters, Mrs. Davies," he replied. "Because Cassandra burned them."

"She what?" Had Celia heard him correctly?

"Burned them," he said. "She told me she intended to get rid of them as soon as she returned from our trip to the geysers. Which she did."

Gad. There hadn't been any ashes in the grate in Elnora's room. But there *had* been in the parlor fireplace.

He was keenly observing her and had noticed her astonishment. "I suppose I should've told Detective Greaves that, Mrs. Davies, but he was annoying me," he said and grinned.

"Cassandra knew about your wife, and wanted to help you remove the evidence of her existence."

"She did. Foolish girl."

Foolish? Celia contemplated the man seated on the cot. Even though Dennis Merrill was rumpled and dirty, he remained handsome, confident, and defiantly charming. Far more handsome and charming than Thaddeus Thompson, the man Hiram Weaver had chosen for his daughter. A man she may have attempted to love, despite not actually wanting to.

"What *was* in that envelope?" she wondered aloud.

"I have no idea, Mrs. Davies. You'd have to ask Gabriella," Mr. Merrill replied. "Or Mr. Thompson."

"He'll not ever want to speak with me again."

"Come now, Mrs. Davies, have you upset him?"

"I may have done, Mr. Merrill. And I do not regret it," she replied, a response that made him chuckle.

"I rather like you, Mrs. Davies," he said.

Her cheeks heated. An entirely inappropriate response.

The warden's snoring grew loud enough to startle himself awake, and he glared when he spotted Celia standing outside Mr. Merrill's cell. "What're you doing there?"

"I am visiting Mr. Merrill," she replied. "Christian charity on a Sunday."

"Hmph," he grumbled and resumed dozing.

"Do you think it's possible that Thaddeus Thompson killed Elnora, Mr. Merrill?" she asked more quietly. "He lied to me about being near the geysers that morning, but I feel positive that he was there."

He leaned toward her. "How can you be sure?"

"I have a very reliable witness."

He laughed. Not the reaction she'd expected, and one that threatened to rouse the warden again.

"Oh, thank God," he said. "Pardon my language, Mrs. Davies, but thank God, because I thought Cassandra was responsible."

"So had I, at one point, Mr. Merrill. Along with you, because this witness smelled the distinctive aroma of your cigarillo smoke," she said. "But you'd given Mr. Thompson a few, even though you'd argued with him."

"A peace offering," he explained. "However, if your suspicion that Mr. Thompson might've killed my aunt is correct, I wouldn't advise confronting him. Let your good friend Detective Greaves do that."

Approaching Thaddeus Thompson would probably be pointless. He'd already had her tossed from a restaurant for trying to question him.

"Do you know where I might be able to find Gabriella?" she asked.

"I don't. Believe it or not, we haven't kept in touch," he said. "Which is why I was surprised to see her in the city."

"Come now, Mr. Merrill, you have to admit you were flirting outrageously with her at the hotel."

He smiled. "That I was. But you probably shouldn't confront her, either, Mrs. Davies," he said. "Because if she'd stolen an incriminating item from Young, she might've killed him to do so."

She perked her chin. "Thank you for your advice."

He cocked his head to one side and considered her. "Has Mr. Greaves ever told you that you're reckless?"

"All the time, Mr. Merrill," she replied. "All the time."

• • •

"I am not lying, Detective," Gabriella said, folding her arms. A dirty window above the front door of her relatives' house barely lit the hallway she stood in. It did, however, provide enough light to see the worried pinch of skin between her eyes. "I saw Mr. Merrill near Mr. Young's boardinghouse. Friday morning."

"All right, Miss Raas," Nick said. "You did see him, but not exactly where you told me you had. A good two or three blocks away from Young's place is more like it. Also, you spotted him *after* you'd been to Young's room. Didn't you?"

A baby crying in a back room of the four-room house she was staying in distracted her. "You should leave. My nephew needs to sleep."

"Why lie to me?" he asked. "The only reason I can figure is that you're trying to protect yourself. Because *you* killed Young."

"Shh!" she said, pushing him backward. "My sister does not need to hear this."

"Have you explained to her why you're in San Francisco?" he asked.

"Or did you claim you just wanted to come and visit family? Did you even explain why you're not working at the Geyser Hotel anymore, or have you told her you'll be going back there soon, and for her to not worry?"

"Please leave."

"Did you kill Young because he refused to give you the money you thought he owed you?" he asked. "We didn't find any cash in his room. Just a nickel he'd dropped on the floor. Because you'd cleaned his place out, didn't you?"

"I told you he was dead when I got there," she said. "I ran. I didn't take anything."

"What if I tell you that I don't believe you any longer?"

She reached for the front door and threw it open, a shaft of light breaking across the hallway. Illuminating a leather bag tucked underneath a stool shoved against the wall.

"Get out!" she yelled.

"Gabriella?" her sister called. The baby wailed.

"I'm okay. He is leaving," she called back.

Nick pushed into the house and grabbed the saddlebag. "Care to explain why you have Mr. Young's saddlebag?" he asked. "His initials are stamped right here. *PY.*"

"No!" she cried, before turning and sprinting for the back of the house.

"Damn it!" he shouted and chased after her.

• • •

Shoot, thought Owen. Should he continue looking into this Miss Gabriella Raas, or should he go back to his boardinghouse and get lunch? His stomach rumbled right then, trying to answer the question for him. He'd gone to Mrs. Davies's house, hoping for some of Addie's cooking, but both she and Miss Barbara were getting ready to head out with Mr. Taylor and she didn't have time to feed him.

Maybe Miss Raas wasn't a suspect. Just a witness. But Miss Barbara thought it was significant that she'd been spotted in San Francisco, and Mr. Taylor had written her name and address down on a piece of paper. So she had to be a suspect in Mr. Young's death. Didn't she?

Maybe she came to town to kill Mr. Young. Miss Barbara had said something about him causing Miss Raas to get fired. Heck, Owen had been fired a bunch of times and never thought to kill somebody because of it. Especially when one of those times it had sorta been Mrs. Davies's fault.

Miss Raas's address wasn't far from Owen's boardinghouse, though, and a side trip to see who she was and what she might have to say for herself didn't seem like much of a bother.

He was turning the corner when he spotted a fellow running full chisel down the street, chasing after a woman. The fellow looked an awful lot like Mr. Greaves. *Shoot.* It *was* Mr. Greaves.

"Hey!" Owen shouted and started running, too. A boy in too-short pants watched him pass, barely getting out of his way in time. "Hey, Mr. Greaves!"

Mr. Greaves skidded to a halt. "Cassidy, what the he . . . what are you doing here?"

"Helping you."

"Dear God. Well, at least you're not Celia," he muttered. "Go that way. Quickly, before Gabriella gets away."

He pointed to a gap between the fence at the rear of a house and a store at an angle to it. He sprinted off, leaving Owen to run down the passage made by the buildings on either side.

What'll I do if I find her first? What'll I do?

Just then, Gabriella burst into the passage through a chink between two buildings. She spotted Owen and ran for a fence at the end of the corridor. Leaping, she grabbed the top and was halfway over when her skirt snagged on a sliver of wood broken off from one of the pickets.

"Hey, stop!" Owen shouted. "Stop!"

She hopped back down and struggled to free her skirt. It tore just as he reached her.

"Stop!" he demanded, grabbing the young woman around the waist and tackling her to the ground.

"Get off me!" she shouted, reaching back to hit him. He didn't like having to tackle a lady, but it might not count as being improper if she was stronger and bigger than Owen. Heck, maybe he *was* just a skinny kid, because it was taking all he had to keep her pinned to the ground.

"Stop struggling!"

She was thrashing around like a short-tailed bull in fly-time. That was a saying one of the fellows at his boardinghouse liked. Owen never used to understand it, until now. Although maybe he still didn't exactly understand it, having minimal experience of bulls.

"C'mon, please stop struggling," he said, resorting to begging.

"Get off me!"

She was inches from breaking free when Mr. Greaves dropped to the ground alongside them.

"Thank you, Cassidy," he said, seizing one of Gabriella's arms. "I think I've got her."

Panting, Owen collapsed backward onto the gravel, careless of what he might be lying in. Although it felt like . . . *shoot*. Dung. He bolted upright again.

"Gabriella Raas, I am arresting you for the murder of Mr. Young," Mr. Greaves was saying, pulling a pair of handcuffs from inside his coat and fixing them around her wrists.

"I did not kill him," she insisted, glancing over at Owen as if looking for sympathy. Or wondering what a kid was doing helping a cop.

"I'm arresting you anyway," Mr. Greaves said, hauling her to her feet. "For thievery, if nothing else."

• • •

A trip to Nicholas's accommodations had resulted in Celia learning from Mrs. Jewett that he was not at home. But Celia was welcome to come inside for some tea, if she'd like, which represented how greatly Mrs. Jewett's opinion of Celia had improved.

Back at her own house, she found the front door secured. Addie must have already left on her walk with Mr. Taylor. She fished around in her reticule for the key and unlocked the door.

"Barbara?" Celia removed her bonnet and hung it on its hook. "Barbara, I'm back."

There was no response. The house was heavy with silence, aside from the gentle ticking of various clocks.

She sat on the bench in the entry hall and stripped off her half-boots. Her cousin's parasol was not propped against the entry hall table, where she tended to leave it, and her bonnet was missing too. However, there was a folded piece of paper on the table. It was from Barbara, announcing that she'd gone with Addie and Mr. Taylor on their stroll around Washington Square and telling Celia to enjoy the peace and quiet. An addendum in Addie's hand indicated that she'd left the kettle on the hob for Celia and they'd be back soon.

"Well," she said, returning the note to the table.

She retrieved some hot water for tea—noticing that Barbara had forgotten her parasol and left it behind on Addie's worktable in the kitchen—and strolled into her clinic. She supposed she could update her patient notes, which she'd neglected, while she waited for Nicholas. She'd left a message for him at the station, requesting that he come to see her, and another with Mrs. Jewett. Eventually, he would turn up.

She sat at her desk and scanned the notes she'd already made on the files she'd left out, reading and rereading the same passages multiple times over. Not absorbing a single word. A neighbor's dog took to barking. The clock in the hall chimed the hour. A horse and its rider slowly clopped up the road.

"Gad." She pushed the files to one side. "I'll go mad waiting for him."

She needed to confront Gabriella, even if Mr. Merrill thought it unwise. Even if she'd been warned in a telegram to mind her own business. Only two people could explain about the envelope she'd handed to Mr. Thompson so surreptitiously. One would never remotely consent to speak with her again. But the other . . .

"I have no clue where she is staying."

Blast. She'd simply have to wait for Nicholas. Patience, however, was not her strong suit. She could search through the city directory, but what would that gain her? Gabriella was not a regular resident of San Francisco. She returned to her notes and made no more progress than before.

She stood and grabbed her gone-cold cup of tea. Tea was the solution to all of life's ills as well as to her inability to concentrate. She crossed the examining room and pushed open the door that connected her clinic to the kitchen.

And walked straight into the barrel of an upraised gun.

⚥ CHAPTER 21 ⚥

Owen strode along Vallejo with his shoulders back and his head high. Mrs. Davies was gonna be amazed when he told her about helping Mr. Greaves arrest Gabriella Raas. What a story it was. That he'd run fast as a jackrabbit in order to grab her and tackle her to the ground. True, he *had* landed in a pile of dung in the passageway, but he thought he'd gotten most of it off his coat. He sure hoped so, because he wouldn't be allowed inside the house if he hadn't. And since he'd missed lunch at his boardinghouse, he was hoping there was food in the kitchen. Although Addie might not be back from her walk with Mr. Taylor yet. She would've left something for Mrs. Davies to eat, though, wouldn't she? And if there was food for Mrs. Davies, there would be food for him. The thought made him smile, and his stomach grumble. Again.

He was only a few doors away from her house when he noticed a young woman in a nice blue dress hurrying up the street. The blond curls peeking out from beneath her bonnet bounced as she rushed along. From the back, she looked an awful lot like Cassandra Weaver. But he'd only seen her a couple of times, so he couldn't be sure. Was she heading for Mrs. Davies's house, too? But Miss Barbara might not be at home, either.

Well, heck, he thought, picking up his pace to catch up to her.

"Miss Weaver!" he called, hoping she'd hear him and stop.

But she didn't stop. In fact, it looked like she picked up speed.

Shoot. This was not good. Not good at all, he thought. And started running.

• • •

"I did *not* kill Mr. Young," Gabriella said. Nick had located the nearest beat cop, who'd commandeered a buckboard and bundled her onto the bed. "I did not," she insisted, for maybe the sixth or seventh time. Or had it been more? Nick had lost track.

The cop, driving the wagon to the station, must have thought she was overdoing it too, because Nick caught him rolling his eyes.

Nick turned on the seat to look at her.

"You had his saddlebag." At least the question of where it had disappeared to was answered. "Is that why you were seen coming out

211

of his room at the Geyser Hotel that morning? Because you were trying to steal it then?"

She reluctantly nodded. "Yes, but I heard someone coming and I was not able to."

"You succeeded in San Francisco, though. Stole it from Young then killed him."

"I did take the saddlebag, but he was already dead," she insisted. "I told you. Ask the woman across the street. She must have seen his killer."

"Don't know why you're bothering to talk to her, Detective," the officer said, turning the wagon onto Kearny. "She's admitted she's a thief. Not trustworthy."

She dropped her chin to her chest. "I was wrong to steal. I know."

"What was inside the saddlebag that you wanted so badly, Gabriella?" Nick asked. "Don't think you took it for the clothes and hair pomade he'd packed in there." The saddlebag sat at Nick's feet. He'd examined the contents when they'd started for the station.

She stared at her lap as if the rip in her skirt was the most interesting thing in the world and refused to answer.

"Was he carrying a lot of money with him, and that's what you were after?" Nick asked.

"She just steals things, Detective, that's all. And kills folks," the beat cop said, offering his opinion.

Which Nick didn't need.

"What was in the saddlebag, Gabriella?" he asked again. "If somebody paid you to steal it, confessing that now might help your case."

She looked up at him. "An old newspaper article. From Virginia City."

Her answer wasn't what he'd been anticipating. "Who paid you, Gabriella?"

She took a few breaths before answering. "Mr. Thompson."

"Thompson."

"Yes."

"What was so important about that article?"

"It was about arrests for a riot," she answered. "Mr. Thompson was named. So was Mr. Young. And many others."

Damn.

The cop slowed the wagon as they approached the station. Being

212

Sunday, there were spots at the curb in the absence of the cabs usually parked there, and he took one. The wagon's abrupt stop rocked Gabriella back against the side of the bed. She grunted in frustration that her handcuffed wrists kept her from steadying herself.

"They did know each other already," Nick said.

"Mr. Young did not think that Mr. Thompson remembered him," she said. "Mr. Thompson is not a good man. He escaped punishment. And he did not pay me what he'd promised. Not for stealing the saddlebag. Not for searching for a telegram in Mrs. Davies's room. He was worried she'd found out about the article."

Brake set, the cop jumped down from the wagon and went around to lower the tailboard.

Nick climbed down too. "How much did he claim he'd pay you to kill Young, Gabriella?"

"I did not kill Mr. Young, Detective," she said wearily. "He was already dead."

"I know. I know. Because Mr. Merrill had killed him." How many times did they have to have this conversation?

She squeezed her eyes shut, and sighed. When she opened her eyes again, they were almost devoid of expression, as flat and dark as a dead-calm sea.

"No, I do not know that he killed Mr. Young," she said. "I lied about where I saw him. I wanted you to not think I was responsible."

"Lies. Of course," the beat cop said, climbing up onto the bed and yanking her off the wagon. "What else were you expecting, Detective?"

For a minute, Nick thought she was going to say more. Tell him who'd killed Young, maybe. But she didn't say more, and he let the officer drag her off into the station. Nick had other business to attend to. Namely, locating Thaddeus Thompson and asking him about a damning newspaper article.

· · ·

He will shoot me without compunction, here in my empty house.

And Barbara and Addie would discover her corpse on the kitchen floor, the victim of an error in judgment. She had been so focused on first Mr. Merrill, then Thaddeus Thompson, and then Gabriella that she'd discounted a man with his own reasons to commit murder.

But he'd not shot her yet. Instead, he'd chosen to spend the endless minutes since she'd found him in her kitchen berating her for asking too many questions and upsetting Cassandra.

"I did not intend to upset your daughter, Mr. Weaver," she said, proud that she almost sounded calm. "You have to believe me."

Why, though, might he believe her this time any more than the multiple times she'd already asked him to?

"But you *have* upset her, Mrs. Davies," he stated. "And you're done prying into our affairs."

"You've decided to stop me by sneaking into my house and confronting me with a weapon?"

"I did not need to sneak in, Mrs. Davies. The door wasn't locked," he replied coolly. "And I'm glad that I correctly guessed that any of your servants would be out, since it's Sunday. Leaving us alone. Makes it so much easier."

"Ah," she replied, hearing the uneasy catch in her voice. "Well, Mr. Weaver, although it may have seemed like irritating prying, my chief concern was proving who caused your sister-in-law's death. As well as who may have murdered Mr. Young."

"We know who's responsible for Elnora's death," he said flatly. Unfortunately for Celia, he was doing a remarkable job of keeping the gun steady and pointed straight at her chest. "Parker Young."

"Perhaps you're blaming the rather obvious Mr. Young because *you* were the one who'd pushed Elnora into a hot spring that fatally scalded her, Mr. Weaver."

He scoffed. "Why would I want to harm Elnora?" he asked. "Because she thought that I'd bought off Julius Thompson? Why on earth would I bother over that? Nobody would have listened to her claims."

The words of a female, after all.

Outside, the neighbor's dog took to barking again. This time, though, it was the friendly yip it reserved for Addie and sometimes for Owen. Unlike its earlier barking, which had indicated a stranger in the area. The stranger having been Mr. Weaver. *Do be careful.* Please *be careful.*

"Would people have listened to Mr. Young's claim that you'd paid a city official to grant you a contract?" she asked. "Is that why the two of you had an argument the night before Elnora died? Because he'd found out?"

He narrowed his gaze. Not to better examine her, but to better examine his memory of that evening. "We'd argued because of his outrageous allegations about Thaddeus. That he is . . ." He hesitated to finish the sentence.

"A fraud, Mr. Merrill called him."

"It's all lies. It has to be," he insisted. "But Young's allegations risked everything I'd worked hard for. I told him to leave my family and the Thompsons alone. I stupidly thought he'd listen."

Probably because Hiram Weaver was a man used to having people obey his directives without question.

"Did Mr. Young continue to harass you once you'd returned to San Francisco?" She was playing for time, hoping that someone would intervene. But who would? Addie? Owen? The thought of either of them attempting to rescue her made her blood run cold. "The note that was sent to your house the morning of his murder had alerted you to the fact he'd returned—astonishingly—to the city."

"He requested that we meet. The gall," he said. "I was in a coffeehouse waiting for him at the time he was killed, though. I told Detective Greaves that, as well. Young never showed up."

Nicholas had to have confirmed his alibi or else Mr. Weaver would be in jail and not Dennis Merrill. Which begged a critical question . . .

"Mr. Weaver, why are you pointing a gun at me if you are innocent in the deaths of both Elnora and Mr. Young?" she asked. "Simply to get me to cease annoying you and your family and acquaintances?"

"It's as good a reason as any, Mrs. Davies."

Was it? "Unless you are actually seeking to shield the person who *is* responsible," she guessed. "An individual you deeply love. Cassandra."

A flicker of emotion passed too quickly over his face for her to interpret it. But the fact that what she'd said had given him pause made her realize she was nearing the truth. There had been clues indicating his daughter's guilt. The yellow streak on her shoe heel, which she'd not explained. Her frantic insistence that Elnora's death had been an accident. Her false tale about following her aunt up the hill.

"She had nothing to do with Young's murder, Mrs. Davies."

"No, she did not, because she was with Mr. Merrill at the time," Celia said, noticing his shocked reaction. "But as for Elnora . . . perhaps Cassandra did not intend to harm her. An argument that got out of hand. She should have informed the police, though. They would have believed an innocent young woman like her."

Muscles tightened along the edge of his jaw. "Would they have?"

Celia heard the creak of a floorboard out in the dining room. Mr. Weaver did not appear to have noticed the sound.

"Are you saying the police would not have believed her because you think it was not an accident?" she asked. "That Cassandra intentionally shoved Elnora, resulting in her death?"

"It doesn't matter now. Young is dead. It's all taken care of."

And with those words, everything moved into place, like the interweaving of gears and wheels that had been stuck but were now freed up.

"You *did* kill him," she said, feeling a rush of prickles. "Because he'd seen what had happened. He'd seen Cassandra with Elnora and told you that he had. You needed to protect her from scrutiny, so he had to be silenced."

He raised the gun again, which had momentarily sagged during their conversation. The muzzle was no more than a foot from Celia's chest. He'd not miss if he fired. "I told you I was waiting for him in a coffeehouse at the time."

"Oh, I suspect we will be able to find the holes in your carefully woven tale, Mr. Weaver."

"And I think you won't have the chance to, Mrs. Davies."

"No, Father! No!" Cassandra Weaver shouted, bursting into the kitchen from the direction of the dining room.

He spun to face her, and as he did, the revolver went off. Dropping her to the ground.

ℬ CHAPTER 22 ℛ

"Shoot!" Owen exclaimed. The sound of a pistol firing was definitely not good.

He hadn't caught up to Miss Weaver before she'd barged into the house. He should've followed her straight inside, rather than decide to go around the back. Except the gunshot had come from inside the kitchen, and his impulsive decision had turned out to be smart. Unless, of course, the gunman shot him, too.

"Here goes," Owen murmured to himself, climbed the back steps, and threw open the door. Afraid he'd find Mrs. Davies bleeding on the floor.

Instead, it was Cassandra Weaver, a stain of dark red soaking the left sleeve of her nice blue dress, her father crouched next to her and repeatedly telling her he was sorry.

"Ah, Owen. I am happy to see you. Please help me, if you will," Mrs. Davies said, returning to the kitchen with plasters and a basin in her hand. "Fill this with warm water. There is a kettle on the hob."

Owen did as he was instructed.

"Killing her wouldn't have helped any of us, Father," Miss Weaver sobbed.

Owen looked over his shoulder at her and her father. She'd managed to sit upright. Her hand was clasped over the gunshot wound, trying to stanch the bleeding.

"I just wanted to protect you, Cassandra. That's all."

"But you didn't. I could've died!"

"What's going on here?" asked Mr. Taylor, storming into the kitchen.

Owen could hear Addie in the dining room shouting at him to be careful. "And you, too, Mrs. Davies!"

"Thank you, Addie. Barbara, bring clean towels and my needle and silk thread." Mrs. Davies knelt on the floor next to Miss Weaver. "And thank goodness you are here, Mr. Taylor. You need to arrest Mr. Weaver. For the murder of Mr. Young."

• • •

217

"Taylor, what are you doing at my house on a Sunday afternoon?" Nick asked, trudging up the steps of Mrs. Jewett's place. He'd wasted at least an hour hunting for Thaddeus Thompson. Nobody had answered the door at his house, and he hadn't been visiting Cassandra Weaver at the Weavers' place, which had also been strangely deserted. "I thought you went for a stroll with Miss Ferguson."

"I did, sir. But it's Mr. Weaver, sir. He's shot his daughter," he said, his words coming out in a rush.

"What?"

"When I took Addie home, I found that Mr. Weaver had shot his daughter in Mrs. Davies's kitchen," he said. "He killed Mr. Young. He tried to shoot Mrs. Davies. Accidentally shot his daughter, instead."

"Damn it, Taylor!" He turned and ran back down the steps.

"She's okay, sir!" his assistant shouted after him. "You don't need to go there."

"Hell, yes, I do," he shouted back.

• • •

"I am so sorry, Mrs. Davies," Cassandra said, propped up in the bed that Celia's uncle had once used. It had accommodated other invalids, as well. "I should've been honest with you."

Celia leaned over her to inspect the bandaging covering her wound. She was fortunate that the bullet had passed through the muscles near her shoulder and not hit bone or lodged in her arm. The damage, nonetheless, was significant. The far wall of their dining room had not fared well, either.

"I do wish you'd explained what had happened with Elnora, Cassandra." Celia was pleased to see that the young woman's stitches were holding, and she sat back. "Rather than tell me you'd followed her up the hill out of curiosity. You were already at the mineral pools, waiting for Mr. Thompson, weren't you?" She wondered if Mr. Merrill had noticed her climbing the trail that morning. His comments to Celia had vaguely implied as much.

"I was, but . . . It all went so horribly wrong, Mrs. Davies."

"You *did* push her?" *Gad.*

"It happened in a blur," she stammered, curling her fingers around the edge of the coverlet. "She was so angry with me for telling Father that I intended to accept Thaddeus. She didn't like him at all. And when she found out that Denny has a wife and I couldn't marry him, like she preferred . . ." Her voice trailed off. "She thought I was making a terrible mistake."

"Your argument got out of control and you unthinkingly shoved her away."

"She became so upset that she began to shake," she said. "She turned away, but she wasn't being careful where she stepped. She twisted her ankle and stumbled. I tried to grab her wrist and stop her from falling, but I wasn't strong enough."

The cause of the bruise Celia had observed on the woman's arm.

"She didn't even scream as she stumbled into the pool. She must've had a heart attack straight away." Cassandra drew in a shaky breath. "It was terrible."

"Do you know why your aunt had gone up there early?"

"Probably to meet with Mr. Young. About the note you found in her pocket," she said. "The one that was meant for Denny."

"That was why you'd come into the shed." Interrupting Celia's examination of the woman's body. "You were looking for it."

She did not confirm Celia's suspicion; she didn't need to.

"I shouldn't have argued with her, Mrs. Davies. If we hadn't argued, she'd still be alive."

She might still be alive; Celia could not reassure Cassandra otherwise.

"You should have told the coroner what had taken place," she said.

"Thaddeus said I'd have to admit that we'd been arguing and what our quarrel had been about. He said it would look bad for all of us. He also thought I'd never convince anybody that I hadn't pushed her on purpose," she said. "Because to him it hadn't looked like an accident."

"He was there when she fell."

"He'd climbed the trail just as I . . . just as she tripped." The tears collecting in Cassandra's eyes began to slip down her cheeks. "He demanded that I keep quiet about it. To let Mr. Young take the blame. I didn't want him to be blamed, though. He was innocent. But I stayed quiet, just like Thaddeus said to."

Cassandra Weaver, young and naïve and obedient.

"I did try to warn you to be careful, though," Cassandra said.

"The telegram. *You* sent it to me."

"I did. I'm sorry if it scared you."

Celia considered her. "Were you afraid Mr. Thompson might hurt me?" she asked softly.

She drew in a trembling breath. "I didn't know what he might do, Mrs. Davies. Maybe."

Gad.

"Unfortunately, Miss Weaver, I find it very difficult to mind my own business," Celia responded. "And even if I had, as Mr. Shakespeare would say, 'the truth will out.'"

"Like a splinter eventually squeezing out of skin."

An apt metaphor.

Celia rested her fingers upon Cassandra's bare forearm and gave it a gentle squeeze. "You should have told me the truth, Cassandra. I would have believed you."

"But nobody else would have. Even Father suspected me."

Even Dennis Merrill as well. A man who'd done his best to protect her.

"When did you first suspect that your father had killed Mr. Young?" Celia asked.

"As soon as you told me he was dead," she answered, swiping the tears off her cheeks. "Mr. Young did send that note to our house. I read it before Mary gave it to Father. His message said that he'd seen me with Elnora. That he was going to tell the police I'd pushed her if my father didn't give him two hundred and fifty dollars. But why would the police ever trust the word of that awful man?"

"They might not have done, Cassandra, but your father probably had not wanted to risk an investigation into the man's accusation," she replied. "You went to Mr. Merrill after you read that note."

"I couldn't think of anybody else to turn to except Denny," she said. "He'd tell me what to do. He didn't think my father would harm Mr. Young, though. He thought he'd pay him off. I wanted so badly to believe him. But I should've told you, told Detective Greaves. My father tried to kill you, Mrs. Davies. I saw him take the Smith and Wesson . . . I followed him here because I was afraid of what he planned to do."

"It is all right, Cassandra."

"But he wanted to kill you, and I could have prevented that," she insisted. "Just like I could've prevented my aunt from dying if I'd kept my head."

"I do not blame you."

Fresh tears rolled down the young woman's face. "What will I do now, Mrs. Davies? Where will I go?" she asked. "I can't marry Thaddeus. I don't love him. And I don't think he actually loves me, either."

"We shall find a solution," Celia replied. "I promise."

"Ma'am," Addie quietly said from the doorway. "Mr. Greaves is here to see you."

Celia gently patted Cassandra's hand and went downstairs. He was waiting in the entry hall, his hands strangling the brim of his hat.

"Celia? Are you . . . ? Damn, Celia, are you okay?"

"I am fine," she said. "I am . . . Oh, Nicholas." The tremors that overtook her prevented her from saying more, and she stepped into his open arms. Into the warmth and strength of his embrace.

• • •

"Mr. Merrill practically skipped out of his jail cell this morning, Celia," Nick said, leaning back in his chair. It squeaked.

She sat in the seat on the opposite side of his desk, looking as though not much had occurred yesterday. As if she hadn't had a near brush with death. A near brush that could've been avoided if he'd been a better detective.

The wound in his arm burned, and he reached up to rub it, her gaze following the gesture.

"Nicholas, I am all right," she said. "I told you yesterday that I was, and I meant it."

But she hadn't been "all right" yesterday and had stood shaking in his arms for a very long time, until the terror of what had almost happened to her finally subsided. He would've held her for an eternity, if necessary. Just to be her strength.

"Don't think I'll stop feeling bad about how things unfolded for quite a while, Mrs. Davies."

"There is no need to feel bad, Mr. Greaves."

She smiled, and he almost forgave himself.

"Although *I* feel bad about how much time I wasted focusing on those blasted letters from Mrs. Gannon and Mr. Merrill's culpability, Nicholas," she said. "I missed the obvious."

"It's all right, Celia. I wanted Merrill to be guilty, too." The charming Dennis Merrill. Nick hoped they'd heard the last of him.

"I suppose his plans to start a baseball team will have to be scotched." She smiled over the look of confusion on Nick's face. "The least of his concerns, I know. Mrs. Gannon's sister being a primary one. Mr. Taylor informed me, when he stopped by the house this morning, that Mrs. Gannon had visited Mr. Merrill while he was still in his jail cell. I was surprised to hear she'd not left town."

He'd been surprised, too. "She'd intended to leave sooner, after Mrs. Merrill threatened her and Mr. Merrill's response to the message she'd left at his house had been, let's say, less than pleasant," he said. "However, the ferry that will connect her to a train home doesn't leave until later today. She was forced to stick around."

"Clearly, his less-than-pleasant response did not fully put her off a visit."

"She must've figured he couldn't hurt her while locked away in a cell."

"And what of Mr. Weaver?"

"He presently has a cell two down from Gabriella Raas's," he replied. "She admitted to stealing Young's saddlebag in order to retrieve that envelope you saw her hand to Thompson. It contained a newspaper article listing several men arrested for rioting in Virginia City. Two of those men were Thompson and Young."

She sat forward on her chair. "They *were* acquainted."

"Not well, apparently," he said. "But, according to Gabriella, when Young moved to San Francisco and one day spotted Thaddeus Thompson at an Odd Fellows' meeting, the prospect of earning some cash presented itself. You see, Thompson had evaded punishment for his crime."

"He's a wanted man?"

He nodded. "The Virginia City police have informed us that Thompson has a lengthy list of offenses. Drunkenness, fighting in a public street, in addition to rioting," he said. "They thought he'd fled to Cincinnati to join his brother. They didn't realize he'd come to San Francisco, instead."

"I wonder if his father knows of his past."

"He has to," he replied. But sometimes family could be blind to the sins of their loved ones. God only knew Nick had been blind to his Uncle Asa's crimes. "I also gather that Thompson has a reputation in

Virginia City for all sorts of excesses."

He'd more than simply sown some wild oats.

"Ah," Celia said, frowning. "His father must have hoped that a marriage to Cassandra would encourage Thaddeus to settle down. Quiet any storm of rumors swirling around his head."

"She's frankly lucky to have escaped that marriage," he replied.

"Elnora was correct to be concerned about Thaddeus Thompson, wasn't she? He is every bit a fraud," she said. "Worse than a fraud."

Nick shifted on his chair. Making it squeak again. "As for Weaver, I'm waiting to hear if our witness has identified him as the man she spotted outside Young's boardinghouse Friday morning."

She sighed. "I should have more seriously suspected him as Mr. Young's killer, Nicholas."

"There was no reason to, Celia. He had a supposedly watertight alibi," Nick said. "But Mullahey and Taylor returned to that coffeehouse and got the proprietor to admit that Weaver had slipped him ten dollars to lie about when he was there."

"Hiram Weaver is fond of handing out money to get his way, isn't he?"

"It might've worked, if he hadn't panicked over the questions we both kept asking," he replied. "He must've been afraid that Miss Weaver would eventually reveal her suspicions about him."

"The deceit was gnawing at her, but she loves her father. Her only living parent," she said. "And given her part in Elnora's accidental death, Cassandra likely simply wished the entire situation would vanish and be forgotten. Until she recognized the very real threat he posed to me."

Why Weaver thought he'd get away with shooting Celia, Nick couldn't figure. However, heated emotions didn't lend themselves to clearheaded decision-making.

"How is Miss Weaver doing?" he asked.

"She is bearing up rather well," she replied. "Jane has offered to find her a place at the young ladies' college that Grace attends in Benicia. Miss Weaver has inherited funds from Elnora that will pay her way. A substantial sum, it turns out. And it strikes me that Mr. Merrill's assertion that his stepmother was a spendthrift was a ruse to keep us from concluding that Cassandra might have killed Elnora for her money."

Knuckles rapped on the doorframe, and Taylor stepped through the opening. He nodded a greeting at Celia before turning to Nick.

"The, umm . . ." He cleared his throat. "The woman who lives across the street from Mr. Young's place has finished having a look at Mr. Weaver, sir. She confirms that he is the fellow she saw outside the boardinghouse."

Would a jury believe a prostitute, though? "Thank you, Taylor."

"Glad to see you're doing okay, ma'am," his assistant said to Celia.

"And I am equally glad."

He left and closed the door. The officers out in the station would start gossiping any second, guaranteed.

"Addie has told me they have decided upon an October wedding," she said. "I told her she did not need to wait that long, but she wants to make certain that I have found an acceptable maid-of-all-work to help out. Addie will not be living with us any longer after she and Mr. Taylor marry, obviously, but has promised to cook our evening meals. Because no one else's food will suffice, she says."

"This won't be easy for you, will it?" he asked quietly.

"No, it will not," she admitted, her expression turning melancholy. "Addie has been with me since when I lived in London. I am losing a dear friend. Barbara is too distressed to even mention the wedding, even though it is months in the future."

She tried to smile, but this time, she couldn't get it to stick. He hated to see her unhappy, but she was strong. Too strong to need his help. Hell, maybe *he* was the one who needed help. The one who needed to fill the hole in his heart that he'd let fester ever since a friend had taken a bullet for him during the war.

Now. He should ask her now.

"Celia . . ."

Her brows perked. "Yes?"

"Would you con—"

"Ah, Greaves, entertaining a guest?" Briggs asked, barging into the office with a stupid smirk on his face. "Mrs. Davies, heard you caught a killer. Well done."

"Thank you, Mr. Briggs." She got to her feet. Nick had lost his chance. "I should return home, Mr. Greaves. I have a patient to attend to."

With a "good day," she departed the detectives' office. Leaving Nick with a tittering Briggs and a sinking feeling he might never again screw up the courage to propose to her.

• • •

"I did not have the opportunity to ask you how your trip to visit Frank's parents went, Jane," Celia said, handing a fresh cup of tea— oolong, as usual—to her friend. Yesterday, Jane had paid her a call just in time to see Hiram Weaver hauled off by Mr. Taylor. "How is his mother's health?"

"How our trip went is unimportant compared to how *you* are doing," Jane said. "I'm worried about you."

Celia smiled. It was the only response that might wipe the look of concern off Jane's face. But both she and Nicholas were right to be concerned; if not for Cassandra Weaver's intervention, Celia might be dead.

"I am a trifle shaken but otherwise fine," she answered. "So, your trip?"

Jane scanned Celia, checking for any sign that she was concealing injuries, either physical or mental, before continuing. "Well, Mrs. Hutchinson's health was amazingly restored by the time we arrived. So, compared to your holiday, Celia, ours was uneventful. I'd be happy to never repeat that train ride, though. I think I was covered in soot half the time," she said, relaxing against the settee cushions. She'd brought her stepdaughter, Grace, with her, and she and Barbara had gone up to visit with Cassandra. The murmur of their voices floated down the stairs and into the parlor, causing Jane to glance in the direction of the sound. "How terrible. To have witnessed your aunt's death and been shot by your own father."

"Thank you for offering to find her a place at Grace's ladies' seminary."

"It's the least I can do for her," she said, sipping some of her tea. "What are you going to do, Celia?"

"Take care of Cassandra as long as is necessary. We have room here and she is a welcome guest," she said. "And attempt to stay out of trouble. I doubt my nerves can withstand another encounter with a weapon anytime soon."

"That's not what I'm referring to, Celia, and you know it," she said, setting down the cup. "I mean what are you going to do about Mr. Greaves?"

"Ah." She'd told Jane that she was positive he'd nearly asked her to marry him that morning at the station. That she'd felt equally scared and thrilled by the prospect. But he hadn't asked, had he? "We shall go on as we have done so far. And should he ever think to ask again, I will . . ." *What* will *I do?*

"You will say yes, Celia. I won't allow any other reply."

She laughed. "Yes, Mrs. Hutchinson."

Jane gave a brisk nod. "Good."

There was a knock on the front door, and Addie hurried through to answer it.

"I confess I'm surprised that Frank allowed you to come visit me, Jane." Her husband had previously banned her, judging Celia to be too dangerous for his wife to associate with.

"He hasn't read the newspapers yet, so he hasn't found out about your involvement in this latest case," she said. "He probably will again attempt to ban me, once he has found out."

"Ma'am," Addie said from the parlor doorway. "It's Mrs. Gannon here to see you."

Lifting an eyebrow, Celia glanced at Jane. "Show her in, Addie."

The freckled woman from outside the hotel entered the room. "I don't mean to be interruptin', ma'am."

"You are not," she replied. "I am glad to finally put a name to the face. Jane, this is the sister of Dennis Merrill's wife. The woman at the center of a mystery. I was quite convinced, Mrs. Gannon, that the letters you sent to Elnora Merrill were a motive for murder."

"Oh." She looked abashed, her fingers tightening around the ties of the net purse she carried. "Oh, dear."

"But they were not," Celia quickly added. "How might I help you?"

"I saw your name in the newspaper, and I came to see how you were farin'," she answered. "After the accident with the horsecar, and all. I felt awful I didn't tell you then that I saw the fellah who pushed you in front of it. I didn't want to get involved."

Out of the corner of her eye, Celia noticed Jane's startled expression. "What did he look like?"

"A tall, blond fellah," she said. "Do you know him?"

Thaddeus Thompson. *Well, well.* He must have spotted her leaving the Weavers' house and followed her, taking advantage of an approaching horsecar to possibly put a halt to her investigation. Stop her from one day uncovering damaging secrets about him.

"I believe I do know him, Mrs. Gannon," she replied. "Thank you for telling me, and I am recovered from the incident."

"Good. Well, I have a ferry to catch," she said. "Oh, before I go, you might be interested in learnin', since Denny tells me you know him, that he'll be takin' back me sister."

Celia hoped Mr. Merrill would make amends to his wife for abandoning her. Something Patrick Davies had never done.

"Take care of yourself, Mrs. Gannon."

She wished them both well and left, crossing paths with Nicholas, whom Addie had let into the house. He cast a questioning glance at the woman.

"Mrs. Gannon came here to inform me that Mr. Thompson very likely was the individual who pushed me in front of that horsecar, Nicholas," Celia said. "And, also, that Mr. Merrill's wife will be joining him in San Francisco."

"The unfortunate woman," he said.

Jane stood and pulled on the gloves she'd discarded. "I shall be taking my leave, Celia. There's no need for you to get up and show me out."

"You don't have to go because I've turned up, Mrs. Hutchinson."

"Oh, I think I do." She crossed the room, pausing alongside Nicholas long enough to rest one gloved hand atop his. "I told her to accept, Mr. Greaves, should you ever finally ask her to marry you. Hope you don't mind."

"Jane!" Celia exclaimed.

"Now, Celia, you know you want to," she said, laughing. "Good day to you both."

The front door clicked shut behind her, and the house fell into quietude. Aside from the soothing sounds of Addie humming in the kitchen and the girls chattering upstairs.

"Nicholas, what brings you here?" Celia asked, her pulse skipping.

"I need a reason?"

"We saw each other only a few hours ago."

"If you want me to leave—"

"Certainly not," she interrupted, smiling.

He sat down next to her. "I wanted to tell you that Julius Thompson has already been indicted for accepting a bribe," he said. "A year minimum in state prison if he's convicted. The same would apply to Weaver for offering the bribe."

"Except he may hang for murder, instead. All to protect Cassandra."

"At the very least he'll face jail time for threatening you with a deadly weapon and shooting his daughter," he said. "And Thaddeus Thompson is on his way to Virginia City to answer for his crimes there. Should I bring a charge against him for pushing you in front of that horsecar? You could've been seriously injured, Celia."

"Our only witness to that offense is probably halfway up the street by now," she said. "And it's not necessary."

"But still—"

"I am fine," she said, gazing into those brown eyes she so dearly loved. "Truly, I am fine. You do not need to keep prodding me."

"What? You're not going to quote Shakespeare?"

"'All's well that ends well'?" she asked. "There. How is that?"

He gathered her fingers in his hands and pressed them to his chest. "You are incorrigible, Mrs. Davies."

"I suppose I should inform you that I am unlikely to ever change," she said, feeling the pulse of his heart through his clothing. "Even if I become Mrs. Greaves."

"I wouldn't want you to ever change," he whispered, releasing her hands to trace his fingers along the outline of her jaw. His touch sent tingles across her skin and down her spine. "Ever."

✳ AUTHOR'S NOTE ✳

In 1847, during John Fremont's survey of the Sierra Mountains, he came upon an area in the mountains northwest of Calistoga that were given the name the Geysers. An active zone of fumaroles and mineral springs, developers soon became interested in founding a spa there for tourists to use. Mineral springs have long been popular attractions for folks seeking treatment for all sorts of afflictions—arthritis, rashes and other skin diseases, even general sluggishness. By 1854, the Geysers Resort Hotel was founded, and numerous famous people visited, including Mark Twain and Ulysses Grant. The natural beauty of its surroundings, along with the excitement of seeing the geysers and the mineral pools, were part of its attraction. An even bigger attraction was the journey itself when Clark Foss was the man driving the carriage. A colorful character and famous throughout America, his handling of the horses was notorious and considered by many to be more thrilling than the geysers themselves.

During the next decades, the resort's popularity rose and fell, its remoteness likely a factor. Mr. Shafer, the actual proprietor in 1868, was one of many who owned and operated the property over the years. Sadly, the resort's decline was steady and inevitable. Interest in the area increased, however, when engineers developed the ability to harness geothermal energy and produce electricity. The first geothermal wells were drilled in the 1950s, with many more to follow. The era of the Geysers as a tourist destination finally came to an end in 1980 when the resort hotel was demolished.

Dennis Merrill's interest in forming a baseball team reflects the growing interest in the relatively new sport. Baseball had already spread to California by 1860, when the first games were played in San Francisco. By 1868, there were multiple clubs organized in the state. In 1869, the nationally famous Cincinnati Red Stockings made a much-lauded trip to California to play some of the fledgling teams. Unfortunately, the local clubs did not fare well. In one game, for example, the final score was 76 to 5.

Lastly, as ever, a word to my readers—Celia and Nick and all the folks who inhabit these books would not exist without your support. Thank you.

ABOUT THE AUTHOR

Nancy Herriman left an engineering career to take up the pen and has never looked back. She is the author of the Mysteries of Old San Francisco, the Bess Ellyott Mysteries, and several stand-alone novels. A winner of the Daphne du Maurier Award, when she's not writing, she enjoys singing, gabbing about writing, and eating dark chocolate. After two decades in Arizona, she now lives in her home state of Ohio with her family.